Deliver Us from Evil
by
Richard Davidson

The Lord's Prayer Mystery Series
Volume V

Richard Davidson

"Deliver Us from Evil," by Richard Davidson.
ISBN 978-0-9829160-3-2.
The Lord's Prayer Mystery Series, Volume V of V

Published 2013 by RADMAR Publishing Group, P.O. Box 425, Northbrook, IL 60065, U.S.A. Copyright 2013, Richard Davidson. All rights reserved. No part of this publication may be reproduced, stored in a retrieval system, or transmitted in any form or by any means, electronic, mechanical, recording, or otherwise, without the prior written permission of Richard Davidson.

Manufactured in the United States of America.

Yea, though I walk through the valley of the shadow of death, I will fear no evil: for thou art with me ...
The Bible, Psalm 23, King James Version

CHAPTER 1 – WEDDING

It was the kind of wedding where everyone expected something to go wrong. Parkville United Methodist Church buzzed and bustled its way through early afternoon preparations for the ceremony that everyone had anticipated; but few had considered likely to happen. Today's ritual would be the climax of four years of the bride's increasingly focused campaign to overcome the groom's resistance to marriage. The groom, Pastor Arthur Blake, had secretly enjoyed his bride's premarital crusade even while continuing to delay the inevitable by concentrating on his church duties and his sideline investigative interests. Now that the big day had arrived, they both knew their growing interdependence had prepared them well for their special transition.

Many members of this northwest Illinois congregation had correctly predicted that District Superintendent Angela King would perform the ceremony uniting in marriage their unique pastor, Arthur Blake with the former County Medical Examiner, Irma Custis. Other attendees expressed surprise that Angela, Arthur's chief critic within the church hierarchy, would even want to attend this event, let alone preside over it.

Pastor Arthur Blake had been married once before while working as a trouble-shooting engineer within NASA's space program. When his project preparation and spaceflight duration duties had made him only infrequently available to her, his wife Cindy had rebelled and left him for a local weather forecaster who offered her a more stable home life.

This would be the first wedding ceremony for Irma Custis. She had remained single into her fourth decade, declining past marriage opportunities, while concentrating on her medical career. She had grown up believing that we each have one perfect partner, and had demonstrated sufficient patience to wait for her unique mate. She had first encountered Arthur while the two investigated the death of his predecessor pastor at Parkville UMC. Shortly afterward Irma decided that she had found her destiny.

The guest list for today's event included a curious blend of local church members, Parkville police and fire officers, academics, elderly war veterans, federal investigators, a congressman and his family from Florida, and even the Bishop of the Northern Illinois Conference. Many of these people had been somehow involved in mysteries investigated by Arthur Blake and Irma Custis, usually through the ABC Consultants group that she had created after resigning as County Medical Examiner. The presence of these guests emphasized their appreciation of the couple's past investigative assistances.

The conversations of people awaiting the beginning of the ceremony dealt mainly with the identities and relative prestige of those in attendance. Occasional random discussions shifted to the red carpet runner upon which the wedding party would make their ceremonial approach to the altar. This carpet had been a well-publicized gift to Parkville UMC from Peter and Janice Blake, Arthur's parents. Peter was an antiques dealer, and he had certified that this red runner had graced an old Virginia church for special events during the period when George and Martha Washington had worshipped there.

As the ushers escorted family members and special guests to their reserved front pews, the conversations tapered off to respectful silence. The organist played the processional music, and people pivoted slightly in their seats to better watch the entrance of the several couples in the wedding party. Per Arthur's preference, the groomsmen, Wally Sanborn and Bill Martin, were dressed in dark suits rather than tuxedos as they ushered the more formally dressed bridesmaids, Penny Gonzalez and Renee Andrews, toward the altar, where Reverend Angela King, adorned in ornate clerical robes, awaited them. To the right of the altar stood Arthur Blake and his best man, Police Chief Bobby Andrews, each attempting to relax while still maintaining good posture.

The organist began to play *Here Comes the Bride.* The congregation stood and turned to watch as Irma made her grand entrance, escorted by Arthur's father, Peter Blake, in the absence of her deceased parents. Arthur and Bobby relaxed slightly as they watched the final sequence of the wedding drama unfold. Arthur thought that Irma looked elegant in her understated tailored wedding gown. Peter had disregarded Arthur's informality instructions by proudly wearing a tuxedo as he prepared to give the bride away.

Irma and Peter had completed only one quarter of their journey down the aisle, the focus of everyone's gaze, when a loud crash and thud from the direction of the altar disrupted the scene's serenity. The music stopped abruptly, and the bride broke into a run toward the altar, startling the congregation. When people pivoted their heads to follow her movement, they realized that her target was Angela King, the District Superintendent, who had collapsed. Several firefighters in the congregation also rushed forward. After a brief period of consternation and several radio transmissions, they carried Angela out of the sanctuary to the church's upper parking lot, reaching it just as paramedics in a Fire Department ambulance arrived. Paramedic Allison Whitney took charge of the situation and soon had Angela secured in the truck for the trip to Parkville Care Center.

The church filled with murmurs and movement as people who had assisted Angela returned to their seats. Arthur stood in the main aisle and called for silence.

"I've learned that Reverend King is now being transported to the hospital. She regained consciousness as they loaded her into the ambulance. Please pray that she will have a quick and complete recovery...Irma probably suspects that I'm somehow involved in this disruption of our wedding. I want to tell her and all of you that we are going to continue the ceremony. Bishop Howard Chandler has graciously volunteered to perform the ritual.

"Everyone please return to your seats, and in five minutes we will restart the bride's procession down the aisle." He looked toward Irma and saw her blowing kisses at him from the back of the sanctuary.

Under Bishop Chandler's well-polished leadership, *take two* of the wedding ceremony proceeded smoothly. All present were pleased to hear the Bishop intone his final blessing:

"...Send therefore your blessing upon Irma and Arthur that they may surely keep their marriage covenant, and so grow in love and godliness together that their home may be a haven of blessing and peace; through Jesus Christ our Lord...Amen."

Following the usual round of introductions, congratulations, and kisses in the receiving line, the wedding party returned to the sanctuary for formal photographs. Everyone else adjourned to House of Ming for a grand party, hosted by that restaurant's owner and Arthur's good friend, Tony Fleming. His use of the last syllable of his family name to sound Chinese was a well-received joke around Parkville. As they prepared to depart the church, few people noticed Arthur and Irma conferring in a corner of Fellowship Hall between kisses and hugs. Fewer still noticed that after the photography session, Irma drove alone to the reception, while Arthur departed for Parkville Care Center to check on Angela King's condition.

CHAPTER 2 – ANGELA

Two hours after the conclusion of the early afternoon ceremony, as he approached Angela King's room at Parkville Care Center, Arthur encountered Dr. Bernard Miggles in the hallway.

"Hello, Bernie; I'm here to visit Angela King if she's well enough. Have you figured out what caused her collapse?"

"Good to see you again, Arthur; her case is a little puzzling. She may have had a cardiac event, but if so, it was mild and shouldn't have caused her to lose consciousness. We're monitoring her and taking more tests. She was awake and lucid when she arrived in the ambulance and appears to be close to normal now."

Arthur thanked Dr. Miggles for the information. Then he entered the private room and found Angela reclining in the uptilted bed, encumbered by several fluid-conveying tubes and snake-like links to monitoring devices.

"Hello, Angela; are you well enough to talk with me? Do you know what caused your problem?"

"Thanks for coming, Arthur. I'm feeling much better, but I'm mortified that I disrupted your wedding. Will you have to reschedule it?"

"Nope, we're legally hitched; I'm wearing my wedding ring. After they took you away in the ambulance, Bishop Chandler stepped in to perform the ceremony. You don't have to worry about our status. I'm just concerned about you."

Angela shifted to a slightly more comfortable position. "They're still running tests, but they think I had a minor heart attack. I'm sure I know what happened. I had my worst panic attack ever, due to guilt feelings. I lost control and blacked out."

"What do you mean by guilt feelings?"

"Our conflicts during the past four years have been pretty intense. I didn't think you were suitable to be pastor here – I even argued with Bishop Chandler about it - and yet I was about to perform your wedding service. Didn't that seem strange to you? I tensed up about the improbable circumstances as I stood waiting for Irma to join you at the altar. Then I recognized someone in the congregation whose unexpected presence shocked me."

Arthur adopted a more serious tone. "Now that we're openly discussing the basics of our relationship, I have to admit that I wondered about your change of heart toward me a few months ago. You suddenly started showering me with compliments and hugs. Then you insisted on officiating at our wedding. I couldn't decide whether you had completely changed your attitude toward me, or if your actions indicated a hidden underlying motive."

"That was very astute of you. The truth lies in a mixture of those two possibilities. It's time for us to talk about it."

"Are you sure you're up to this right now?"

Angela nodded, adjusted her hospital gown, and pushed the button to raise her bed a little higher. She wanted to look Arthur in the eyes as they talked. "I told you pretty early in the game that your engineering background bothered me. I had been married to an engineer, and he had left me. Charlie preferred participation in some new startup venture to married life with me. Then you came along with your history of suddenly switching from engineering to the ministry, and I pegged you as being the same type as Charlie, likely to leave the ministry for something else."

"My decision to prepare for the ministry evolved over several years; it wasn't sudden."

"That's not important right now. There's a lot about my relationship with Charlie that needs telling, even if it means the end of my career or worse."

9

"That sounds ominous. I thought we were talking about our relationship. Don't let your medications make you say anything you'll regret later."

"They won't, and my dealings with Charlie affected how I dealt with you." Angela snapped at him. "There's a lot more to my life than my official duties!"

Arthur said nothing but leaned forward to assure Angela that he was focusing on her story.

"I told you the truth when I said that Charlie had decided to move on to other ventures, but what I didn't tell you is that he was also running away from something. Charlie is a chronic gambler, and he had lost a lot of money. He owed more than he could possibly afford, and some tough characters had threatened him with physical beatings if he didn't repay the money soon.

"As you know, the United Methodist Church takes a strong stand against gambling, so Charlie saw me as looking down on him for his failures. He didn't realize that my outward show of support for all of the church's positions was a façade and one of my tactics for gaining advancement. I had hopes of becoming a Bishop. That goal will be behind me after you hear the rest of my story. Anyway, after he heard me give a sermon endorsing the United Methodist Church position against gambling, Charlie left for destinations unknown."

"I'm sure you could have found resources for helping him."

"It was too late to do anything. He left because the bad guys were pursuing him, and also because he resented my churchliness...He never did understand me."

"I don't see how this relates to your collapse, Angela."

"I've only told you the first half of the story, Arthur. Earlier this year, he returned. He said that his debts were behind him and that he wanted to get back together with me. I wanted to believe him, so I agreed to take a vacation with him in Canada, a fishing trip. It mirrored an outing we took when we first got married, and I took it as a romantic gesture. We drove to some place far off the main road up there; there was no one within miles of us. While we were fishing from the bank of a lake one evening, we had too much to drink...

"Angela, throw me another beer."

"Charlie, we've had enough to drink. We're supposed to be trying to catch fish, not get sick from too much drinking."

"You look pretty good for yourself, almost as though you didn't age since I left. I thought it might be due to your mellowing up while I was gone, but you're just as prudish as ever: no booze, no gambling, and no sex. Relax, and be a loose woman out here. There's no one in these woods to see whether you're human after all."

"I think you're looking at me through beer-plus-vodka eyes, Charlie. What happened to you while you were away? I'd like to say you look the same, but it wouldn't be true. You look as though you've been squeezed through a wringer a few times."

"That's not a bad analogy. Those collection thugs caught up with me and squeezed me for every buck I could scrape up from every source I could find. I pacified them for a while though. I have another month before they call on me again. They won't find me at that same address, and if you'll come with me, we can go out west where I have some connections."

"I thought you said you stopped gambling and didn't owe any money."

"No more gambling – I only bet on sure things. I've been working for a bookie, which means that I get a cut of the money that other slobs lose."

"You lied to me, Charlie. You said no gambling and no debt. What happened to that technical opportunity you talked about?"

"The venture turned out to be a bust. It folded two months after I arrived. My debts aren't much more than I owed before. Beside, when you let me have money from our joint accounts, I'll pay it all off."

11

"I thought this was supposed to be a rekindling of the romantic flames, Charlie. You didn't bring me here for the dreamy setting or sex in the wilderness. You just came back to hit me up for more money...Well, it's not going to work! Get an honest job so that you can be proud of yourself again. I don't need any bloodsuckers. There are no more joint accounts. I put everything in my name right after you left. This started as a good day until the real you showed up to ruin it. They should label that vodka as truth serum."

Charlie sat down on a rock and opened his bottle of vodka. He took a lengthy drink from it. "Well, my dear, it's time for you to unbuckle that account and help your old Charlie wipe out his debts. That money you hid came out of our joint accounts, so you owe me half of it. You're still legally my wife. I could sue for my share."

"You could try, but you couldn't afford a lawyer good enough to get you anything. My friend, Judge Frobacher, has wanted me to file for divorce based on your having abandoned me. I think it's time for me to take him up on it."

"Now you're playing the Holier Than Thou card. Get off that soapbox. I know there are things in your past that say your Angela name is a joke."

"Let's talk about things in my past. I want you to be one of them. As soon as we're both sober, we're getting out of here, and you're going to take me home and then disappear, once and for all."

Charlie, obviously angry, stood up and glared down at her. "Right now we're still man and wife. I could leave you here without any phone or way to get home, and you'd starve to death before you reached civilization. Preachers don't know the ways of the wilderness. Wild animals might even eat you. You deserve a fate like that, picking on a nice guy like me."

"Charlie, you're even more of a loser now than you were when you left me earlier. Get rid of that vodka, and we'll head back to civilization as soon as you sober up. I *won't give you money, and I will file for divorce. You are bad news for me and my career."*

Charlie responded by chugging the last two inches of vodka in the bottle. "I'll get rid of the vodka, all right!" He threw the bottle at her, missing her right shoulder by three inches. The bottle bounced off a tree trunk and smashed on a boulder below. "Angela, you always were a self-satisfied, superior, holier-than-thou bitch. I should leave you here alone, but I won't because I don't want your death on my conscience. Unlike your pontificating self, I actually have a conscience."

"If you want to play rough, Charlie, I can do that too." She ran over to the fishing gear and pulled Charlie's serrated-blade fish-cleaning knife from its sheath. Charlie approached just as she grasped the knife.

"You don't scare me, you church-witch. Your rules say you can't judge, and you have to turn the other cheek. You're a fraud!"

Without another word, she walked forward, bringing her eyes within eight inches of Charlie's.

Angela plunged the blade into Charlie's left side. Then she withdrew it quickly and stabbed him a second time, thrusting the blade upward. She smiled at the amazement she saw in his eyes.

"I'm turning my cheek away from you and going far, far away. Enjoy spending eternity here, Charlie. It's time for you to make your peace with God."

...I grabbed my gear, took the car keys, and drove away. I didn't look back."

Arthur saw more passion in her face than ever before. "Did you kill him?"

Angela refocused on Arthur, and the fire in her eyes dimmed. "I thought so, but I didn't stick around to find out. I left him bleeding by the lake and drove away feeling satisfied that I had surgically removed him from my life. I didn't care about whether he lived or died; I just wanted to get away from there. I must have gone down a dozen unpaved intersecting trails before I finally reached a paved road."

"I'll guess that your return home marked the time when you began to treat me differently."

"That's right, Arthur; I had looked down on your church qualifications before that point, but after I stabbed Charlie, I began to fear you. You solved crimes, and I was a murderer. I thought my only chance for safety was to become so close to you that you would overlook my evil."

"I suspected that your change of attitude masked a hidden motive, but I didn't see you as a criminal. I thought it had something to do with your campaigning for a new church position. What triggered your collapse today?"

"I saw a teacher friend of mine, Julie Wyandt, in the congregation. She attended a conference in Denver about two months ago. She said she saw Charlie there and went up to greet him. When she called out to him, he denied being Charlie King. He identified himself as Oliver Parkworth and said that he was a science teacher in a junior high school. Julie said she was sure that it had been Charlie. After that, I couldn't decide whether I had killed him or not. When I saw Julie at your wedding, I became certain that Charlie had to be there too. I expected him to jump up from his seat and attack me.

"Whether he's dead or not, I'm a murderer. I enjoyed stabbing him and leaving him to bleed to death. I tried my best to kill him. My conscience tells me that I'll have to accept the consequences."

"If Charlie were still alive, wouldn't he have come back here earlier, either to confront you or to have you arrested?"

"You forget that the gamblers were still after him. He may have thought I did him a favor by causing Charlie King to die so that Oliver Parkworth might live in peace."

CHAPTER 3 – RECEPTION

When Arthur entered the banquet room at House of Ming, he found everyone seated at their tables, surrounding empty platters from Chinese appetizers. Joe Gonzalez was the first to spot Arthur; he stood and launched into a rendition, quickly joined by others, of *Here Comes the Groom*. Arthur responded with applause and thanks as he moved from table to table to greet the guests. He found Irma talking with Bishop Chandler. Arthur put his arm around her and addressed the Bishop.

"Howard, thanks so much for stepping in and making our marriage a reality. I really feel enhanced by being married to this beautiful woman."

Irma kissed him, and people throughout the hall started striking their glasses with their forks. Encouraged by all of the chiming sounds she kissed him again. "Arthur, I do believe that you're romantic after all."

He laughed and kissed her again.

Bishop Chandler said, "Arthur, fill me in on Angela's condition before I leave you two lovebirds. I've been thinking about retiring soon, and I need to know whether she'll be healthy enough for me to nominate her to be my successor."

"The tentative diagnosis is that she suffered a minor heart attack. She should fully recover before long, but I don't believe that she will remain a candidate for the episcopacy based on information she gave me. I suggest that you give her a few days for additional tests and then discuss her status and future with her personally."

Bishop Chandler frowned. "Is there a problem?"

Arthur looked at both Howard Chandler and Irma before responding. "There's a very large problem, and I'll be advising you about it after we return from our

15

honeymoon. In the meantime, I repeat my suggestion that you have a confidential discussion with Angela."

Arthur shook hands with the Bishop, and walked away holding hands with Irma.

She said, "I know that look, and I hope it doesn't mean that we've lost our honeymoon."

"No, Mrs. Blake, our time alone together will definitely go according to schedule; just plan to do some intense investigative work after we return."

"I like that Mrs. Blake part. Are you going to give me details soon?"

"Let's round up Penny and Joe for a briefing at the corner table in the back of the room. I think we'll need their help."

"Hold up a bit, Arthur; we'll have that discussion after we do some celebrating. This is our wedding reception, and you arrived late. For now, we'll convene at the head table and let Bobby Andrews perform his best man's toast. Renee says he's been working on it for several days."

"Sorry about that, Irma. You're right. There's a time and place for everything, and this reception has been a long time coming. Bring on the festivities."

Irma led Arthur by the hand over to the head table, pausing along the way to greet and exchange pleasantries with guests at the other tables. At one point, Arthur started to take a separate path, but Irma tugged at his hand, indicating that he was to stay with her.

"I've been waiting a long time for this evening, Arthur, so for at least a little while, we're going to be a couple instead of two individuals. Stay with me, and follow my lead."

"Yes, ma'am; I knew I married a strong assertive woman. This is going to be fun."

Together, they meandered among all of the occupied tables, greeting their guests, and then they departed the array of round tables for the long head table occupied by members of the wedding party. As they sat in their centered seats, the chiming of forks striking water and wine glasses rang out again. Irma and Arthur obliged their guests with a sensuous and lengthy kiss, drawing equally lengthy applause. Then Bobby Andrews stood up and the room eased into silence, both in honor of the ceremonial duty he was about to perform and in respect for the massive physical presence of the police chief in his black suit.

"I want to thank you all for attending the ceremony and this reception. Many of you know that this marriage was the culmination of a long period during which we watched the relationship between Arthur and Irma develop from a tiny spark to an ember and then on to a flickering and then a blazing flame. Talk like this used to bring a blush to Pastor Arthur's cheeks, but the lack of that reaction now shows how much he is enjoying his newfound marital bliss. At this time, please raise your glasses to Irma and Arthur. They are not only a well-matched couple, but they are best friends and colleagues too...Long may your love for each other grow and blossom, as an emerging seedling thrives and bears fruit over many years, withstanding many assaults from nature and man. We have great confidence that your life together will be an inspiration for the rest of us, and we hope that you will continue to dwell in our midst and be our friends. We drink to your health and the unlimited prospects for your life together."

Choruses of "Hear! Hear!" and similar salutes rang out from the various tables, punctuated at first by the clink of toasting glasses and then by the persistent clanging of forks against the sides of glasses. Irma and Arthur complied by kissing each other, and then Irma stood up to respond.

"Thank you all for coming to help us celebrate our special day. We want to especially thank you, Bobby, for your kind and upbeat toast. In the interest of some brevity, I'm offering my words rather than allowing Arthur to preach a sermon. Tony Fleming's staff will bring us our main courses following these speeches. I have only two comments. This day has been fun, except for the unfortunate collapse of Angela King at the church; we pray for her prompt recovery. My second comment is that ever since I was a little girl, I dreamed of this day – I guess all girls do – but I held out for Prince Charming, and I got him!"

Everyone applauded. Bobby Andrews stood up and said, "Disregard my previous words. Arthur's blushing again."

After the laughter died down, servers appeared from both ends of the room pushing stainless steel carts full of Chinese delicacies. Light instrumental music at a subdued level mixed with the conversations to suggest the murmurings of several small streams merging in turbulence. Arthur stood and walked over to thank Tony Fleming for the fine job he was doing on the food and atmospherics. As he passed the table occupied by Penny and Joe Gonzalez, his friends and associates from a covert government agency, he slipped Joe a folded note.

Joe unfolded the note on his lap and spread it out so that Penny could see it too. *Meet Irma and me at the back corner table when they serve dessert.*

CHAPTER 4 – ASSOCIATES

The village of Parkville, nestled in the northwest quadrant of Illinois, served as the base of operations for Pastor Arthur Blake and his associates whenever they faced a strange event that begged examination or a crime that required a solution. The odd circumstance is that most of these deviations from normal social behavior somehow involved his Parkville United Methodist church, a somewhat oversized institution that had expanded to its current size during the years following World War II when local residents incorrectly expected returning Chicago veterans and their families to move to the remote Parkville area. The church itself, located at the X-shaped intersection of Main and Jeffers, was a combination of a quaint original building, now used as a museum, backed up by a large two-story edifice combining the American colonial influences of its exterior, with British Anglican interior design concepts. Because its long dimension terraced across a hillside, it had an upper level parking lot on the Main Street side of the building and a lower level parking lot accessed from Jeffers Street. Across Jeffers from the church, Mallard Lake offered quiet vistas, hiking and jogging trails, and occasionally good fishing.

Against this restful backdrop, Pastor Arthur Blake operated to solve a wide range of mysteries and other problems while still attending to his pastoral duties at the church. Most members of his congregation considered his crime-solving activities a vicarious honor rather than a problem – even when their pastor's investigative challenges temporarily removed him from their presence at the church.

Arthur's strengths in attempting to unravel the tangled threads of a mystery lay in his creative thinking and well-honed sense of logic, tempered by his social and religious sensitivities to the thoughts and outlooks of people from many backgrounds. These talents stemmed from his experience as a trouble-shooting NASA spaceflight engineer along with his training and practice as a counseling pastor.

During the course of investigating the history and sudden death of his unique predecessor as pastor of Parkville UMC, Arthur had become friends with Parkville Police Chief Bobby Andrews and Irma Custis, then serving as County Medical Examiner. Together they worked on local aspects of the case and later, when their investigation revealed interstate and international complications, they joined forces with Penny and Joe Gonzalez, principals in a small covert government agency, who had been working on a related inquiry. Their small agency thrived by undertaking special federal assignments while not appearing on any government organization chart.

As time and additional investigations ensued, friendships and interdependencies among these five individuals strengthened. They grew into a team of associates, contributing their respective expertise and resources as the nature of an investigation and its jurisdiction demanded. Over the course of several years of assisting each other, Arthur and Irma had morphed into associates for life.

CHAPTER 5 – HUDDLE

The sound level within the banquet hall rapidly increased from the relative quiet of the main course, as servers materialized from several directions, clearing dishes and depositing desserts in one seamless operation. No one noticed the bride and groom departing their mingling routine for seats at a corner table in the rear of the hall. Penny and Joe Gonzalez left their table for the same destination, each grabbing two desserts from the closest trays along their route.

As they reached their target table, Penny said, "We love intrigue and surreptitiously passed notes, but we also love desserts, so we brought some for all of us. Does this gathering mean you want us to help you escape for your honeymoon trip? You do look spectacular, Irma, I hope they've taken lots of pictures of you two."

"Thanks for the compliment, Penny. I really do feel special. Unfortunately, Arthur has roped us into this little huddle because he has some non-wedding information to pass along, which will require us to ask a favor of you. Go ahead, Arthur; get this over with, so that we can concentrate on dancing."

"Thanks for joining us. I have this nasty habit of finding disturbing developments in apparently normal situations."

Joe said, "What do you mean? That sounds ominous."

"I arrived late at this reception because I stopped at Parkville Care Center to see how Angela King was doing. She suffered a minor heart attack from which she should fully recover. That part is the good news. The bad news is the story she told me about the events underlying the triggering shock that caused her collapse. In summary, Angela's husband Charlie left her several years ago due to a conflict over his gambling habits and the enforcers who were after him to make good on his debts. A few months ago, Charlie reappeared saying he had paid his debts and wanted to come back to her. They took a romantic fishing trip to Canada, but one night had too much to drink, and when Angela realized Charlie had only returned to look for money and still had the gambling collectors after him, she stabbed him. She thought she had killed him and had no qualms about it as she left for home, putting all thoughts of him behind her."

Irma said, "Wow, she's a lot tougher than I had thought."

Arthur made a T with his hands to ask for time out. "We'll have time to discuss this after I finish telling you Angela's story."

Joe shook his head. "You just blew it, Arthur. You're married to Irma now; don't cut her off."

"I'm minimizing the interruptions so that we can get to dancing and an early start on our honeymoon; is that acceptable, Irma?"

She laughed. "Joe, you have to admit he's a smooth talker. Go ahead with your story, Arthur. You have my blessing."

"I was amazed that Angela had been angry enough to stab her ex-husband, but the story gets more interesting. A couple of months ago at an educational conference in Denver Angela's friend Julie saw Charlie apparently quite well. She went up to him and called him by name. He said that he was not Charlie King. He called himself Oliver Parkworth and said that he was a science teacher at a junior high school. Angela didn't want to believe Julie's story, so she ignored it, but when she saw Julie at the wedding, Angela remembered the false identity tale, and the shock triggered her heart attack. That's the whole story...Penny and Joe, I'm hoping that you won't mind checking out the facts of her story while Irma and I enjoy our ritual vacation. I'm sure you wouldn't want us to have to stop everything in order to check it ourselves."

Penny said, "You're right, Irma, he is a smooth talker. You two deserve a honeymoon. Go in peace, and enjoy it. You may consider this an additional wedding gift from us."

Irma said, "Hear that, Arthur. They're giving us something else, too...Seriously; I really want to thank you for handling this one. I've had visions of Arthur running into something that needs investigation and forgetting about both the honeymoon and me. I have to admit that his setting up this little discussion shows that he is trying."

"Just to show you how much I'm trying, stand up for a minute."

Irma and the others looked puzzled, but she stood as requested. Arthur reached up and waved his right hand with a horizontal circular motion. The click of a switch in the speakers resulted.

Tony Fleming's voice emerged from the speakers. "Ladies and gentlemen, honored guests, please direct your attention to the rear corner of the room as our bride and groom step forward for their first dance as a married couple. Please welcome Pastor and Mrs. Arthur Blake."

The guests applauded, and Arthur offered Irma his arm. The very traditional Anniversary Waltz started playing. As they walked forward, Irma jabbed Arthur with her finger. "We didn't practice a waltz."

"Just follow my lead. I took lessons from some of the older ladies at church."

Apparently, those lessons succeeded, because Irma and Arthur were soon rotating around the dance floor in high style, nodding to the various guests as they passed them. Then the music stopped, and Tony invited the bride and groom to pick new partners for the beginning of the chain of dance numbers that would soon have everyone moving. Irma next danced with Arthur's father, Peter Blake, while Arthur danced with his mother, Janice. The original two dancers became four, and after relatively short musical selections, they changed sequentially to eight, sixteen, and thirty-two people on the dance floor. After that, Tony let the music continue longer and invited everyone else to join the dance party.

As they twirled around the floor, Penny removed her head from Joe's shoulder. "What do you think about the supposedly-murdered man who recovered and took on another identity rather than reporting the crime or looking for revenge?"

"That guy has to have a very big desire to disappear. I worry about people like that. He could turn out to be a potential terrorist."

"Then you're not buying the story about his running away from gangsters trying to collect gambling debts?"

"That sounds too much like a bad crime novel or movie. I'll be very surprised if it turns out to be true. Nowadays, gambling interests try to collect through the courts. Charlie King's wife is a wealthy church official, and no one has tried to collect a dime from her. What do you think, Penny?"

"I think Charlie King became Oliver Parkworth a long time ago, not when he recovered from the stab wound. You don't become a science teacher eligible to attend an education conference overnight."

CHAPTER 6 – HONEYMOON

As Irma prepared for their honeymoon trip, she spent a few minutes walking throughout her apartment and studying everything around her. "When we get back, we'll have to pack everything for our move to the parsonage."

Arthur looked up from the brochure he had been studying. "You don't have to give up this place. We can keep it as the office for our ABC Consultants investigating business. We'd only have to make a few changes to the furniture."

"I know that's one possibility, but it seems wasteful to have two places now that we're married."

"It would be a business expense if we used this place for that dedicated purpose. Also, there will be times when we won't want all the folks at church to know what we're doing."

"That sounds deceptive, but I understand what you mean. I'm happy to delay the decision for a while. Top priority is the honeymoon anyway. Did you tell anyone where we're going?"

"Not a single one – I let everyone think we were still planning to go to Guatemala, per our discussions a while back."

"We can still go there, if it's important to you."

"No, Irma, I think your idea is great and more practical too. In Guatemala, we'd be reliving some of the events of our last case. Let's go where we'll have more fun. We need a break from anything to do with investigations."

"That sounds great to me. What's our schedule?"

"We drive to Rockford early tomorrow morning to catch the 5:00 AM airport bus. That gets us to the O'Hare terminal at 6:30 AM in time to go through security, snack, and take an 8:30 AM flight."

"See, I'm changing you already, Arthur. You do know how to plan ahead."

"That's because I'm looking forward to getting away with you."

"That schedule and your refreshingly romantic attitude say that we had better head for bed early tonight. Would you prefer here in my apartment or the parsonage? We have a choice now."

"I heard myself telling you a few minutes ago that there will be times when we won't want the church folks to know what we're doing. This is definitely one of them."

CHAPTER 7 – CHARLIE OR OLIVER

Joe stood up and stretched. He had been searching online for thirty minutes, and he needed a break. As he walked to the kitchen for some coffee, he wondered whether his recent increase in consumption of that bean brew was due to his friendship with Arthur Blake. Arthur's passion for coffee was a running joke among his close friends. Joe walked behind Penny who was working on a Sudoku puzzle, and massaged her shoulders.

"Oh, that feels good. The combination of having time to work on a recreational puzzle in our own house and having your loving touch, make me completely sure that we did the right thing in exchanging our Washington apartment for this small-town home."

"I agree, Penny. The cases stemming from Arthur's church and family kept us commuting to Parkville anyway. It's rewarding to have a place of our own, and yes, I'm beginning to join you in thinking about children as well. This will be a much better atmosphere than DC for raising them."

"Thanks, Joe; I've been very careful to avoid that subject since we transplanted ourselves here. You went along with me on the house, so I wanted to give you the option of discussing children or not. Now that you've brought it up, we'll be able to discuss the topic from time to time, right?"

"Sure, Penny, all aspects of raising a family will be open for discussion. Right now, though, I'd like your input on Charlie King and whether he's now alive and well, playing the role of Oliver Parkworth."

"You sound as though you have doubts."

"I'm frustrated because Charles King is such a common name that I found three hundred and seventy-

27

eight million entries for it on Google Search. Even though I haven't covered all of them, I've scanned enough to suggest that I may not find anything appreciable about Angela's ex-husband. I'm supposed to be finding out whether Charlie King took on the new identity of Oliver Parkworth, but I'm not even convinced that Charlie King is a real person. That may have been an earlier assumed identity."

"Now that's an interesting speculation. Maybe Angela couldn't kill him because he's a vampire or some other paranormal being."

"I won't go that far, but it's possible that he has gone through several identities. Angela said he had an engineering degree from a small school in Rhode Island, but I checked every school I could find, and I came up empty."

"Do you think he's a criminal?"

"Right now, I'm guessing that he's either a con man working some kind of fraud, a spy for another country, or a terrorist sleeper agent."

Penny said, "Well, even if he's a con man, he's working in multiple states, so we should have no trouble establishing federal jurisdiction."

"Then you agree that our favor to Arthur and Irma is likely to result in a case for us?"

"I'm afraid so; we have to find this guy and discover his scheme. Potentially, any failure to check him out could result in a terrorism disaster. How did you fare on checking the Oliver Parkworth persona?"

"That's my next step. I hope that I'll discover more useful information than I did with Charlie. At least we know that he's a science teacher in a junior high school."

"No, we only know that he gave Angela's friend, Julie Wyandt, that story."

CHAPTER 8 – FUN TIME

Irma looked radiant as they left the Haunted Mansion ride. Disney World's magic temporarily removed years from their chronological ages. They held hands as they walked toward the Hall of Presidents.

"You appear to have really enjoyed the ghosts, Irma."

"I felt as though I was among old friends. I did enough autopsies as medical examiner to at least occasionally wonder about ghosts and the afterlife."

"Are you saying that you believe in ghosts?"

"Not exactly, but I do believe that the dead remain alive in some sense so long as people keep remembering them. It's not exactly the biblical version of what happens, but I'm comfortable with that."

"I think your view is compatible with traditional church thinking. We say that the body dies, but the soul lives on. It's difficult to define the soul. In a very real sense I consider a vibrant memory of a deceased person to be a glimpse of his or her soul."

"I'm not sure that all theologians would agree with you on that view, but it's pleasant to have you share some of my opinions. I don't expect you to agree with all of them. What did you like most about the Haunted Mansion?"

"You're going to think I'm unimaginative, but I admire the clever engineering they use to produce effects like the stretching room and the dancing ghosts. The first time I came here I accepted everything at face value, but now I like to analyze how they do things."

"I'm not at all surprised by your being analytical; it's part of who you are. I didn't know that you had been here before. There's still a lot we don't know about each other. For the record, this is my first visit here."

"Well, then I'll have to admit that I have been here six times, and every trip is equally pleasant – from a tourist point of view. This visit is the most special because you're with me and we're married. Nothing is more special than that."

She squeezed his hand as they walked. "I should have expected that information. You did work for NASA at Cape Canaveral, so this place was just down the road. Newcomers or old-timers, we are special together."

"I'll try not to spoil your fun at the Hall of Presidents by talking about the engineering that went into that show."

"It doesn't matter. We're here together, and we don't have to think about church problems, investigations, or anything else. We'll just enjoy the park and do some people watching. That's one of my favorite things that I haven't told you about."

"I'm a people-watcher too. At a place like this, I especially like to watch and listen to the kids. We have fun here as adults, but it was designed for children, especially those who accept everything as being real."

"Not all of them are joyful. Look at that family over there. The parents are having a hard time getting their children to try things. Let's drift by them and see what we can overhear."

Irma and Arthur did their best to act casual and exchange trivial comments as they passed within earshot of the two adults and three children. The oldest child, a boy, appeared to be about nine years old, while his two younger sisters looked to be seven-year-old twins. The red-haired boy protested loudly, while the blond girls held hands and edged farther away from the adult couple.

"You can't bribe us with trips to places like this. You aren't our real parents. They put us up for foster care because Dad left home, and Mom is sick, but they're both still alive, and when I get older, I'm going to find a way to put our family back together."

The woman said, "We know that you still love your birth parents, but we want you to think of us as your second set of parents, we want to do the best we can for you. This is a famous and wonderful place. Don't you think you could relax and enjoy it, at least a little bit?"

The girls started to cry, and the boy said, "You can't be our second set of parents. They pay you to take care of us. We want to go back home."

The tall man bent down toward the boy and said, "You'd better learn to make the best of this. We're trying to treat you as though you were our own children. Your mother is not going to get well, and no one even knows where your father is. This is the best deal you'll get from now on. At least we were willing to care for all three of you. Anyone else would have split you up."

The boy stood silent and sullen for a few seconds. Then he walked over to his sisters and put his arms around them. "You can't split us up. We're the only family we have left."

The woman addressed the boy, "Don't worry, Alan; we'll work this out. Let's all go get some ice cream, and then we'll let each of you choose something you'd like to do. Would that be all right?"

Alan looked at his sisters; they stopped crying and nodded. Then he took their hands and slowly followed the woman. The tall man followed at the rear of the procession.

As the group moved farther away, Arthur said to Irma, "That was a classic case of good-cop/bad-cop as applied to controlling children."

Irma continued to watch the family as they walked toward the restaurants. "We've talked about adopting children, but we haven't considered whether they would come to think of us as their real family, or if they would just tolerate us. I'm beginning to worry."

"First of all, we're still on our honeymoon, and not quite ready for parenthood. Second, there's not a child in the world who could resist your attentiveness as a mother. Those children are in foster care. That's a potentially unstable relationship. We would be looking to adopt and make a lifetime commitment. That makes a much different impression on a child. We all long for stability, both parents and children, and we're in a great position to offer that. Right now, I want to follow that woman's lead and offer you some ice cream or a soda. How do you feel about the old-fashioned picture of one drink with two straws as a token of my sharing everything with you?"

"Oh, that would be a delight. You might turn out to be an acceptable husband after all."

"And this evening we'll head for Epcot where I'll wine and dine you at restaurants from several different countries."

"I'm not sure we'll enjoy all of that weight gain. How about making the rounds for appetizers and drinks only?"

"That sounds good to me. Then we'll head back to the hotel for some just-the-two-of-us time."

"That sounds like a great menu for the evening. I wouldn't even mind if we skipped some of the early courses and headed straight for our dessert together.

CHAPTER 9 – ANGELA'S STORY

They had removed some of the tubes and had declared her to be in stable condition. She would have to remain in the hospital for only one more day prior to transfer to a rehabilitation center. Still, Angela felt edgy. Bishop Chandler had telephoned and said he would visit her shortly. She didn't have to consult her vital signs monitor to know that her pulse rate and blood pressure had accelerated following that call. What would she tell the Bishop? How much had Arthur told him? She assumed that it would have been enough to keep her from reversing field and claiming innocence. She would have to tell the truth, both because of her religious convictions and because Arthur and Charlie could come forward and expose her lies.

She heard a knock on the half-open door, and a smiling Bishop Chandler entered. "Hello, Angela; it's good to see you looking so well after your ordeal. You had us all worried."

Angela gave up any pretense of hope for advancement. "Howard, I don't know what Arthur told you, but it's time for us to have a frank discussion. I'm no longer in the running to succeed you after you retire. I doubt that I'm even suitable for keeping my own job."

"Arthur declined to get into the details of your problems until after his honeymoon, but I have plenty of time to sit with you and receive your story first-hand."

"Fair enough...I have a tale that will shock you more than just a little."

Howard Chandler nodded in acceptance of her statement, but he refrained from showing any emotion. "Would you mind giving me the detailed story?"

Angela debated internally for what seemed a long time before responding. "Four years ago, my husband, Charlie, left me for the stated purpose of joining a small engineering company to work on a new product venture. Because Charlie was an engineer and had abandoned his local engineering career in favor of something flashy and new somewhere else, I attacked Arthur Blake with my frustrations when he arrived in Parkville. I saw Arthur, another engineer, as a latecomer to the ministry who might decide to abandon it when offered some new tempting incentive in the future. I learned later that the underlying reason for Charlie's departure was the combination of his gambling debts and my denouncing from the pulpit those who gamble."

"Did you change your opinion of Arthur and his engineering background after you learned about Charlie's gambling problem?"

"No, Bishop, I tried to have it both ways. I continued to blame Arthur because of my feelings about the ways of engineers, even after I learned about the gambling debt angle on why Charlie had left."

"Might we have guided Charlie through church agencies for support?"

"That was not an option. By the time I realized Charlie's problem was the gambling losses, he had gone and left no contact information."

"Sorry for the interruptions...please continue your story."

"Charlie had been out of my life for almost four years, when he suddenly reappeared and said that he wanted to re-enter my life. He told me that his gambling ways were behind him and that he had eliminated his indebtedness. At first, I rejected his appeals, but he used his smooth-talking romantic ways to convince me that we could have a healthy relationship. I softened my objections, and after a few passionate evenings, we felt certain that we would be able to resume our married relationship."

"I take it that you had not taken any legal steps after Charlie left."

Angela raised her back support on her bed and gave the Bishop a slightly stern look. *Why does he keep interrupting me?* "I had thought about filing for divorce on a few occasions, but since I had no other man in my life, I kept putting it off. Anyway, he suggested that we should repeat the fishing trip we had taken for our honeymoon, and I took it as him showing me his romantic side. I agreed, and we set off for Canada. We flew to North Bay, Ontario and then rented a Jeep for exploring farther north. We didn't have a preselected destination, but kept driving until we found a remote spot with good fishing potential. It felt like an adventure, romance in the great northwoods."

"But it didn't turn out the way you expected?"

"Didn't Arthur tell you the whole story?"

"He indicated that something bad had happened that would affect your future, but he wanted to withhold the details until he returned from his honeymoon."

"He's more sympathetic than I would have guessed. When he told you that, he made sure you would hear everything directly from me, so that he wouldn't distort anything.

"Anyway, we drove north for about half a day and then wandered the side roads until we found a perfect spot. We set up our tent and did some successful fishing. The first day turned out very well; it even included several rounds of the passion I had missed for so long. After that, I was pretty much at peace with Charlie and the world around me.

"That evening we brought out the beer and the bottles of vodka that we had purchased in North Bay. We had a party. Everything went very well until the alcohol loosened Charlie's lips and removed his inhibitions while we sat by the campfire...

Angela repeated a slightly more detailed version of the story she had told Arthur, deleting a few of the more disturbing slang quotations in deference to the Bishop's spiritual position.

...so, you see that I'm about as bad as possible. I've broken the sixth commandment. I murdered my husband."

Bishop Howard Chandler mumbled a brief prayer for her physical and spiritual recovery and left Angela's hospital room silently, his head and shoulders slumped forward.

CHAPTER 10 – JULIE WYANDT

Julie answered her front doorbell, but using caution, she opened the door only a few inches so that she could slam the door shut if she found danger on her doorstep. Through the narrow slit, she saw a man and a woman in business attire. The woman held up an open leather folder displaying an identification card and a badge.

"Mrs. Wyandt, my name is Penny Gonzalez, and this is my husband Joe. We represent a government agency, and we would like to ask you a few questions if you have a little time."

Julie opened the door halfway. "It's Miss; I'm not married. Am I in trouble for something?"

Penny smiled to ease Julie's apprehension. "There's no problem at all; we're just looking for some information from you. May we come in?"

Julie thought about it for a few seconds, and then she opened the door the rest of the way. "We can talk in the kitchen if you don't mind. I reduce housework by staying out of the more formal rooms."

Penny continued to smile as she entered the house. "That would be fine, Miss Wyandt, we don't want to interfere with your normal routine."

They all walked past the stairway and through a swinging door into a bright yellow kitchen. Julie motioned for them to sit at the high table and then joined them, pulling over an extra stool from its storage space under a counter.

Penny noted that their host did not offer them coffee or tea. She was still being cautious and wanted to keep this interview short. "Julie, we're here because Angela King informed Pastor Blake that you had seen her estranged husband at an education conference where he claimed to be someone else. We'd like to learn some more details about that encounter, but we also want to inform you that Angela is recovering well from her collapse at Arthur and Irma's wedding. I understand you were there as were we. Arthur is our close friend."

Julie visibly relaxed. "You're saying that this isn't entirely an official visit. I feel better now that I know you're friends with Pastor Blake and were at the wedding. I decided to attend at the last minute, not because I'm close to either Arthur or Irma, but because of my long friendship with Angela. In all of the years of our friendship, I had never seen her ministering at a church, so I thought I would do so on this happy occasion. As it turned out, Angela's collapse kept me from seeing her officiate this time, also."

Joe had deferred to Penny up to this point, but he wanted to keep the conversation on track. "Miss Wyandt, what was it about the person you saw at that conference that convinced you he was Charlie King?"

"As I said, Angela and I go way back together, and I recognized both his face and that nervous habit he has of holding his left arm behind his back while he stands and talks with people. Most folks either keep both arms at their sides or both behind them, but Charlie keeps returning to a stance with only his left hand behind him."

"Did he show any surprise when he saw you?"

"No, Mr. Gonzalez, he didn't. For a while, his calm demeanor had me thinking that I must have made a mistake, but then I caught him ordering a margarita made with vodka instead of tequila. That was always Charlie's signature drink; it would have been too much of a coincidence for a similar-looking stranger to fancy the same unusual drink."

Penny asked, "Who did he say he was?"

"He identified himself as Oliver Parkworth and said that he was a science teacher. If he told me where he was from or the name of the school where he taught, it didn't register. I was still confused by his saying he wasn't Charlie."

Joe asked, "Do you feel 100 percent sure that he was Charlie King?"

"I'll say that I'm at least ninety percent sure. I'm not infallible, but I was and am convinced he was Charlie."

Penny said, "I have just two more questions. Was he part of a group, and did many people appear to know him?"

"Thank you for asking that question. There was something strange about him that had bothered me, but I couldn't quite identify it - the way he interacted with others. He appeared to be alone, but wherever he went, people gathered around him and wanted to get his attention and talk with him. He appeared to be a celebrity, or at least very well known. I only managed to speak with him after working my way through the crowd around him. I still don't know why he was the center of attention."

Penny looked at Joe, and he nodded in response to her unasked question. Then she thanked Julie for her assistance. They stood and prepared to leave. As they approached the front door, Julie said, "If you see Angela, please give her my best wishes for a full recovery. I haven't seen her that much lately because of all her important church work. Rumor has it that she's in line to become the next Bishop of her church conference."

CHAPTER 11 – NEWLYWEDS

Irma unlocked the door to her apartment and froze in the doorway staring forward. She could hear thumps and grunts behind her, but she gave them little attention. She was jarred out of her reverie by Arthur's voice.

"Irma, I'm carrying a lot of luggage, and I have to set it down somewhere, would you mind going inside so that I'll have some room?"

She walked into the apartment and looked around. "Sorry, Arthur, but when you get in here you'll understand why I stopped. I thought I had entered the wrong unit."

"What do you mean?" Arthur came through the door carrying two suitcases and wearing a backpack. He looked around and answered his own question. "We've been reverse robbed. Instead of taking things out, they brought stuff in."

Someone had stacked their old furniture into the far end of the combination living and dining room. They stepped forward to confront a massive cherry wood antique dining table with eight chairs, a matching china display cabinet, two antique wooden desks, and a side table from a similar period.

Irma said, "There are cards on each piece of furniture." She opened the card on the dining room table and read it aloud. "Welcome home, Lovebirds. We remembered Arthur saying that he wanted to wait for antiques until he was living somewhere other than the parsonage, so enjoy this dining set with our blessings. We'll expect some dinner invitations...Love, Mom and Dad."

Arthur opened the envelope on one of the desks. "This one says, 'We think you should have a real desk instead of the dining room table...Love, Penny and Joe.'"

"Is the other desk from them too? Check it out, Arthur."

"The card on the second desk says, 'Ditto...Love, Renee, Bobby, and Thelma Lou Andrews.' How did they know I would open the other card first so that they could just echo the sentiment?"

"It must be the kind of insight that comes from being a police chief. Look at the card on the table."

Arthur opened the card, read it, and laughed. "You require a proper side table to display your one-year supply of weekly pastry shipments from our bakery...Love, Shirley, Walter, and Jeremy Hadley."

He walked over to Irma, put his arms around her, and gave her a kiss. "Welcome home, Irma. Our friends have helped us decide to live here and restrict the use of the parsonage to church business. I think that's a wise choice."

"I do, too. Newlyweds deserve some privacy. Can we still use this place as our ABC Consultants headquarters?"

"We'll have to do that. We each have an antique desk, and Jeremy gets the side table."

"That should work, Arthur, but remind Jeremy to call us first before any morning visits."

"They must have had a big crew to get all this heavy furniture up here. We'll have to get them to come back and help us move the old pieces to the parsonage."

"And I'm going to have to get started on writing thank you notes and planning parties. We're going to be busy."

Arthur opened two more envelopes he had found on the kitchen table. "We will be busy indeed. The first note says that Penny and Joe have started their inquiries about Charlie King, and they've already had intriguing results."

"What's the second envelope?"

"The Bishop wants me to meet with him as soon as possible."

CHAPTER 12 – BISHOP CHANDLER

The Rockford Northern Illinois Conference office served as the Bishop's headquarters when he ventured out from Chicago to work with the northwestern districts. Sarah, the receptionist, greeted Arthur and led him into a small meeting room where he would await the Bishop. She promised to return shortly with coffee. Arthur expected this meeting to be about Angela King, but there was always the possibility that the Bishop wanted to discuss a new appointment for him to a different church. Arthur would not welcome that development so soon after getting married.

Sarah returned with mugs of coffee for him and the Bishop. She set them down on opposite sides of the meeting table and left just as Bishop Chandler arrived.

"Good morning, Arthur; I hope I haven't kept you waiting. I selected this room so we'd have fewer distractions, and so I wouldn't be tempted to answer phone calls."

"I've been here only a few minutes, Bishop."

Bishop Chandler sat down, placing an ominous-looking file folder on the table. Arthur recognized it as his personnel file.

"Arthur, I've enjoyed following your career, in part because it has shown how the tools of the ministry are well suited to solving unconventional problems. Someday we'll have to assign you to recruiting new candidates for the ministry. You would be able to dispel any notions that it is a boring career."

"Is that recruiting project the reason for this meeting?"

"No, Arthur, we need to have a confidential discussion about the information we've each learned from Angela King. She said that her account to me of the events on her

Canadian fishing trip was more detailed than the one she gave to you on your wedding day, but she also indicated that you know of subsequent events that you might want to share with me. It's a very disturbing matter, both for the sake of the church's reputation and for Angela's future."

"Did she try to justify her actions to you or to back away from her admission to me of violence against her estranged husband?"

"No, she gave me a detailed account of how she stabbed him after she discovered that he had come back to her looking for money rather than love."

"Did she argue that she acted in self-defense?"

"I'd give a 'not really' answer to that one. A good attorney might be able to build on that argument, but I had the feeling that while Charlie did threaten her with abandonment in the woods, he carefully avoided any suggestions of physical harm to her. What did she mean by saying that I should talk with you about later events?"

"According to Angela, months after the incident in Canada, her teacher friend, Julie Wyandt, went to an education conference in Denver and saw someone she swore was Charlie, and this individual was in good health. When Julie approached him, he said that she had made a mistake and that he was a science teacher named Oliver Parkworth. I've had some associates attempting to confirm Julie Wyandt's information, but I haven't been home long enough to check with them."

Bishop Chandler leaned back in his chair. "Then there's at least a chance that Charlie is alive, and Angela isn't a murderer."

"Angela still considers herself a murderer, even if she flubbed her attempt."

"What would the law say?"

"That's a very interesting question. The only evidence of a crime we have is Angela's confession to it. She'll make it increasingly difficult to avoid prosecution if she keeps

43

telling her story to others. The supposed crime took place in another country, out of U.S. jurisdiction. Charlie might be alive, but if he were using an alias, he wouldn't be able to press charges without revealing it. If he indeed survived and is healthy, he may not even want to charge Angela."

"What if Angela decided that the incident in Canada never happened?"

"If someone convinced her to take that stance, that person could be charged with effectively destroying evidence of a crime. On the other hand, if Angela were to decide that she had recounted a dream, it would be difficult to prove that a crime had occurred. It would be like the old Zen Koan: 'If a tree falls in the forest, and there is no one there to hear it, does it make any noise?'"

CHAPTER 13 – PARKVILLE UMC

Arthur and Irma drove to the church and entered from the lower parking lot. They climbed the stairs to the sanctuary and offices, each wondering whether the staff and congregation would treat them differently, now that they were married. That question disappeared as soon as they encountered the secretary, Shirley Hadley, in the church office.

"Welcome home, you two; I hope your journey and stay were pleasant. I hate to say this, Arthur, but with all of your past investigations, we've learned to keep things going quite well during your absences. You don't have to worry about any of your pet procedures having been disrupted, but I will give you some updates."

Arthur said, "As long as we are having everything run on automatic pilot, I will thank you and have a piece of your day-old pastry from Hadley's Bakery. I missed you too, Shirley."

"Don't say that; your wife will get jealous. Irma, you're going to have to teach him how to behave like a married man."

"I'm not worried if he flirts. He's a typical pastor – seldom practices what he preaches. Anyway, the honeymoon was great, but it's good to be back."

Arthur said, "And thanks for all of those surprises we found in Irma's apartment, both furniture and pastry subscription. Who moved all of that stuff in there?"

"First of all, Arthur, you're going to have to watch your phrasing; that apartment belongs to both of you now. I hope we did the proper thing, assuming you would settle in there rather than the parsonage. When we all decided on antique furniture, your dad told us that you wanted your antiques to be in a real home and not the parsonage.

If you change your mind, we can move things again. The main movers were Bobby Andrews, Joe Gonzalez, Wally Sanborn, and our son Jeremy. I went along to make sure they didn't leave a mess, and your father made sure that they didn't scratch any of the antiques. Those pieces are almost living creatures to him – a case of true love."

Irma said, "It sounds as though you did everything perfectly, Shirley. Yes, we have decided to live in our apartment. We hope the church folks won't think we want to distance ourselves from them, but it feels right to have a place of our own."

"I think you two are being smart. Arthur should be available to the congregation, but not too available. Anyway, things are going smoothly. Wally Sanborn did one of his "Appreciate Those Who Serve" sermons in anticipation of Veterans Day. He invited several active-duty soldiers who were home on leave, and we had a contingent from the Veterans Group Residence next door. After the service we had a potluck luncheon, and it turned into a real party."

Arthur said, "That's great. The best churches run themselves, with the laity needing only minor guidance from their pastors. Your celebration also relieves me of any guilt feelings I might have harbored for not having been here."

Shirley came over to them and gave them each a hug. "Thanks to both of you for all you have done for this place and my family. We're all looking forward to some special times with you as a couple. Irma, thank you especially for letting Jeremy join your ABC Consultants investigation group. He feels that he's found his ideal career, whether it is with you or with some official organization."

Irma said, "Shirley, he's a natural for investigations, and he has been a great help. Everything appears to have gone very well in our absence. Are you sure that you didn't have any problems at all?"

"Well, there might be a couple of matters that require Arthur's attention."

Arthur had been thinking about something else while the women talked, but he refocused his thoughts at the mention of his name. "What kind of matters, Shirley?"

"Sue Willoughby had a knee replacement operation after she damaged her left knee in a jogging fall. That surgery didn't go well. Bill Martin says that the church furnace is beyond repair and that we need a new one as soon as possible. Ed Jensen's wife Martha has been having more health problems that they don't completely understand, and Ed would like the two of you to help them review what the doctors have told them."

Arthur said, "Maybe I am needed around here after all. Is there anything else, Shirley?"

"We had a couple of drifters come by looking for assistance a few days ago. I gave them some leftover food from the last meeting of the quilting group, and I gave them some clothing from the upcoming rummage sale. After they left, Wally and I discovered that some of the collection money from the desk in the counting room had disappeared. I don't know for sure that those drifters took it, but the loss coincided with the timing of their visit."

"You did have an interesting week. How much money was missing?"

"We think it was about seventy-five dollars."

"That amount won't break us, and it's the church's mission to support the poor, but I'll look into it. I don't want to blame those two without checking on it. Were there any messages that require an immediate follow-up?"

"Not really, but Penny Gonzalez called and said that they would be in Iowa visiting Bob Caspar and his family for a day or two. She'll call you when they return."

CHAPTER 14 – BOBBY ANDREWS

Parkville Police Chief Bobby Andrews had long been a good friend and investigation partner for Pastor Arthur Blake, but their relationship had grown even closer after Bobby's wife, Renee, gave birth to their daughter, Thelma Lou. Her premature birth had led to early medical problems that a unique specialist had successfully treated. Prior to their successful resolution, Arthur and Irma had been reliable supporters offering encouragement and prayers for their family. Bobby reminisced about his pride at being their best man while he waited for Arthur to arrive at his office. A knock on the office doorpost interrupted Bobby's thoughts.

"Hello, Arthur; welcome back from your honeymoon. Are you getting back to a normal schedule, or will things never again be normal, now that you're a married man?"

"I guess I'm as normal as I'll ever be, Bobby. I came by because the church had a minor crime, and I wanted to find out whether this was something isolated or if there have been others like it."

"Stop right there, Arthur. Was your church visited by a couple of homeless people or itinerants?"

"Shirley called them drifters."

"And did your people try to be good to them and give them something?"

"Shirley said she gave them leftover food and clothing items from the pending rummage sale."

"And did she subsequently find that some money was missing?"

"You are psychic. I take it that this has happened before."

"These guys travel all over this part of the state. They appear to be homeless, and church people always want to

48

help them. While Shirley was getting food and clothes for them, one of them was going through desk drawers and cabinets looking for valuables. The Illinois State Police have put out a bulletin on them. They'll catch those guys sometime, but don't expect to get your money back. At least so far, they've been smart enough to hit each town only once. They probably won't be back here any time soon, but if they return we'll be ready for them."

"Do they drive from town to town?"

"They have an old car they use for more remote places like Parkville, but they travel by train when one serves their target town. They typically go from church to church and then take a train back to Chicago. You don't have to feel that your church was unusually susceptible to this scheme. They got away with money plus a pair of silver candlesticks from the Catholic church."

"I guess church people are too trusting. We'll post notices for everyone at our church to be on alert for this in the future.

"While I'm here, I wanted to thank you for your part in the delivery of antique furniture to our apartment. I'm sure that stuff was very heavy."

"No problem, Arthur; your dad ran the show and told us exactly how to handle each piece. He really knows his furniture. I already told him to look out for a nice piece for me to give Renee for our anniversary."

"Have you heard anything more about the state of Angela King's health? Is she still at that rehab facility?"

"I think she is, but I haven't been following her situation. It's time for me to concentrate on police matters. She doesn't fall into that category, does she?"

"Let's say not at the present time, and not within your jurisdiction. I'll advise you if that status changes."

CHAPTER 15 – JOE AND PENNY

Penny and Joe Gonzalez had just returned from visiting their old friends Bob and Paula Caspar and Bob's Aunt Bertha in Monticello, Iowa. They were tired; so they left their luggage and jackets in the hallway and relaxed on the living room couch before unpacking.

Joe said, "You've convinced me once again that our move to Parkville from DC was a good plan. I'm going to enjoy the convenience of exchanging visits with the Caspar crowd. We go way back together, and it will be fun to keep our relationship active."

"If it hadn't been for the Caspars and the mystery of Aunt Bertha's father's actions during World War II, we might not have met Arthur and Irma, or ended up moving here."

"I think we were destined to meet them, Penny. Don't forget that our personal favors for Bob Caspar's Aunt Bertha, and our professional interest in tracking lost World War II treasures both led us to this town and Arthur's church. I often wonder how much of our life planning is due to free will and how much is guided from above or by pure destiny."

"I'm not sure I know what pure destiny is, but I follow your thinking. Once we started working with Arthur, we discovered a chain of interesting cases."

"They didn't all start with him. During that first one, we were working on our own, and he helped us solve it. Do you think that destiny pulled the two of us together, Penny?"

"Heck, no; I selected you and kept all the competitors away while I worked to get you to notice me."

"You didn't have to work very hard; I noticed your Anglo sophistication right away. Your version does convince me that you and Irma were destined to be friends. You each knew what man you wanted and went after him."

"Thanks, Joe; you just said that you were attracted to me because of a racial stereotype. Would you like to withdraw that statement?"

"Sure, I'll revise it to having been attracted to you because of a sexy stereotype." Joe reached over to Penny and pulled her toward him. The conversation transitioned into mutual physical expressions of affection that ended only when the telephone rang. Joe tried unsuccessfully to keep Penny from leaving the couch to answer the telephone.

"Hello...Yes, Arthur, we've just returned from visiting Bob and Paula Caspar. They, their Aunt Bertha, and their kids all send their greetings and congratulations to you and Irma...

"Yes, we interviewed Julie Wyandt, and we'll have feedback for you about our visit with her when we next get together...I'll tell you right now that there are several mysteries surrounding Charlie King. We have people in Washington working on them. Come over here tomorrow mid-morning, and we'll fill you in on the investigation status. You can tell us about your honeymoon trip." Penny replaced the handset on its cradle and returned to the couch. She smoothed her disarrayed hair with her hand.

"Now, Joe, what were we doing when we were interrupted?"

CHAPTER 16 – DRIFTERS

Their so-called office was the back room of Winoski's Tavern. Stan Winoski let them use it and occasionally sleep there for fifteen percent of their take. George Felkis, better known as *Feckless* sat at a card table counting paper money and change he had emptied from ten plastic grocery bags. He wrote a total on a sticky-note pad and yelled over to *Grumpy* Horrigan, "We did better than yesterday. We ended up with one hundred eighty-seven dollars and sixty-three cents. That's close to thirty-five dollars per church. We could have had more if so many people didn't donate by checks. How did we do on the stuff they gave us? Can we sell much of it?"

Grumpy reached over to a pile of clothing and retrieved a brown tweed sport jacket. "The only good stuff today was clothing. We can usually get about ten dollars for a suit and five dollars for a sport jacket, but this tweed jacket should be worth more. I think it's your size if you want to keep it. I figure we can make about sixty dollars by selling the rest of the clothes and the other junk."

Feckless said, "Yeah, I'll try that coat. It'll be good for when we go to the racetrack. With your stuff, we pulled in close to two hundred and fifty dollars. If we could do that every day, we'd be golden. The trouble is that we have to keep moving to new areas so that we don't hit the same church more than once a year. Maybe we should go to veterans' halls and talk up our military backgrounds while we look for contributions."

"Just be sure to avoid talking about our being kicked out of the Army for going AWOL and then getting picked up by the police in a drug raid."

"We'd just say that we got out, but couldn't land jobs because of psychological problems. That's almost the truth."

"We couldn't get jobs because we don't like to work hard."

"Grumpy, not liking to work or stick to a schedule is a psychological problem. Anyway, this jacket fits me pretty well. There are some papers in the inside pocket. I hope they're worth something."

"Are they stocks or bonds?"

Feckless opened the envelope and examined the papers. Then he gave out a low whistle. "These may be worth as much as stocks or bonds. The envelope's marked for someone named Charles King in one of those small towns we hit today. This must have been his jacket. Anyway, the envelope contains birth certificates for six different people. They look genuine."

"How are they worth money?"

"I have a strong feeling that if we contact this King guy, he's going to want to buy them back."

CHAPTER 17 – BRUNCH MEETING

Joe opened the front door wide and gestured with a sweeping arm motion for his guests to enter. "Come on in, newlyweds. Throw your jackets on the couch; we're all set up for brunch and discussions."

In the dining room, the array of goodies greeted Irma and Arthur with the mixed aromas of coffee, bacon, orange slices, eggs, plus a few unidentifiable blends. Penny had prepared a royal array of food offerings on a long side table while leaving the dining room table clear for eating and discussion space.

Irma said, "I thought this was going to be something simple like pastry and coffee. Now that you have a home of your own, Penny, you're showing off your hostess skills."

"Actually, Joe helped with a lot of it. He's starting to play with cooking too. We just felt that our first reunion after your honeymoon should be a little special. We figured we'd enjoy ourselves while we listened to your tales from Guatemala."

Arthur had been pouring a cup of coffee, and he almost spilled it when he rapidly turned to face Penny. "Double oops – one for the coffee I came close to dripping on your carpet, and one for the fact that we didn't clue you in about our honeymoon."

Joe said, "Here's a napkin for the coffee that spilled into your saucer. What's the confusion about your trip?"

Arthur paused and shrugged his shoulders while looking at Irma. "We changed our plans at the last moment. We decided we didn't want to go to a place that had been involved in one of our cases."

Irma said, "Arthur and I were looking for a spot that would let us just relax and not think about cases, corpses, or churches."

Joe said, "You managed to avoid entangling yourselves in the three C's. What romantic getaway did you select, Irma?"

"The most romantic of all – Disney World; Arthur was a good sport about going somewhere he had visited many times in the past, but we did have fun there."

Penny said, "You would have had fun anywhere, but I can appreciate your wanting to stay away from investigations and crime. That stuff is never far from our minds. Should we head down there sometime, Joe?"

"I'm all for that, but first you'd better check to be sure that Arthur didn't run into a new potential case while he was down there. Our pastor friend finds cases everywhere he goes."

Arthur said, "Thanks for the vote of confidence, but this time I only had eyes for Irma. We entrusted you with the gumshoe department while we removed ourselves from the scene. Do you have any findings to share?"

Penny said, "Don't answer that question, Joe. Before we talk about anything serious, join us for some of our food. Newlyweds, please share the lighter side of your trip. You had to feel young and full of imagination in that place."

The next twenty minutes were devoted to eating, plus Irma ribbing Arthur about his fascination with the engineering side of the Disney attractions. Arthur returned the favor by commenting on the several times Irma had volunteered to help large families by accompanying one or more of their children on rides. He also pointed out how Irma had tended to talk with families about their child-raising experiences, while he had cornered Disney management people to learn about the mechanics of running a tourist attraction. Joe and Penny both commented that the newlyweds had focused their interests in exactly the ways they would have expected. After they had all eaten, Penny cleared all of the dishes except for coffee cups and glasses so that they would have space to sprawl a bit while they talked about other matters.

Joe placed a file of papers on the table and initiated the discussion. "While you were gone, we did some background checks and interviewed Julie Wyandt about her encounter with Charlie King in his Oliver Parkworth guise."

Irma said, "Then you are convinced that they are one and the same person?"

"You phrased that well enough for me to give you an affirmative response, Irma."

"What do you mean by that?"

Penny said, "Joe means that we're not sure that Charlie King existed for very long prior to marrying Angela. He has no background before that event."

Arthur looked amused. "Then Charlie King may be just as fictional as Oliver Parkworth."

Joe removed a sheet of paper from his file folder. "I'm not even sure I can agree with that statement. We have documents indicating the existence of an Oliver Parkworth who was a junior high school science teacher in Indianapolis fifteen years ago. We have no subsequent locations for that person. We also have no evidence of Charlie King's existence prior to his marrying Angela. Oliver may be the real individual, or that might be a fictional identity used more than once."

Penny said, "It's also possible that the Oliver Parkworth from Indianapolis is a totally different person with a similar vocation. We need to do more research."

Arthur had gone back to the food to construct a bacon and egg sandwich on toast. "Penny, your bacon is perfectly crisp. That's exactly the way I like it."

"Thank Joe for that one. He made it that way because he's a crisp-nut too."

Irma said, "I'd better note that for the future. I'm still finding new information about Arthur. It hadn't come up because I've never served him bacon before. I'll start adding that to the shopping list."

Arthur said, "I didn't plan to sidetrack this conversation in the direction of bacon. That was just an off-hand remark. I was about to comment that we should go beyond the question of who was impersonating whom to the matter of motive. If we figure out why this man has had at least two identities, we'll be a lot closer to figuring out what is going on. Irma, you like to analyze things on paper; how about taking notes as we discuss what might be happening?"

"Gladly; my first note is that if Charlie King is Oliver Parkworth or is masquerading as him, them Oliver will have a knife wound in his left side. The survival story bothered me because the weapon was a knife used for fish cleaning, and unless it was new when it was used to stab Charlie, I would have expected the injury to have been complicated by a bad infection."

Joe said, "Add the note that Julie Wyandt might have been wrong in her identification, meaning that there is a definite possibility that Charlie King is dead."

Penny said, "I'll take the approach of believing that Oliver and Charlie are indeed one and the same person, but that Oliver is the original. His teaching techniques attracted national magazine attention. That doesn't happen overnight. Oliver may have used the King identity so that he could lose money gambling and then disappear so that he would not have to repay it. What do you think, Arthur?"

"I find it hard to believe that gambling interests would not have come after Angela King when they couldn't find Charlie. They would have a strong case for her being responsible for her husband's debts. I don't think those gambling debts ever existed."

Joe said, "I said the same thing earlier to Penny."

Irma wrote rapidly on her pad of paper. She held up a hand to call for a pause until she caught up with the comments. "I think I have all the speculations so far. If he didn't owe that money, why did Charlie keep bringing up his fear of those pursuers?"

Arthur said, "He needed a cover story to explain his earlier disappearance, the long time he was away, and his return aimed at getting money from Angela."

Penny showed her growing agitation by leaving the main table to refill her plate with food. "I don't like where this discussion is going. If he didn't flee because of gambling debts, Charlie may have gone off to organize some kind of enterprise, criminal or not. He may or may not have activated it, but he ran out of money, and looked to Angela as his only possibility for additional funding. If he had other resources, he probably would have turned to them first."

Joe said, "Perhaps he did look to others for money, but either couldn't get any, or he ran through funds obtained that way, and had no choice but to play the revived romance card with Angela."

Irma continued to write, burrowing several sheets into her pad of paper. "I'll return to my medical viewpoint. Up to now, everything we've said has depended on Charlie King having operated as a lone wolf individual. I have to suggest that he was part of a larger organization, or at least had such a group supporting him, or he would be dead. It takes a lot of medical expertise to heal someone stabbed in the side with a dirty fish-cleaning knife. When Julie Wyandt met Oliver Parkworth, she detected no health problems at all."

Arthur said, "That also means that this group's plans depended on Charlie. They had to cure him, rather than take the easier path of letting him die and replacing him with someone else."

CHAPTER 18 – PARKVILLE UMC

The telephone rang, interrupting their post-breakfast furniture rearranging. They needed to accommodate several of Arthur's personal pieces from the parsonage. Arthur remained trapped behind Irma's old flowery couch while Irma ran for the telephone.

"Good morning...Hello, Shirley, you sound cheerful this morning...I suppose we could, but you'll have to give us some time to get out of our work clothes...Please make sure that everything is casual...Good, we'll see you then."

"What was that all about, and what commitment did we just make?"

"Arthur, it seems that several members of your congregation decided that their pastor and his new wife need a welcome home party, so they have asked us to stop in at Fellowship Hall in the church later this morning. They've given us a lead-time of two hours, so we don't have to rush. They promised to keep it casual so that we don't have to dress fancy. Is that acceptable to you?"

"That will be fine if you help me get this furniture arranged well enough for us to move around here without falling over things. When we get to the church, you'll have to remember that the pastor's wife always follows two paces behind him and never speaks without permission."

"You're having fantasies again. The truth of the matter is that they've had you around for a long time. They mostly want to spend time with me."

"Now I know why your name is Irma. You must have been a cranky baby who insisted on a name starting with the letter 'I' so that she could always be the center of attention."

"Well, Pastor Blake, I think you're just jealous. This will be a fun gathering, and remember that if I'm close to the church members, I'll be able to take on some of your responsibilities."

"I'll pencil you in for a guest sermon next month."

They found temporary locations for each piece of furniture and ran through a quick cleanup routine. Then they headed for the church. When they climbed the stairs from the lower parking lot, they found themselves greeted by a much larger crowd than they had expected.

Arthur waved and nodded several times in appreciation. "This is a pleasant surprise. I get the feeling that you missed us while we were away. Thank you all for coming over here. I hope you'll all also visit with us each Sunday. You don't get attendance credits for this sort of function."

Wally Sanborn raised his hand to get the attention of the crowd. "It appears that our pastor has lost his bachelor status but not his sense of humor. Many of you have followed both Arthur's church and his investigation exploits, and in the course of so doing, have watched with interest as the relationship and love between Arthur and Irma have grown. Some of you may not have followed these developments and will be sharing in them for the first time today. As one who has been his coffee buddy and occasional co-conspirator, I want to wholeheartedly endorse and welcome Irma in her new status as the pastor's wife. Irma, would you like to say a few words to mark your new relationship with the church?"

"I'd be happy to, Wally, but first, everyone please form a circle around me so that I'll be able to see you all."

Arthur watched with interest and found a place in the circle as it formed around Irma.

Irma said, "Thank you for indulging me. Most of you already know me. Shortly after Arthur and I met, I started to attend this church occasionally while maintaining my membership elsewhere. About two years ago, I became a member here. Since then, I've joined the Parkville UMC church family and staff in many activities. Now that I'm

Arthur's wife, I want you to treat me in exactly the same way as you have in the past. The only change will be that I'll have the opportunity to interact with more of you as I assist your pastor with a few of his efforts on behalf of the church. A long time ago in England, King Arthur formed his round table so that no knight would have the increased status of sitting at the head of it. I have just encouraged you to form Pastor Arthur's circle of faith, so that you might realize that we all make equal contributions to the life of our church here." Irma backed up so that she became part of the circle rather than the person at its center. "Remember this formation of equality, and freely participate in future church activities. If for any reason Arthur is not available when you need his attention, please come to me."

Everyone in the circle applauded. Arthur said, "I thoroughly appreciate Irma's comparing me to King Arthur, and I'll be sure to remind her of that in the future. You'll note that she's already influencing my relationship with you, as I've stayed at the edge of our circular ring of faith, rather than seeking the center. Thank you for this gathering on our behalf. Wally tells me that there is a refreshments table, so please sample the offerings and enjoy yourselves. We'll remain here to mingle with you individually and discuss any and all concerns and interests."

Arthur stepped forward to talk with someone on the other edge of the circle, and Irma followed his example. As people stepped forward, the circle transitioned into a kaleidoscopic rearrangement of people that continued to shift as small group conversations ensued.

Wally Sanborn found his way to Irma's side and motioned her aside for a private conversation during a quiet interval.

"What is it, Wally?"

"I just wanted to mention two things. I've heard a few grumbles among some of the infrequently attending members that Arthur has been away from the church on the weeks they've chosen to attend. I've also learned that we're about to have a new District Superintendent. Angela King is being kicked upstairs on some special assignment for the Bishop."

"You're showing off your intelligence skills again, Wally. You find out church hierarchy information before Arthur hears about it."

"Well, I do want you folks to think of me when one of your cases can use my skills. I also decided that I'm way too young to stop dating, and one of the Bishop's assistants appreciates a man with a career military background."

CHAPTER 19 – WHO AND WHERE

"Joe, this is Arthur calling. Has your agency tracked down Oliver Parkworth and his school?"

"You get one yes and one no in response to that one. We took the information from Julie Wyandt concerning the educational meeting in Denver. Using that, we found the listing for Oliver Parkworth, an eighth grade science teacher at the West Minico Middle School in Paul, Idaho. We then talked with the principal of that school and discovered that Mr. Parkworth requested and received a six-month leave of absence to recover from injuries he suffered in a car accident during his return trip from that Denver conference. We then checked with police agencies along his probable return route and found that Parkworth's car had crashed off Interstate 15 near Pocatello, Idaho, but that emergency people found no one when they searched the car. They assumed that he had hitchhiked to a hospital if he was injured, but we haven't found any records of his reappearance anywhere."

"Would they be able to get a DNA sample from the wreck to compare with a sample for Charlie King, assuming we can get one from something Charlie left behind?"

Joe paused before responding. "Here's where it gets interesting, Arthur. I was thinking along the same line as you, so I asked the Idaho State Police to try to get a sample. They discovered that someone had wiped the car clean of any residues and fingerprints before it crashed. Either the car crashed immediately after it had been through a very good detailing job, or Oliver staged the car crash as a non-controversial means of disappearing. The principal at his school told me that Parkworth had been on probation there due to parental complaints about his gathering personal information from the children."

"Are you suggesting he is a pedophile?"

"No, nothing like that; they just have strict confidentiality rules, and he violated them by asking the children detailed questions about their families."

"Were you able to get a DNA sample for Charlie King?"

"I'm afraid not. Angela let us examine her home, but we came up empty. We couldn't even find fingerprints that didn't belong to a person with normal access. She must be a very efficient housekeeper. The only possibility for his DNA would be that fishing campsite in Ontario, and Angela can't even give us good directions to get there. We still have a phantom."

"You may have two phantoms. You did learn one thing though. Oliver Parkworth is not an innocent bystander, mistakenly identified as Charlie. He's someone who doesn't want to meet with authorities checking on Charlie."

"I'll grant you that, Arthur, but where do we go from here?"

"For starters, you might check the known history of Charles King against that for Oliver Parkworth to see whether they were ever in two different places at the same time. That might tell us whether we should look for one person or two. It would also be interesting to see which one's history goes back farther. They both appeared out of nowhere, but one of them had to be the original character or version."

CHAPTER 20 – ANGELA'S SURPRISE

Angela pondered her controversial situation while she painted her kitchen cabinets. For United Methodist clergy, homes like her townhouse were temporary lodgings due to the tradition of changed appointments every few years. Even so, she wouldn't feel it was home if she didn't maintain it regularly. Angela appreciated Bishop Howard Chandler's decision to put her on special assignment rather than fire her outright. Her new euphemistic status would give her a period of privacy during which she would be able to secure legal representation and to ponder whether she had a future outside of prison. Maybe she would be able to secure a position as a prison chaplain if they didn't convict her. Angela would claim that she stabbed Charlie in self-defense, but it would be an interesting trial. In the absence of his coming forward, she would be the only witness to what had happened, and her lawyer would probably have her hide behind the Constitution's Fifth Amendment that protected her against self-incrimination.

There would be little or no circumstantial evidence. She couldn't remember the exact location where her attack on Charlie occurred. Her angled stance during her knife thrusts into Charlie's side had spared her from most of the blood spatter. She had washed off the small amount adorning her hand and forearm with hand-pumped water at a park alongside the road. The next day she discarded the clothing she had worn at the campsite, not to avoid blood spatter evidence, but because it would forever remind her of the event.

She had submerged the confrontation scene deep within her memory until Julie Wyandt had made it resurface when she returned from that education

65

conference with her encounter story. Angela sometimes wondered whether Julie was even a reliable witness. She actually believed in occult phenomena...Still, no one had told Julie of Charlie's death, so she hadn't been shocked or immersed in the paranormal when she met this very similar individual. It was all very puzzling.

Something else that was puzzling was the pain she had been feeling in her abdomen lately. She had chalked it up to having been due to the stress of recent events, but she knew that she would have to see a doctor soon if it didn't go away.

So many strange things had happened. In addition to her health problems and the question of Julie's encounter in Denver, she had received a telephone call asking for Charlie shortly after she had come home from the hospital. She had told the caller that she hadn't seen Charlie in years, having assumed she was talking to one of his gambling debt collectors. Then that caller had startled her by asking what had happened to Charlie. She hadn't slept for several nights after that.

The doorbell rang twice. Angela wiped her paint-spattered hands on a rag and checked the appearance of the bandanna tied around her head before going to answer it. The bell rang again.

"I'm coming; just a moment."

Angela opened the front door and found two rather seedy-looking men outside. "May I help you?" As she finished voicing this question, she stared at the man closest to her. He was wearing Charlie's tweed sport jacket; it even had the little cross she had given her husband on the lapel.

"My name is George Felkis. My friend and I are looking for Charles King."

"You won't find him here. My husband and I have separated. I would like to know why you are wearing his jacket."

66

Feckless hesitated. Then he said, "I'm glad you recognized it. I purchased this fine jacket at a church rummage sale, and it's actually part of the reason for our being here."

Angela remembered that she had given most of Charlie's belongings to the church, but she knew that the rummage sale was still a week away. Then she remembered what she had heard from sources at several different churches. "I think you'd better rephrase your statement. They haven't held the rummage sale yet. They may have given you that jacket when you asked for a handout from the church, but during that visit, you also helped yourselves to some of the collection money. I've heard about you two, and I think it's time for me to call the police."

Grumpy looked worried, but Feckless said, "I don't think you'll want to call them after I've told you why we're here. I thought I would be dealing with Mr. King, but I'm more than willing to discuss my business with you, Mrs. King."

"What is your business? Make it quick."

"The fact is that this jacket is my property, whether I purchased it or received it as a gift. That makes anything found in its pockets also mine."

"And what did you find in the jacket pockets?"

"I found some official documents that ought to be of some value to you and your family. Mr. King apparently was doing some genealogy searches and obtained copies of some of your relatives' birth certificates, six of them to be precise. I'll sell them to you for twenty-five dollars each."

Charlie had told Angela that he had no family, so she knew that these certificates might reveal family he had wanted to keep hidden, or some other involvement of his. Aloud she said, "Mr. Felkis, they might be worth something to me, but certainly not that much. I'll give you ten dollars each; take it or leave it."

Feckless laughed. "I see that you are a person who is wise in the ways of business. I'll take your offer as an opening bid, and I'll counter that I'd be willing to settle for twenty dollars each." He held the certificates far enough away for her to see their good condition and official character, without allowing her to read their contents.

They did look genuine. "Alright, I'll go as high as fifteen dollars each, but you'll have to let me read them all before we conclude a deal."

"I'll go so far as to allow you to read one of them. I don't want you memorizing the details and then withdrawing your bid; but I won't take a penny less than seventeen-fifty each. That's a total of one hundred and five dollars. Agreed?"

"I'll agree if they look genuine. Show me one."

Feckless randomly cut the stack of documents and held one up to her. She looked at it for about ten seconds and then said, "It's a deal. I'll write you a check."

He shook his head. "It will have to be cash. We don't work with bankers and paper trails."

Angela wasn't sure she had that much cash in the house. "You two stay here while I go inside and see whether I can find that much cash." She went in and closed the door, locking it behind her.

Grumpy said, "I don't like this Feckless. She may call the cops instead of getting the money. We're just standing here asking for trouble. She already figured out that we're the ones taking money from churches."

Feckless knew that he had taken a risk, but he had pegged the woman as someone who wanted the birth certificates badly. He was sure she had a strong reason for bidding and would cooperate.

He patted Grumpy on the back. "I think she'll come across with the money, but to show you I respect your thinking, we'll split if she's not back in ten minutes."

He had hardly completed that statement when the door opened again. Angela reappeared carrying a cloth bag.

"I had to hit the piggy bank, so twenty-five dollars of it is in change. You can count it if you want."

Feckless took the bag and looked into it. "I've done enough money counting to know that you're at least pretty close. Here are the certificates. I'd appreciate it if you leave the police out of our relationship."

"Just don't come back here or to any of the churches in nearby towns, and I won't have to call them. Now get out of here."

As she went back inside, Angela smiled. She guessed that these papers would tell her a lot about Charlie's secret activities. She had also photographed her two visitors through the window. She would give their pictures to the police in the morning.

CHAPTER 21 – ANALYSIS

The telephone rang just as Arthur finished the final sentence of his sermon draft for Sunday. He reached for the phone without looking away from his computer screen.

"Good morning; Pastor Blake speaking."

"Good morning yourself, Arthur, this is your one and only wife speaking. You sound preoccupied."

"Hi, Irma; I'll give you my complete attention now. I just finished the draft of my sermon for Sunday. Its title is *Missionaries to a World that Doesn't Want to Be Bothered.*"

"That's a deep title. I know what you mean though. Too many people think of religion as an add-on rather than a basic part of their lives."

"Irma, you're a basic part of my life, and I like your comment so much that I'd like to add it to the sermon."

"Make sure you give me credit for it, preacher."

"You bet I will! I want everyone to be as impressed by my wife as I am. I assume there's a purpose for your call, or is it that you can't stand being separated from me?"

"Oddly enough I called because someone else wants me to be away from you. I received a call from Angela King, and she asked me to visit her and examine some papers that may help us find Charlie. She specifically requested that I come without you."

"Maybe she doesn't want males around, or perhaps she's once again being critical of my capabilities."

"I won't venture a guess without more information, but this may take a while, so plan on being a full-time pastor today. I'll contact you when the meeting is over or if I have something to report. Give my best to Shirley and the other folks at the church."

They ended the call, and Arthur leaned back in his chair and stared at the ceiling. *What is Angela up to this time?*

Irma parked in front of the townhouse and rang the doorbell. After a brief interval, Angela answered the door in her work clothes.

"Hello, Irma; thanks for coming so quickly. Please excuse my messy place here. I've been painting, but I cleared a space for us to talk and work in the family room."

Irma followed Angela to the family room and put her jacket on a chair. "You didn't say anything on the phone about a work session. Should I have brought something to assist us?"

"No, Irma, I just want to show you some documents I recently obtained and discuss their possible implications."

Angela related in detail her encounter with Feckless and Grumpy during their visit. She described her back-and-forth negotiation for the six birth certificates.

Irma asked, "Why were you willing to pay these scoundrels to obtain the documents?"

"I was pretty sure that they would shed some light on Charlie's activities and enterprises. He's been involved in some very suspicious things - even if it turns out that his alter ego is not that Oliver Parkworth individual that Julie Wyandt met."

"If Julie was mistaken, Charlie may be dead after all. How does that possibility make you feel?"

"I wouldn't mind him being dead at all, but I'd like to understand what he was doing during all of that time when he was away from me."

"Angela, if you don't mind my getting personal, what kind of relationship did you have when you were together? What kind of person was Charlie when you two were husband and wife?"

"Technically, we still are; there was no divorce. Of course, if he's dead, your wording is correct. Anyway, Charlie always presented himself as down-to-earth and good, but I never really felt close to him. I always had the impression that even when he was with me, he was somewhere else at the same time. It was like carrying on a telephone conversation with someone who isn't really listening to you."

"Are you saying that he wasn't interested in your feelings and needs?"

"Irma, it was just the opposite; he was definitely attuned to my wishes, but he also sought out a bunch of other people to learn their needs and desires; that made me feel relatively unimportant."

"You're a minister; don't you attend to other people's needs?"

"Sure, but it's different when your spouse is giving attention to someone else. You want to feel that you can always depend on your husband to give you his primary, if not exclusive, attention. I never had that feeling with Charlie. I was just one of the people he collected along the way."

"That's an interesting way of looking at him and his relationships. You feel that he collected people."

"That's exactly it. I wanted him for my own, but I always had to share him."

Irma noticed how tightly Angela clutched the envelope full of documents. "I expect that you're about to tell me that those birth certificates reveal something interesting. You said that Mr. Felkis showed you only one of them before you agreed to purchase them. I assume that one was significant to you. Whose certificate was it?"

Angela showed her obvious excitement as she said, "I asked you to come alone today because the name on that certificate was Arthur Kipling Blake. There can't be two people with that combination of names."

CHAPTER 22 – PAUL, IDAHO

Arthur climbed the stairs from the education level to the main floor after completing an inspection of the church. His compiled list of maintenance projects would serve as a guideline for Bill Martin's Trustees Committee for priority attention. He approached the church office with his handwritten list, feeling satisfied that the requested projects were relatively minor and doable within the approved budget. He entered the office and handed his clipboard to Shirley.

"This isn't an emergency task that should sidetrack your regular schedule. When you get a chance, please type this project list for the Trustees meeting next Monday evening. The building is in pretty good shape, but I found a fair number of small jobs that need attention."

"I'll have it typed and inserted in Bill Martin's mailbox by the end of the afternoon. In the meantime, please call Irma. She's organizing a meeting that you should attend. Jeremy wanted me to tell you that even though he's back at UW Platteville taking courses this semester, his coop program will allow him to take a break of up to two weeks if you need him on an investigative project. At least he still funnels these requests and reports through me as his mother. I think he feels that I'll have easier access to you than he would if he tried direct contacts."

"Not only that, Shirley, but you'd probably answer the phone anyway. This procedure is more diplomatic because it makes you feel involved in his life. I think he's learned a few points from Professor Middlemiss in Political Science."

"How is Edward? Have you been in touch? That Middlemiss name always reminds me of ancient history around here. Anyway, call your wife before she gets impatient with you."

Arthur returned to his office and made the requested call. "Hi, Irma, I just returned from a dirty-hands job. I don't get to do too many of them around here. Shirley said something about a meeting. What's happening?"

"Thanks for checking in with me. We're due at Penny and Joe's house in an hour. They have some preliminary results from their check on Oliver Parkworth to share with us. I'll add to the discussions with some potentially significant input that I obtained from Angela King. Do you want to come home and then go to Penny's together, or would you rather meet me there?"

"I think I'd better go directly from here. I have a few things to wrap up before I'll be free to leave; no problem with the schedule. I have the feeling that our pooling of data will yield interesting results."

Arthur ended his conversation with Irma and then made one more phone call to obtain the information that he would contribute to the meeting.

By the time Arthur drove up to the Gonzalez house, Irma had already arrived and gone inside. He parked on the street and hopped over the little white chain curbside fence on his way across the lawn to the front door. Penny responded to his knock by opening the door immediately.

"I saw that, Pastor. You cut across our lawn to make up for being late. If you do it again, take a different route so that you don't ruin our grass."

"Sorry, Penny, I forgot how much you treasure this green contrast to the concrete you had outside your Washington apartment. If it's any consolation, letter carriers manage to cut across lawns every day without destroying the grass."

"It's really not a problem, Arthur; I simply wanted to give you a little grief."

"That either means that you're in a good mood because you've learned something significant on the case;

or that I'm misreading your mood, and you really are angry with me."

"Join us at the dining room table, and perhaps you'll gain some enlightenment."

Arthur followed Penny in, waved to Joe, kissed Irma, poured himself a cup of coffee from the carafe on the side table, and sat down.

Irma acted as moderator. "We organized this session on short notice because Joe and Penny report they have significant feedback from their inquiries into Mr. Parkworth. I have some new information received from Angela King that could turn out to be important. What about you, Arthur; do you have anything new to contribute? I know you've been tied up at church today, so I don't expect you to have a presentation prepared."

"I actually do have something new to discuss. I spoke with Bishop Chandler before coming over here. He indicated that he put Angela King on special assignment status to give her time to prepare for future employment and legal disruptions. It was a stalling tactic to assist both Angela and the church's management team. The lawyers he consulted suggest that unless Angela persists in claiming guilt for attacking and perhaps killing her estranged husband, the case against her will be weak. No one has found a corpse; there were no witnesses; and we don't even have an exact location for the campsite where she allegedly stabbed him. Nonetheless, he has accepted her story to the extent of deciding that ethically, she is no longer suitable for holding an active clergy position. His assigned team will attempt to define a staff job for Angela where she won't interact with the public on a regular basis."

Penny said, "That's both forgiving and pragmatic, but it only reflects the evidence as we now know it. If we learn more about what actually happened to Charlie, Bishop Chandler may have to rethink his position."

"He realizes that. As I said, special assignment is a device for stalling and stretching out the acceptable time period before he has to make a firm decision."

Irma said, "That's valuable input, Arthur; I'm sorry I teased you about not having anything to bring to this meeting. I had heard the rumor about special assignment from Wally, but I didn't know exactly what it meant, or about the legalities and strategy behind it...Joe, what has your agency learned about Oliver Parkworth?"

"If you don't mind, I'll stand up and move around while I speak. I'm feeling a little restless today...As I indicated to Arthur earlier, we traced Parkworth to the West Minico Middle School in Paul, Idaho, where his position was eighth grade science teacher. We learned that he wrecked his car on his way home from that Denver educational conference, but that the police found no one in the wreckage. The principal at West Minico School said that Mr. Parkworth telephoned the school after the accident and requested a leave of absence to recover from his injuries. Neither the police nor the principal have heard from Parkworth since that phone call. The principal's name is Aaron Foelsch, and he described Parkworth as an outstanding teacher whose teaching methods had drawn attention in education journals. Despite Parkworth's celebrity, Foelsch had placed him on probation due to parental complaints about his gathering personal information from the children in violation of the school district's confidentiality rules."

Arthur asked, "Have you learned anything about the questions he asked the children and the answers that they supplied?"

"According to the principal, Mr. Parkworth asked general questions about what their parents had taught them at home, family relationships, and at-home training for accepting responsibility for their actions. He spent more time talking with one boy than he did with all the others. That boy had lost his father in the Iraq war, and he had to overcome a difficult period while he and his mother worked their way into a single parent relationship."

"What was the boy's name?"

"His name was Eric Tobias, and he wanted to be an athlete, but he wasn't very good at any of the sports he tried. The school was small enough, though, that they were short on athletes and had to let him play baseball and soccer."

Arthur noticed that Irma was staring at Joe in an unusual way. "Is anything wrong, Irma?"

"Nothing's wrong, but I'm going to do a magic trick for all of you. Joe, I'll bet that the first name of the soldier who died in Iraq was Travis. How did I do?"

Joe searched through his notes, and after looking at several pages, put them down and stared at Irma. "You're absolutely correct. I didn't even remember that I had recorded the soldier's first name. How did you do that?"

Irma related the story of the two men selling Angela the birth certificates that they had found in Charlie's inside jacket pocket. "There were six birth certificates, and Angela passed them on to me because she felt that they had to be significant. She proved that to me by showing me the first one she had looked at during the negotiation. The name on that certificate was Arthur Kipling Blake."

Arthur said, "I never even met Charlie. He left Angela before I arrived."

Irma said, "True, but he had a connection to you. Angela disliked you because she thought your motivations were similar to Charlie's."

Penny had been doodling on a sheet of paper; she stopped and put her pen down. "That's a pretty tenuous connection. Before I met you, I would have been linked to you through other people that we both knew."

"I grant you that the logic is thin. However, there has to be some significance to these birth certificates, and we have found that Charlie or Oliver had affiliations with two of the six: Arthur Blake and Travis Tobias. This certificate indicates that Travis would be twenty-eight years old if he were still alive. He was born in Paul, Idaho, and he may have lived his entire life there prior to his military service."

Arthur said, "Let me examine my certificate."

Irma passed the paper to Penny, who passed it along to Arthur. He looked at it for a long time before he spoke.

"The date is correct, but it says that I was born at the St. Louis Hospital in Berlin, New Hampshire, when I've always been told I was born at the Androscoggin Valley Hospital. I've always filled out official paperwork on that basis."

Penny said, "Then this birth certificate is probably a counterfeit."

"I know that my folks both grew up in Berlin, New Hampshire. I'll go into the other room and call them while you continue here. Hopefully, they'll be able to tell me whether that second hospital existed and which version is correct."

Arthur left the room with his birth certificate, and Irma laid out the other five similar documents on the table. "We've found that two of the people represented by the six birth certificates had some connection to Charlie King, at least indirectly. If we examine the identities and current locations of the other four birth certificate people, we may get an indication of where Charlie is going and what he is doing."

Joe said, "That procedure at least lets us take an active approach and possibly determine where Charlie plans to go in the future. That's a lot better than having to react to something he has done after the fact. What do you think, Penny?"

"I'll go along with both of you. I'm curious to see whether there is a pattern in the identities of the six individuals cited by these documents. I'm also somewhat relieved that at least so far, we haven't detected anything that suggests a terrorist plot."

Irma shook her head. "We're still at the very beginning of this analysis. It's way too early to rule anything in or out concerning his objectives."

Arthur returned from calling his parents and sat down. He threw his birth certificate in the general direction of the others laid out on the table. "I talked with my mother, and I held on while she checked the family records. This certificate is not a fake. In fact, it's more accurate than my parents' memories. The old name of the medical facility in our town was the St. Louis Hospital. It originally had a religious affiliation. In 1971 it was purchased by a community group and was renamed the Androscoggin Valley Hospital. I was born in 1966, so even though my parents always referred to the hospital by its modern name, the certificate is accurate. I was born there before the reorganization and name change. My mother had completely forgotten the timing and the inaccuracy about the name."

Penny said, "If your certificate is accurate, the others are likely to be also. Let's take them all at face value and look for patterns as we try to identify and locate the other people."

Arthur refilled his coffee cup. "I'm still bewildered by my inclusion in this group. If I compare myself to the second individual we identified, we have nothing in common. Travis Tobias is a deceased war veteran; I'm neither deceased nor a veteran. Tobias had a wife and son; I have only recently married and have no child. He grew up in Idaho, and I grew up in Illinois. I'm sure that we never crossed paths, especially since I lived and worked in Florida before coming back to Illinois. Florida and Idaho are pretty far apart."

Irma said, "Arthur, it sounds as though you're bothered by the thought that you may not be in complete control of your life. Destiny, or someone behind the scenes, may have been influencing the directions you've taken."

Richard Davidson

"I accept and welcome the fact that you've redirected my steps through love and marriage, but I don't like even the slightest hint that I've been manipulated by a hidden stranger."

CHAPTER 23 – CERTIFICATES

Irma felt sorry for Arthur as he wrestled with the thought that someone had been looking over his shoulder and perhaps manipulating him in some way. Still, she felt that Arthur had not latched onto the correct significance of his birth certificate's presence among the six that Angela had acquired. She rearranged the matrix of certificates on Penny's dining room table to include Arthur's carelessly thrown document.

"I'd like to set aside the certificates for Arthur and for Travis Tobias and look at the other four. My geometry teacher used to say that two points define a straight line, but it takes three points to define a plane. I think it's going to take more than three data points to make the significance of these birth certificates plain. I apologize for that pun, but I do feel that the solution to our mystery lies in the unknown individuals rather than the two we've already examined.

"The third person in my paper array is different because she's female. The name is Alicia Pavone, and she was born in Little Rock, Arkansas, on March 13, 1950. That makes her the first senior citizen of the group. How does she fit with the others, Penny?"

"I'll follow your lead and say that we need more information on the remaining people. Having seen the first three individuals, I'd say that this appears to be a diverse group in many ways. I had hoped that Arthur's background would be somewhat similar to the others and would act as a key to unlocking the pattern, but so far, the people appear to be a random sample from the overall population. Background checks may help us, but that will take some time."

Joe said, "We can't call these people randomly selected, because Arthur is one of them. There has to be significance to his having been included. Take us to the next step, Irma. Who is the fourth person?"

"The next person in my array is Roger Svenson, born in Wichita, Kansas. I won't call him the fourth person, because I have no idea whether the sequence of these people is important. Roger was born in 1975, so he's thirty-eight years old. In most cases, the birth locations of these people will not be significant. We'll have to do some sleuthing to find where they are now. Joe, I agree with you that each certificate will likely turn out to be significant."

"Thanks, Irma, and just to add some levity, I'll say Roger that; we'll get the background and location checks going as soon as we wrap up this session. Who do you have next?"

"I have Karl Simitski, currently age fifty-eight and born in Joplin, Missouri. The name sounds Eastern European, but we don't know whether ethnicity will play a role in this affair.

"My final person is Geraldine Quig, Geraldine would be forty-three years old now. She was born in Houston, Texas."

Penny had taken notes as Irma reviewed the birth certificates. "My summary shows that we have four men and two women. We have an age range from twenty-six to sixty-three years old. The names reflect a wide variety of ancestries, and modern U.S. birth certificates do not include race information. We will have to investigate each of these people in detail to determine what part, if any, they play in the adventures of Charlie King. We also don't know whether he will show up in any other guises."

Arthur said, "We did learn something, Penny."

"What do we know now that we didn't know before?"

"The inclusion of both Travis Tobias and me in the set of birth certificates suggests that we should consider Charlie King and Oliver Parkworth to be the same person.

Charlie King is linked to me, and Travis Tobias is linked to Oliver Parkworth."

Irma said, "It may suggest that, but we're still a long way from certifying that singularity as a fact. Charlie might have learned about Travis from Oliver while still being a separate person. We need more information before I'll say they're the same."

Penny said, "Joe, I think they're having their first married fight."

CHAPTER 24 – ERIC TOBIAS

At Joe's request, Steve DuBois, an associate from their federal agency in Washington, DC, had flown to Pocatello, Idaho, and then rented a car to drive to the rural town of Paul. He drove past the West Minico Middle School where Oliver Parkworth had taught eighth grade science. Steve thought the school to be surprisingly large for a town with fewer than twelve hundred people, but then he remembered that Minico was a contraction of Minidoka County, implying that the school accepted students who lived well outside the town of Paul. It was late enough in the afternoon for the school to be virtually empty, so Steve drove to the nearby Tobias home on Doris Avenue.

He parked in the driveway of the small blue-roofed house nestled in an arc of large trees that screened the back yard from view, and approached the front door. In the absence of a homeowner's car in the driveway, Steve expected that he would have to come back later. He rang the doorbell anyway, and a gangly young teenager with dark curly hair opened the door.

The boy studied Steve in detail. "Can I help you, Mister? You don't look like anyone I've seen around town."

Steve pulled out his card case with his credentials. "You must be Eric. I'm Steve DuBois, and you wouldn't have seen me around town, because I just arrived from Washington, DC; I work for the government there. Is your mother home?"

"No, she works in the office down at the construction company. Since Dad died, I've been on my own in the afternoons. Say, does that card and badge you just showed me mean that you're a real G-man?"

"It does mean that. I'd like to ask you a few questions, but I think you should call your mother first to get her permission for you to talk with me."

Eric pulled a cell phone out of his pocket. "I'll call her and let you talk with her to prove I met a real G-man."

He hit the contact button for his mother's work number and waited for her response. "Hi, Mom...No, there's nothing wrong, but I have a visitor. Mr. DuBois, who's a G-man from Washington, wants to talk with you...No, not the state – where the government lives. I'll give him the phone."

Steve accepted the phone and hoped he would sound reasonable to Eric's mother. "Mrs. Tobias; I'm Steve DuBois, and I work for a federal investigative agency. I would like to ask Eric a few questions about his former science teacher, Mr. Parkworth. We have him listed as a missing person. I requested that Eric call you to ask your permission for me to talk with him. I won't ask him any questions without your approval...Well, that would be fine with me, if it's not inconvenient for you...I'll give the phone back to Eric so that you can finish the conversation with him."

Eric spoke briefly with his mother, disconnected, and returned the phone to his pocket. "We're supposed to wait for Mom before we start talking. She's only about ten minutes away. Do you like football?"

When Ellen Tobias drove into the driveway, she saw Eric and Steve passing a football back and forth. It both pleased and saddened her because the scene reminded her of the many times Eric had done the same thing with Travis, before he died in that Iraq suicide bombing. Eric had mentioned just last week how much he missed playing catch football with his dad. She climbed down from her pickup truck, instinctively smoothed out her long reddish hair, and walked toward the pair. Steve tucked the football under his left arm and walked over to meet her.

"Mrs. Tobias, as I indicated over the phone, I'm Steve DuBois, and I work for a federal investigative agency. We're looking into the disappearance of Oliver Parkworth, Eric's science teacher." Steve showed Ellen his credentials.

Ellen said, "I guess Eric was correct; you are a G-man. Your job is one of the many that Eric has considered for his future. Why do you feel that Eric can help with your inquiry?"

"It's our understanding that Mr. Parkworth received probationary status because he had been asking too many personal questions of children, violating the school's privacy policy. We learned from Principal Foelsch that Parkworth had spent more time talking with Eric than anyone else. I'd like to ask Eric what they discussed. Their conversations might reveal Parkworth's interests and clues as to his location."

"Why are you trying to locate Mr. Parkworth? Has he done anything illegal?"

"It's not that, Mrs. Tobias. We want to get information from him about someone else who may be involved in a conspiracy. I'm not allowed to give you the specifics of our investigation."

"I understand, Steve, and please call me Ellen. You have my permission to question Eric, but I want to be present. I may even be able to contribute something useful. Why don't we go into our front room? It's a little chilly out here. I'll make some hot chocolate."

Eric said, "Can we play some more football after we talk, Steve?"

"You bet. I haven't passed a football around for a long time."

Ellen gestured for Steve to flip the ball to her, and he complied. She said, "And I might even join you. Let's head inside."

They went into the small frame house and spent two hours discussing Parkworth's conversations, accompanied by hot chocolate, sandwiches, and memories of Travis

Tobias. By the time their discussions and subsequent football session had ended, the sun had set, and Steve had information that would give a new perspective to the investigation.

CHAPTER 25 – MARRIED FOLKS

Irma finished clearing the breakfast dishes and sat again at the table, while Arthur completed his Sudoku puzzle.

"I guess the honeymoon is over. You're finding lots of things to do that don't include me."

"I have a second puzzle book for you. Feel free to try this."

"That's not what I meant, Arthur. In some ways I think we were more of a team before we got married."

"We've been a team for years. The only difference is that now we see more of the placid intervals between our more interesting and exciting projects. We have a case going right now, but we have to sit and wait here in Parkville while Penny and Joe's agency does the distance work. It's probably harder on you because I have my work at the church for filling the interim periods, and you no longer have a second career since you left the medical examiner post."

"I should have recorded that statement, Arthur. You've confirmed my suspicions. Investigations have become your primary focus, while your church work fills in the intervals. Admit it."

Arthur closed his puzzle book. "We're getting back to your recurrent questioning of whether I have enough dedication to my ministry. The last time you raised this issue, I said I'd be willing to discuss it after we got married. I suppose we've reached the appropriate time."

"I don't want to pressure you."

"I don't feel any pressure. I'm quite content with saying that I enjoy our investigations, both because they are challenging and because we tackle them as a team. I don't just want to live with you. I want to share our life interests, and our casework is a vehicle for that. I do appreciate that you walked away from your Medical Examiner career because you thought it might negatively affect our relationship. I'd be equally willing to walk away from being a pastor if I had a good enough reason for doing so. Right now, I don't have that reason, so I'll keep up with my dual career. I'll monitor future developments to see whether they should influence my outlook. Is that enough of a statement for now, Irma?"

"I left my earlier career because of slight glitches in my qualifications that might not have sat well with you, Arthur, had they come to light in the wrong way. You're well qualified for the ministry, but I continue to see you wavering as far as interest and commitment. I'm fine with whichever direction you take, so don't alter your future decisions based on my feelings."

"Thanks for that pledge of support, Irma. Angela King took my change in career from engineering to the ministry to indicate a flaw in my character. I think we all change as we learn more and have new enlightening experiences. A changed person may require an altered focus and commitment more than once in his or her lifetime. That's a sign of continuing to develop and mature – not a character flaw."

"That's good enough for me, Preacher. Somehow I have the feeling that even if you stop being a pastor, I'll be hearing your sermons for the rest of my life."

"Until death do us part...Amen."

CHAPTER 26 – FEEDBACK

Joe greeted Arthur and Irma at his front door and ushered them into the dining room where they found Penny Gonzalez and Steve DuBois arranging table supplies and computers.

Irma said, "I feel slightly usurped. We used to have these meetings at my apartment, which doubles as the ABC Consultants headquarters. Your new home has taken over the function of housing our conferences. Penny, you have all the fun."

"If you feel that way, Irma, I'll yield the next conference to you. We feel more useful if we justify our move to Parkville by having this place serve as our agency's local headquarters as well. We even have Steve staying with us in our spare room."

Steve said, "And they're great hosts; I could hardly believe the brunch they served earlier today. When we have a break in the meeting, we should raid the leftovers...This is the first time I've seen you Blake folks since the wedding. You appear to be thriving as a married couple."

Arthur said, "It feels completely normal. Pretty soon I won't be able to remember my single days."

Irma smiled at Arthur's words and took her place at the table. "Arthur's doing very well as a husband. We're past the initial training period, and he's almost housebroken. That's enough chat about us; I'm looking forward to hearing what Steve learned during his field trip. Let's all sit down and get started."

Arthur said, "I'll be there as soon as I get some of Penny's great coffee. Penny, you don't have to worry about where we locate our meetings. Irma will run them wherever we are. It is good to be working together again."

Joe took his seat. "This impatient gang has spoken. You'd better start reporting on your trip, Steve."

"I'll sit while I speak if you don't mind. I won't be using charts or projections anyway.

"Paul, Idaho, is a complete contrast to Washington DC. It's a small town in a craggy part of the country, where the residents tend to be rugged individualists. Travis Tobias had his personality formed by growing up in this place, and he took his independent thinking with him when he served in Iraq as a military policeman. There, his assignment was security at one of Saddam Hussein's palaces in the Baghdad Green Zone. Occasionally, his unit also inspected other palaces and government buildings outside that zone. During the course of this work he learned to appreciate the biblical history of the area."

Arthur asked, "Do you mean that he started to study the Bible and archeological documents?"

"No, he wasn't a scholar or an intellectual. He appreciated the age of Middle Eastern civilizations and went out of his way to study antiquities and Bible-era artifacts. He also got involved in trying to recover some of the items that were looted from the Iraqi National Museum in April of 2003 during the lawless period between the fall of the government and the arrival and posting of coalition troops."

Joe said, "They lost many unique and priceless artifacts during that looting. We received bulletins describing many of them and requests for us to watch for their appearance in art markets."

Steve resumed his report. "One of Travis Tobias' favorite activities at home had been throwing a football back and forth with his son Eric. Because of this, he couldn't resist setting aside a souvenir that he subsequently took home when he returned on leave. He had found the item in the rubble of a palace building after insurgent rockets had hit it. He told his wife he thought it had fallen out of a cavity in a wall that had crumbled. The artifact was a stone or clay cylinder that resembled a football. It had tapered ends. He was home for two weeks, and during his leave, he showed the object to Eric and even used it to play catch with his son at short distances. By the time of Travis' return to Iraq at the end of his leave, he had transferred the object to someone else for evaluation. Three months later Travis Tobias died during a suicide bomb attack on the Green Zone.

Penny asked, "Do you know who received the object from Tobias?"

"Travis sent it to a friend who is an art appraiser and agent in Kansas. He was supposed to determine if it had value and whether any buyers might be interested in it. Travis' widow, Ellen Tobias, said she hadn't minded her husband's bringing the souvenir home when she considered it a worthless novelty, but she became nervous when his friend in Kansas City started hinting that it might be very valuable."

Arthur said, "I think I know what the object is and why it would fetch a high sale price. It sounds like a cuneiform cylinder from ancient Babylon or Mesopotamia. They aren't stone, although they feel quite hard. They are clay cylinders on which scribes recorded the earliest forms of writing using a reed stylus. After the scribe filled the clay cylinder surface with writing, he would take the object to a kiln or furnace to harden it and make the cuneiform writing permanent."

Joe said, "I'm glad we have a Bible and antiquities scholar in our midst. Does he impress you with this stuff all the time, Irma?"

"Right now, I'm more interested in having Steve tell us the name of the person in Kansas City who received the cylinder from Travis Tobias."

"I have that in my notes, Irma. His name was Roger Svenson."

"People, Roger Svenson's name is on one of those birth certificates that had been in Charlie King's jacket pocket.

He was born in Wichita and apparently has remained nearby in Kansas City."

The room went silent for what seemed like a long time. Then Penny said, "I think it's time we increase the staffing on this project. We're learning that those birth certificates are significant and that something very valuable is involved."

CHAPTER 27 – KANSAS

Using her maiden name, Penny telephoned Roger Svenson at the offices of Inland Associated Art Examiners from her Kansas City hotel room. "Mr. Svenson, this is Penny Greene calling. A friend in St. Louis suggested that you might be the appropriate person to assist me by evaluating a piece of art. It has been in my family for several generations. Could we schedule an appointment in the near future? You're available - splendid. I'll visit your office at three o'clock this afternoon. I'd prefer to show you the item rather than to discuss it by telephone. Thank you very much; I'll see you then."

Penny turned to Joe who had been consulting his laptop computer for background on Roger Svenson and his company. "Is this guy legitimate, or questionable? How should I slant the conversation during our meeting?"

"He appears to run a clean business, but his ethics may be slightly elastic. A few of his clients have complained that he uses a contract that bases his fee on a percentage of his appraisal figure rather than the selling price. That gives him a conflict of interest and encourages him to overvalue each piece of art because that procedure increases his income."

"I'll spot that weak point in his contract and see how he responds to my objection. I'm more concerned with his reaction to my art object than I am with his contract. We can't sell the Egyptian artifact we borrowed from the Smithsonian anyway. The main objective is to see how he plans to dispose of something with a questionable history and, if possible, to identify his contacts for a private sale."

"I'll accompany you as your attorney, so that he doesn't try to take advantage of your being alone. I'll insist that some of his pointed questions are off limits and that you should not answer them. If we play hard-to-get with information, the value of our object may increase in his eyes and in those of his collector clients."

At precisely three o'clock, Penny and Joe entered the lobby of Inland Associated Art Examiners, located on the second floor of a small office building with an unaffiliated art gallery below. As they rode the elevator, Joe suggested that Svenson had selected the space above the art gallery for window dressing. They opened the suite door to find a very young, blond, gum-chewing secretary sitting at the front desk reading a romance novel. She put a pink flowered bookmark in the volume, closed it, and greeted them.

"May I help you?"

"I'm Penny Greene. I have an appointment with Mr. Svenson."

She depressed a key on the intercom telephone. "Roger, you have Penny Greene and an associate here to see you." Turning to the visitors, she said, "He'll be right out." Then she returned to her book.

Joe noted that the offices contained little furniture except for a conference table behind a shoulder-height partition and an oriental carpet in the center of the main area. He discarded his preconception that he would encounter paintings, statues, and plush furnishings for an exclusivity aura. The space projected a wholesale rather than retail image. A narrow door opened at the far end of the outer office, and Roger Svenson stepped into their midst. He was unexpectedly short and bald with wire-rimmed glasses. A red cardigan sweater over a white spread-collar shirt topped his blue jeans.

"Hello, Mrs. Greene. It is Mrs. I assume? You didn't indicate that you would be bringing a companion...Greetings; I'm Roger Svenson."

"Pleased to meet you Roger; I'm Joe Gonzalez, Mrs. Greene's attorney. We work together on changes to her collection."

"I didn't realize, Mrs. Greene, that you have a collection. I had assumed from our telephone conversation that you possessed only a single piece to be evaluated."

"You can call me Penny; and, Roger, we are discussing only a single piece today, but there are others for possible future consideration."

"What is the nature of today's item?"

"Shall we move to your conference table so that we may examine it carefully?"

Roger led the way to the conference area behind the shoulder-height partitions.

Penny nodded to Joe, and he retrieved a leather-covered box from his attaché case. He handed the box to Penny. She removed the cover, unwrapped the enclosed item, and presented it to Roger.

Penny said, "This is a very fine quality Egyptian bronze statue of the god Osiris holding his crook and flail. I've been told that it dates from the period circa 775 to 653 BC."

Roger spent about a minute examining the piece. "This is in very good condition, especially since the feathers have not broken off the atef crown. There are many statues of Osiris in the mummiform pose like this, but this one has extraordinary condition for so old a statue."

Penny said, "Then you think that we should be able to find a buyer for it? Because it has been in the family for so long, I would only sell it to a collector who specializes in antiquities and who will preserve this item for future generations. I am definitely not looking to sell it to a status-seeker who throws money around but doesn't appreciate the historical value of artifacts."

"As one who has assisted in the recovery and preservation of many ancient treasures, I appreciate your position. There aren't many objects of this quality left on the open market, especially since the 1970 UNESCO treaty on trade in antiquities. The world of historic

96

preservation suffers a great loss when one artifact is damaged or mistreated."

"Do you have a buyer who might have an active interest in such an item?"

"As a matter of fact I had recent contact with an agent for just such a buyer."

"Were you in contact with that agent for an Egyptian artifact like this?"

"No, it was for an item of Babylonian origin."

"That is interesting. I don't have anything Babylonian in my collection. Would you mind telling me the nature of this item? I might be willing to consider purchasing it if your other buyer fails to complete the transaction."

"I doubt that you would have that opportunity, but I can tell you that the object is a cuneiform double-tapered cylinder that might even date back to the reign of Nebuchadnezzar."

"That would indeed be interesting. I might consider entering into an auction for such an antiquity. However, I'll first need your opinion on the value of the statue that you have before you today."

"Before I give you an actual appraisal figure, you'll have to sign a form agreeing to my contractual terms. My fee will be ten percent of the appraisal figure."

Joe said, "As Mrs. Greene's attorney, I'll have to advise her that your fee structure is unacceptable. You have an obvious conflict of interest if you calculate your fee based upon your appraisal. Your services deserve compensation, but we will only pay based on the sale price, and we will transfer funds only after this object has changed hands and we have received the payment. You will have to furnish your appraisal to us objectively, in good faith, and without remuneration prior to the sale."

Roger Svenson's composure failed him as he searched for an agreeable compromise solution. "I'm afraid I couldn't work with you on that basis. How do I know that you'll pay me after you have made contact with the buyer's agent or the principal himself?"

Penny noted that Roger had revealed the final buyer to be a man. "Roger, if you can't work with us on the basis of good faith then we'll have to take our Osiris elsewhere. Either way, I've enjoyed meeting you." She stood and started to rewrap the Osiris statue.

Joe said, "It's a much simpler transaction if we sell it to that museum anyway, Penny."

Whether the determining factor was the news of museum interest or the sight of Penny preparing to return the statue to its carrying case, Roger raised his hand in the manner of a police officer stopping traffic. "Please stay. I'll work with you on the basis you suggested. That is a beautiful piece, and I do want to be part of the team that transfers it to a new owner. I would value it at twelve thousand dollars, given the intact feathers on the crown. I've seen other similar statues that have lost their feathers, and they sold for about eight thousand dollars."

Joe and Penny had previously found a similar piece without feathers on sale for less than six thousand dollars, but they showed no reactions as they went along with Roger's inflated price.

Joe said, "That's fine, Roger. We're happy to work with you on that basis. Now as a team member, we expect you to provide the name and location of the agent to whom we will be presenting this piece."

"I assumed that you would leave the statue with me, and I would make the presentation."

Joe said, "Sorry, Roger, but this item does not leave our hands until a sale has been concluded. I will not allow Mrs. Greene to entrust it to anyone who has not paid for it."

"Let me go into my private office and make a few phone calls." Roger left, and the others sat down at the conference table to wait for him. Penny and Joe exchanged a raised eyebrow signal indicating that they would soon know whether Roger would willingly guide their quest to the next person in the network.

CHAPTER 28 – RESEARCH

Irma had decided to put aside her normal busy schedule and spend the entire day with Renee Andrews and her baby, Thelma Lou. Renee was both a close friend and former colleague in ABC Consultants. Arthur had chosen to dedicate this day without Irma to learning more about the type of artifact that Travis Tobias had brought home from Iraq and about the cuneiform writing system. When he arrived at Parkville UMC, he asked Shirley to take messages on all routine calls she received and to clear the day's appointment schedule. Then he settled himself at the study table in his office and prepared to spend the whole day on research.

He started by doing computer searches on cuneiform writing and surviving samples including seals and cylinders. After reviewing these materials, he concluded that this early form of documentation, because of its inefficiencies and the need to fire the clay to make it permanent, served primarily to record important business transactions and archive government data. He found for instance that the Metropolitan Museum of Art had a double-tapered cylinder on which Nebuchadnezzar II had described the rebuilding of the temple of the sun-god Shamash at Sippar. He also found that surviving cuneiform cylinders varied in shape and size, presumably selected to fit the length of the inscribed record.

He next turned to the Old Testament of the Bible as the most reliable and most readily available surviving documentation of the Babylonian period and empire. He found significant references in the books of 2 Kings, 2 Chronicles, and Daniel, plus related background material in Exodus. He had set up a large sheet of paper with columns and headings into which he would enter the

Bible texts he judged to be important. The telephone rang, startling him out of his intense concentration.

Arthur reached for the telephone, knowing that it would be a necessary call, or Shirley would not have put it through to him. "Parkville United Methodist Church, Pastor Blake speaking; may I help you?"

"It's Howard Chandler, Arthur. Something dreadful has happened. We need your help right away."

"Slow down please, Bishop. I'll need some details. What exactly has happened?"

Arthur could hear the Bishop take three deep breaths before he responded. "Sorry, Arthur, I'm not as used to traumatic events as you are. As you know, I put Angela King on special assignment status to give us time to decide how to handle her reported attempt to kill her ex-husband. As part of that arrangement, we rented an office suite in Parkville for her to use as she wished, and I loaned her my secretary from the Rockford office to assist her. That secretary, Joyce Jennings, just telephoned. She was crying and said that she found Angela dead in her office. Joyce doesn't know whether it was suicide or an accident."

"Did you or Joyce call the police? Did she touch the body?"

"I told Joyce to stay outside of Angela's private office and to refrain from touching anything. I'm that much in line with police procedures from television. I called you before calling the police. Will you please handle it? If possible, try to keep anything that might be detrimental to the church out of the media."

"I'll take care of everything, Howard. What's the address?"

"The office is at 536 Main Street, room 22. It's on the second floor, one block past the Ford dealership."

"I'll call you after examining the scene, as soon as we have something to report."

Arthur ended the call, took his own deep breath, and then called Chief Bobby Andrews at the Police Department on his direct access number. "Hello, Bobby, it's Arthur. You'd better scramble your troops to 536 Main Street, room 22. I just received a call from Bishop Chandler saying that Angela King has been found dead there. They don't know whether it was a suicide, accident, or murder. A secretary, Joyce Jennings, found the body, and she's there now. I'll meet you there in ten minutes."

Bobby said, "Thanks for the summary; we'll get right on it. I'll see you there."

Ten minutes later, Arthur pulled into the parking lot behind 536 Main Street. Two marked and one unmarked police cars plus the paramedic ambulance had already arrived, and two of Bobby's new recruits kept the Main Street traffic moving. Sergeant Al Gomez opened the building's back door to admit him.

"Thanks, Al; Is Bobby upstairs already?"

"He's interviewing the woman who found the body, while Detectives Gene Murphy and Hank Robbins are examining the crime scene."

Arthur thanked Al and paused at the foot of the stairs to call Irma and tell her what had happened. He suggested she grab her forensics gear and come over before Gene and Hank disturbed too much evidence. He knew that they were old school cops who weren't forensically inclined when it came to investigations. John Pugh, the Medical Examiner who had replaced Irma had his office and laboratory in Rockford so that he could cover two counties, and Arthur knew it would take a while before he arrived.

There were too many people in the small two-room suite. Bobby sat interviewing Joyce in the outer office, while Gene, Hank, and two paramedics stood looking at Angela's body in the private room. Arthur went over to Bobby and whispered a few things to him. Bobby nodded and went into the other room while Arthur sat with Joyce Jennings to comfort her and listen to her summary of how she had found the body.

A few minutes later, the paramedics plus Hank went downstairs while Gene remained in the outer office. Bobby had arranged for the technicians to return for the body later if the Medical Examiner requested their assistance. He had also told Gene and Hank that Irma would soon arrive to provide technical consultation and make a forensic sweep of the offices.

Bobby returned to the outer office and joined Arthur and Joyce.

Arthur said, "So, Joyce, you didn't hear anything before you went in and found Angela dead. What prompted you to go in there at that particular time?"

"Angela had asked me to download a document from the conference website regarding the duties of the District Superintendent. Then I was supposed to print it out for her. I think she was reviewing the job's official duties so that she would be able to make a well-informed recommendation for someone to be her successor. I also had to use the copier downstairs to make twenty copies of her resume. When I came back upstairs and opened the door, I saw her lying on the floor in an unusual position. Her eyes were open, and they looked strange. I just dropped the papers. A few went into the room with her, and the rest are still on the floor in this room."

Bobby asked, "How did you know that she was dead and not just injured?"

"I tried to detect a pulse in her wrist, but here wasn't any, and her hand looked burned. When I let go of her hand, it just flopped down as though it had no life or feeling."

Arthur asked, "Which hand did you touch?"

"It was the left one. Her other arm was under her body, and I didn't want to move her from her strange position. If she were alive, she would have been very uncomfortable."

"Joyce, I know that this is a difficult time for you, and we'll let you think of other things as quickly as possible, but can you tell us anything about Angela's mood before she went into that office?"

"She seemed fine to me, Arthur. She may have been preoccupied because she was concentrating on her task, but she was cheerful when she told me how she liked her coffee earlier."

"And how did she have you prepare it?"

"She took it black with two spoons of sugar. Her coffee mug was still on the desk when I found her."

"Did she take any files or other objects into that office with her?"

"No, I don't remember any – just her purse."

Arthur said, "Those are all the questions I have, Bobby. Do you want to ask Joyce anything else?"

"No, there's no need to extend this session. Joyce, I'd like you to see Al Gomez downstairs. He'll give you a statement form to fill out and sign. It will cover the same information we discussed, but we like to get things down on paper while they're fresh in your mind."

Joyce left the outer office, and Bobby remarked to Arthur, "It's unsettling for someone who has never witnessed a crime to discover a murder victim. It will probably take several days for her to feel normal again."

"She gave me the impression of having her emotions under control."

The door from the hallway opened, and Irma entered, leaning slightly to the right to compensate for the burden of the heavy evidence kit suspended from a strap over her left shoulder.

"Hello, you two gumshoes. Aim me toward the crime scene, and I'll do my forensics examination."

Bobby said, "Welcome, Irma; too bad you had to lug that gear up to the second floor."

"Don't worry about me. I stay in shape by running around with that amateur sleuth friend of yours. Will you assist me with analyzing the death evidence, Arthur?"

"I wouldn't miss it; we work as a team now, except for lugging the heavy equipment. I leave that to you."

Bobby laughed. "I'm removing myself from the middle of any spats you two may have. Let me know when you reach some conclusions." He left and went downstairs, taking Gene Murphy along.

Irma gave Arthur a hug and said, "Let's get in there."

They hesitated at the doorway to the inner office, in order to grasp the overall layout of the scene. Angela lay on the floor near the desk in a semi-fetal position with her right arm underneath her body and her left arm outstretched. The desk had moved backward from its normal position, and the steel straight chair upon which she had been sitting lay on its side behind the body. Several sheets of paper and some items that had been on the desktop scatter-accented the floor like an abstract painting.

Arthur spoke first. "It looks like a straightforward case of murder by electrocution to me. What's your first impression, Irma?"

"No fair; you're reaching a conclusion before I even start my act. I'll be a little more systematic before I agree or disagree with you. First, I'll indicate that she pushed herself away from the desk with great force, causing the desk to move backward, especially on the right-hand side, and the chair to fly in the opposite direction as her body rebounded backward to the floor. Her distorted position on the floor is consistent with electrocution as are the burn on her outstretched left hand and the discoloration, probably due to burning, of her corneas."

"Joyce Jennings said that Angela's eyes looked strange to her when she entered, and the left hand looked burned."

"I'll have to agree with you that it looks like a case of electrocution. Now we have to ask whether it was an accident or murder. It is unlikely that it was suicide. There are more convenient and less painful ways to take your own life."

"Oh, this was premeditated murder and definitely not an accident."

"Why do you say that, Arthur?"

"I'll begin by pointing out the careful setup for it. There are only straight-back steel chairs in here, while there are wooden chairs in the outer office."

"And just to show you that I notice things too, the floor protector under the desk is made of metal rather than the usual plastic. I also noticed that the lamp's electrical cord is frayed a bit and runs under the metal floor protector mat."

"If you have a voltmeter in your kit, I'll wager that we'll be able to measure line voltage between the outer metal shell of that desk lamp and the floor mat. Be careful when taking that measurement; I'm not ready to lose you."

"Thank you for your sweet sentiment, Arthur. I won't take your wager. I show no voltage in that measurement now, and none at the wall socket, because the electrocution of Angela blew the fuse or tripped the circuit breaker. However, the office lights are still on, so someone may have prepared this arrangement using a power outlet that was on a separate circuit to avoid immediate detection of the crime."

Irma had been writing notes throughout their conversation. She added a final sentence and then said, "We agree on what happened here. All we need is to figure out who did it and why."

"I already know who the murderer is. I'm still working on the motive."

CHAPTER 29 – BOBBY

Chief Bobby Andrews leaned back against his black unmarked car behind the building where Angela King had died. He stared skeptically at Pastor Arthur Blake.

"You're telling me that you and Irma spent ten minutes at the death scene, determined it was a murder rather than an accident, and also solved the crime?"

Irma said, "I was part of the ten minutes thing, but Arthur's the one who says he knows the identity of the murderer. I bet he'll enlighten us if we give him just a little encouragement."

"All right, you two; I'll tell you who did it. That part is easy. The hard part will be to determine the motive. I have a feeling that the reason for the crime will help us to understand many other things."

Bobby put his arm around Arthur's shoulder. "I realize that you're enjoying this, but I have this recurring feeling that the world would be a better place if the professionals solved the crimes while the amateurs appreciated them and applauded. Ever since I first met you, I've found it to work the other way. I'm even getting used to it now, so please stop stalling and give me another reason to appreciate your insights...Who murdered Angela?"

"Joyce Jennings did it. She had the opportunity, and her story of how she found the body contained several lies. We'll have to learn more about her and her past relationships in order to discern the motive."

Bobby said, "I'll grant you that we cops are always suspicious of the person who finds the body, but what evidence do you have that she lied and did it?"

"I'll start by questioning her statement that she was away from Angela for just the time it takes to print a document several pages long and to make some copies.

She said that she didn't hear anything, but simply opened the door and found Angela dead. Bobby, you know that a Tasered criminal usually thrashes around, and if in an office would make significant noise after a shock. What's your opinion, Irma?"

"I would have expected Angela's involuntary reflexes to have kicked in, making her pull her hand away from the shock point on the lamp very rapidly. I would also suggest that the setup in that office would not be a very reliable way to electrocute someone. There would be too much chance of a minor shock that caused little damage."

Arthur said, "Thanks for that insight. I had been concerned about the reliability aspect, and I'll wager that right after the initial shock, Joyce went into the office and finished Angela off with a Taser or another shocking device set to a high level. Irma, you or the current Medical examiner should check for evidence of a shock site on the neck or head."

Bobby said, "What's your reasoning on that one?"

"The shock from the lamp burned Angela's hand, which is reasonable to expect. However, both Joyce's description and our observation showed that Angela's had burned corneas. That indicates a shock site on or near the head. It wouldn't be a likely thing to happen from a shock on an extended hand. Nothing in that office setup should have shocked her head, so I concluded that it was a deliberate follow-up event with some kind of hand-held device. Joyce would have had plenty of time to hide or get rid of it before she decided that it was safe to report the death."

Irma said, "I'll have to agree with you as far as a shock site needing to be near the burnt corneas. What other evidence do you have against Joyce?"

"You guys like to kid me about my love of coffee, but some of the strongest evidence against Joyce relates to coffee."

Bobby said, "What do you mean? How does coffee prove she's the murderer?"

"First, we have Joyce's statement that she gave Angela coffee before she went to make document copies. When Angela felt the shock, she pushed away from the lamp and desk, moving the desk backward and toppling herself backward along with the steel chair. Yet, the cup of coffee on the desk did not spill at all. Therefore, it was placed on the desk after Angela hit the floor in order to make the desk setup look more normal."

Irma said, "You're right. I thought there was something unusual about the desktop, but I couldn't quite figure it out."

"That's not all. The most damning evidence about the coffee is that Angela never asked Joyce for coffee at any time. Joyce said that Angela asked her for black coffee with two spoonfuls of sugar. Because I am such a fan of the brown brew, I always invite my guests to have coffee with me in my office. Angela liked hers with a little creamer but no sugar. Joyce had no idea how Angela liked it, so she created her own formula. Is that enough evidence for you, Bobby?"

"I'm convinced, but move on to the question of motive. What possibilities have you considered?"

"I haven't come up with any reasons that I'd give a high probability rating. She could have been in love with the Bishop and was seeking vengeance for Angela having embarrassed him through her attempted murder confession."

Irma said, "Passion does strange things to people, but we'd have to know more about Joyce to analyze the probability of that one."

"Another possibility is that she had a personal conflict due to something Angela did as District Superintendent. What do you think of that one, Irma?"

"That sounds more reasonable but still pretty drastic unless Joyce felt she had been very badly wronged."

Bobby said, "I have a suggestion, but we'd have to do some research to check it out. What if Joyce Jennings turned out to be Charlie King's relative or lover?"

Arthur said, "You mean someone seeking revenge for Charlie? Why take that approach?"

"Joyce executed Angela in an electric chair."

CHAPTER 30 – AGENT

Alicia Pavone completed her telephone conversation with Roger Svenson and updated her calendar to show that in two days he was to send her one of his clients who had an outstanding Egyptian artifact. She assumed that the piece must be special for Roger to have taken such an aggressive posture in talking with her about it. When they had met to discuss that earlier cuneiform piece, she had found him to be quite sheepish and wimpy. Perhaps he hadn't previously handled such an unusual antiquity, and once having been through the process, he felt more secure about himself. Roger was a bit of a strange character. She liked the idea of meeting his clients without him being along. If the artifact turned out to be of unique value and condition, she would gladly arrange a second meeting with her principal. The nearly completed purchase of the previous item had welded her relationship with a major buyer who insisted on shrouding his identity.

Alicia had stumbled into the art agent field ten years ago after briefly working at the Art Institute of Chicago as a Jill-of-all-trades assistant. While there, a young sculptor had approached her and asked whether she would be willing to help him get publicity and sell a few of his works. She would have taken it for a pick-up line if she hadn't been so many years his elder. Once she visited his studio and realized that he really did have unusual talent, she turned her full attention to promoting his work and made an unexpectedly large amount of money in the process. That taste of success in the art world had been intoxicating for her. It convinced her that she had found her niche in life, albeit at a relatively senior age. Since then her sales expertise had earned her familiarity status with a surprising number of well-known artists, collectors, and galleries.

If she played her cards well, her newest client would be the crowning achievement of her art career. His collection inventory surpassed those of many museums with regard to quality and, in certain specialty categories, even quantity. They had met through a third party confidante and had become close, even intimate, friends. She hoped to become his public spokesperson, allowing him to enjoy the anonymity he cherished. It would not be out of the question to consider a marriage with the great collector; but she hesitated to think openly about that. A premature push in that direction could backfire and ruin her career. She would have to be patient and see what developed over the course of multiple transactions.

CHAPTER 31 – JOYCE JENNINGS

Chief Bobby Andrews sat across his conference table from the Blakes. He explained some of the difficulties he saw with the case of Angela's murder. "I have to proceed carefully and build a strong case against her. Our initial checks show that Joyce Jennings has no criminal record of any kind. She served for several years as Bishop Chandler's secretary in his Rockford office, but there is no evidence or even a suspicion of romance between them. We tried to link her to Charlie King, but we have not been able to find any connection at all between those two. I don't think Joyce even met Charlie. He never accompanied his wife when she attended church functions."

Irma said, "I hear your frustration. We all agree that she is the most likely person to have planned and carried out this murder, but if you arrest her without significant evidence, a good lawyer will get her an acquittal. She wouldn't be able to be retried later based on new additional evidence because of the Constitution's double jeopardy clause."

Arthur said, "If we can prove that she's the only one who had the access and opportunity to install that electrocution death-trap, you might have enough evidence to arrest her. We took pictures showing that the coffee didn't spill despite the sudden movement of the desk. However, that would only prove that she lied when she said she brought the coffee into the office before Angela died. Bobby, what does the law say about setting a trap so that the victim's death is self-triggered?"

"We can get a conviction if we show deliberate preparation of the trap with intent to kill. It would be useful to have the motive in order to present a convincing case to the jury, but you can get a murder conviction without showing the motive."

Irma said, "Regardless of the courtroom benefits, I'd like to know the motive, both to convince myself that we have the correct person and to better understand her thinking. What's your breakdown of Joyce's possible motives, Arthur?"

"I told you at the crime scene that I was having a problem working out the motive. It's still a bit of a problem for me, but I'll walk through my thinking.

"Bobby's people have determined that there was no obvious connection between Joyce Jennings and Charlie King, and they could not find any past criminality or immorality for Joyce. Those facts suggest that the motive might be based on something in the present or the future, rather than the past."

Irma said, "That might include things like jealousy or competition for the same job."

Bobby shook his head. "I don't want to be negative during a brainstorming session, but those don't sound like things that would stir up enough passion to murder someone. I'm going to disagree with you, Arthur, and say we should look into the past, but beyond the recent past. I'd like to know more about Joyce's life history, not just whether she has a criminal record."

Irma nodded. "I think you're on track with that thought. I'll second your thinking. Joyce Jennings is someone we encountered at the crime scene, but we know very little about her. Her background may help us to understand what happened. Will you go along with that, Arthur?"

"I'll go you one better. While you two are looking into Joyce's past life, I'll examine Angela's background. They may have had some prior history or friction between them. Joyce has served as Bishop Chandler's secretary in the Rockford office for quite a while. Let's do our homework and then revisit our motive discussion."

Irma said, "I'll tell Joe and Penny about Angela's murder and ask for their assistance on deep background checks."

CHAPTER 32 – ALICIA

Their search had led them to one of the older St. Louis office buildings on Washington Avenue. After entering, they ascended in an old-fashioned elevator that took what felt like five minutes to reach the fourth floor. Upon exiting that scrollwork cage, Penny and Joe read the directions on the opposite wall and turned left toward Suite 416. Upon reaching their destination, they realized that Alicia Pavone presented a much higher level of hospitality to her clients and visitors than did Roger Svenson. Roger's offices had a bare bones feeling with minimal furniture and furnishings. Everything in Alicia's suite was first class and welcoming. A young man in a pinstriped suit and tie strode briskly toward them within ten seconds of their arrival.

"You must be Mrs. Greene and Mr. Gonzalez. I'm Jeffrey Melton. Alicia asked me to tend to your needs until she finishes her telephone conversation. Would you like anything to drink? We have coffee, tea, sodas, and wine. We also have assortments of biscuits and fruit. Those items are all on the counter in the conference room to your right. There is also a projector and screen in there, in case you have something on your computer that you will want to project during your meeting."

Penny said, "Thank you, Jeffrey; that is very thoughtful of you, but we've just come from another meeting where refreshments were served. Perhaps we'll sample something later, depending on the length of our discussions with Alicia. We'll get settled at the conference table and wait for her to join us."

They were both surprised when they entered the conference room and Jeffrey closed the door behind them. However, his reason became clear a few minutes later when Alicia Pavone joined them through a different door in the rear of the room.

"Greetings to both of you; I hope that my tardiness didn't inconvenience you. I had a negotiation for a delightful miniature painting that I was able to conclude by telephone."

Penny said, "I'm glad you were successful. It's always enjoyable to meet with someone who has recently concluded a satisfactory transaction. Congratulations to you."

"Thank you very much, Mrs. Greene; I hope that our business today will be equally satisfying. I'm pleased to meet you also, Mr. Gonzalez. Please make yourselves comfortable and we'll review the purpose of your visit. I received a brief summary from Roger Svenson, but, where possible, I always prefer to receive an explanation directly from the principals."

Joe nodded to Penny, and she took the lead. "My family has gathered a small collection of art objects, primarily antiquities, and we regularly look to sell a few of the more conventional pieces in order to fund our acquisition of some new items for which the market may not yet have been established. This technique has worked well for us and has allowed us to expand our little collection."

"I understand your approach, and it is quite laudable. Essentially, you are trying to buy low and sell high. That is always a worthwhile strategy, so long as you do not acquire too many pieces that fail to increase in value. I assume you have had at least a few of those, Penny."

"We do have two parchment scrolls that had not received proper care prior to our purchase of them. We are currently debating whether we will be able to afford commissioning someone to recondition them and whether that process would even be successful. Antiquities are wonderful because they allow you to reach across the centuries to those who helped found our civilization, but by definition they are so old that they might fall apart despite the best handling and intentions."

Alicia brightened at the opportunity to discuss one of her favorite topics. "I thoroughly understand. We're currently in negotiations for a unique cuneiform cylinder."

Joe said, "That would be the double-tapered item that Roger mentioned when we visited with him. Such a piece would be of interest to us also."

Alicia stiffened at Joe's comment. "Svenson didn't show good judgment in discussing an object that is currently the subject of negotiations. We are acting for a collector who remains anonymous and does not care to broadcast his holdings or interests. He is a unique individual who requires unquestioning support and loyalty from those who assist his efforts."

Penny said, "You wouldn't be interested in discussing that piece even if we were talking about a much higher price than the one you have discussed?"

"As I said, the relationship with this potential buyer is of utmost importance. He would be a potential buyer for many artifacts."

Joe chose his words carefully. "Even such a collector must concern himself with the ownership history of an artifact and the legality of his purchase."

"Are you suggesting that there might be a problem with the piece that Svenson brought to us? If so, the burden is on him; he certified that his client had free and clear ownership of that cylinder...And who are you to raise that question?" Alicia did not like the direction this conversation was taking.

Penny stood and said, "I'm afraid that we really don't have anything to sell you today. The statue we brought to discuss is on loan to us from the Smithsonian. It is a true treasure. We did misrepresent ourselves somewhat. Joe and I are principals, all right, but the entity we represent is a federal government investigative agency. That cuneiform cylinder may be the property of the Iraqi

National Museum. We're searching out items looted during the early stages of the war in Iraq." Penny and Joe each displayed their federal credentials.

Joe said, "We're going to have to ask you to return that artifact so that we may determine its ownership, or you may face possible prosecution for dealing in stolen property."

"I no longer have it. It's in the hands of the collector for whom I'm working, and per the terms of our contract, I'm not allowed to reveal his identity."

"You'll either reveal his identity, or we'll have to arrest you. Which would you prefer?"

Alicia felt sweat trickling down her back and moistening her designer dress. "Your demand would ruin my business. If I tell you, none of my clients will consider me trustworthy. I also want the opportunity for continuing work with this client on non-controversial artworks. I absolutely will not reveal my client's name."

Penny said, "Perhaps I can assist you in solving your dilemma. You don't have to reveal his name. Simply confirm whether I already have the correct name. Is that agreeable to you?"

Alicia wondered whether they were trying to trick her, but she nodded.

"Do you confirm that the principal you represent is Karl Simitski?"

Alicia looked shocked, but she nodded. Her eyes had a blank stare as they led her out of the room. In the outer office, she recovered enough to tell Jeffrey to lock up and take the rest of the day off, while she left with her visitors to meet with some of their associates.

CHAPTER 33 – ANGELA'S HISTORY

Arthur arrived a few minutes early for his meeting with Bishop Howard Chandler and used that time to pour some coffee and scan the office where Joyce Jennings normally worked. She had been given time off to recover from her traumatic experience of finding Angela's body. The police had been very quiet about their suspicions, so all of the officials of the UMC Northern Illinois Conference assumed that Angela's death had been a tragic accident. When Bishop Chandler came out of his office to greet Arthur, he found him looking at some of Joyce's family photographs.

"Hello, Arthur; I set aside a block of time so that we won't have to rush our conversations. Angela's death was such a shock. Thank you so much for handling the interface with the police for us."

"That's one burden I'm suited to remove from your shoulders, Howard. I was just looking at some of Joyce's pictures. I know very little about her background. Is she married and a mother?"

"No, those are pictures of some of her extended family members. She is single, but from a family that had adopted six children from varying backgrounds. She calls her family a miniature United Nations. I've found that background very useful to the church when we are entertaining international visitors. Joyce can usually come up with some family member or friend with an appropriate ethnicity or cultural knowledge. Let's make ourselves comfortable in my office for privacy while we discuss Angela's demise."

Bishop Chandler closed the office door behind them. Then he motioned for Arthur to join him in the two chairs in front of the fireplace.

"Now, Arthur, please tell me what happened to Angela. I didn't ask Joyce because I want her to avoid reliving that experience."

"The basic facts are that Angela died as the result of an electric shock when she reached to turn on a lamp that had a short circuit."

"Then it was an accident?"

"The police are still investigating all aspects of the case and haven't reached any conclusions. They asked me to refrain from expressing any personal opinions until they completed their work...I did want to ask you how much you know about Angela's personal background."

"Do you mean relatively recent information or all the way back to when she was a child?"

"Until fairly recently I had only interacted with her on an official basis. I would like to get a feeling for her entire history, as you know it. She should have the benefit of being remembered as a complete person and not just as a professional."

"That's compassionate thinking, and it also fits with my feeling that you should perform the memorial service when we have one. I've had my staff trying to locate any of Angela's family members. It would be up to them to schedule the service."

"Have you found any family members yet?"

"None so far, but we're still hopeful. I'll tell you what I know about her, but some details may not be correct. I'll be talking off the top of my head, without records or notes."

"That will be fine, Howard. I'll take a few notes from your comments, and then we'll check them against her official records later."

"To start with, Angela's maiden name was Melrose, and she grew up in Los Angeles. Her mother did name her after the city. She once told me that she was a little wild as a teenager, but she didn't tell me much more about that period. She said that at one time she wanted to be an airline flight attendant, but that when that didn't work out she went into social services, working with abused and unwed mothers at a childcare center. During her social services work, she met several church clergy people who convinced her that she should continue her formal studies and eventually enter the seminary. Once she took that route, she discovered that she was a better student than many of her more conventionally educated peers, and she graduated from the seminary with honors. She was also very fortunate in that she emerged from training at the time when our church was searching for good female candidates for local church ministry and staff positions."

"Did she have her own congregations?"

"Angela served as an associate pastor in two California churches and then became pastor of a church in Las Vegas. After several years there, she asked for a transfer to the Northern Illinois Conference because she had an elderly Aunt in Rockford who needed her assistance. That aunt died six years later."

"Was Angela serving in a church while she cared for her aunt?"

"The conference gave her an appointment as associate pastor of one of the larger Rockford churches, so that she would be able to spend a portion of her time assisting her aunt. After the Aunt died, Angela served as pastor of a church in Mt. Morris. From there she moved up to become District Superintendent."

"Was Charlie King her first husband?"

"That's an interesting question. She never talked about a previous marriage, but she came into our conference as Angela Markham rather than Angela Melrose. I would assume that either she had married earlier, or she had legally changed her name for some reason. Will that be important to your understanding her better?"

"No, Bishop, I think I have more than enough information to prepare for the memorial service. Thank you, and let me know when you want to schedule it. I'll keep you advised on any official statements issued by the police."

Arthur left Bishop Chandler's office with an emphatic mental note to check on the significance of Angela's use of the Markham name.

CHAPTER 34 – PSYCHIC POWER

During her interview at the St. Louis Federal Building, Alicia had cooperated in providing a recorded statement to Penny and Joe about her business relationship with Karl Simitski. She kept the personal and intimate portion of their relationship to herself. Once Penny had told her that she knew about Karl, Alicia considered herself to have been relieved of her confidentiality obligations. Penny's knowledge of Karl was mysterious, but Alicia respected the intelligence-gathering capabilities of the federal government and assumed that his name had resulted from a second parallel investigation. She felt relieved when they told her that she would be free to leave as soon as she signed her transcribed statement plus a pledge that she would not reveal any information about her interview when she contacted Karl. Having feared an arrest for dealing in stolen artifacts, Alicia was more than willing to sacrifice her possible relationship with Karl for freedom and the ability to pursue her business interests elsewhere. If they were going to arrest Karl, she would stay far away from him.

After Alicia left, Joe congratulated Penny on the effectiveness of her surprise statement to Alicia. "I didn't expect you to take that approach. What if your guess had been wrong?"

"I was pretty confident that it deserved more than a *guess* rating. I'm hardly psychic, but I finally figured out that those birth certificates constitute a treasure map for us. It took a while to determine the nature of the treasure, but once we had covered the first couple of stops along the trail, the pattern started to emerge."

"Explain yourself."

"The first stop on this trail had to be Travis Tobias, both because he had died in the war and because his home town was where Charlie King or Oliver Parkworth had last been sighted. Steve's conversations with Ellen Tobias led us to the cuneiform cylinder treasure item and identified Roger Svenson as the second link in the chain. Roger connected us with Alicia Pavone, leaving three remaining possible connections from the mysterious set of six birth certificates: Karl Simitski, Arthur Blake, and Geraldine Quig. One of these had to be the buyer for whom Alicia was working. Arthur has no money for purchasing such items. I had previously checked Geraldine Quig and found that she is an academic who would want to study the cylinder, but couldn't afford to buy it. That left Karl Simitski, who in addition to being an art collector, is the right age for a love tryst with Alicia. Her loyalty in trying to mask his identity suggested to me that theirs was more than a business relationship."

"That logic suggests that some of Arthur's deductive talent is rubbing off on you. Do you think that either Roger Svenson or Alicia is innocently entangled in this web?"

"Not a chance; those two are both pros at finding and profiting from artifacts. It wouldn't take a huge intellect to understand that a soldier spiriting an antiquity out of Iraq, had probably *liberated* rather than purchased it. Roger and Alicia could have refused to seek a buyer for an undocumented item of suspicious origin, but they didn't. They took a risk, and they may pay for it before this affair comes to an end."

Joe settled back in his desk chair. "Even if that artifact was not looted from the museum, we can relax a bit. When we thought we were chasing Charlie King, we expected to encounter a terrorism plot. Now it's obvious that we're uncovering schemes of greed, not terror."

"Don't get too comfortable with that thinking. We still don't know what happened to Charlie King. The fact that those birth certificates came from his jacket pocket might suggest that we're following a path he set out for us. It may turn out that he's looking over our shoulders as we seek the treasure that he was pursuing."

"I'll pull myself out of my complacency."

CHAPTER 35 – YOUNG JOYCE

Penny glanced at the incoming caller identification on her phone and answered it. "Hi, Irma; have you missed us while we've been following leads?"

"You bet we have, Penny. I hope that the trail of breadcrumbs you've been tracking hasn't disappeared."

"So far we've done a good job of following that trail, but I have a feeling that the next stage will be more challenging. Those birth certificates are artwork dots that we have to connect in order to see the hidden picture. Is there anything we can do to assist you in solving your part of the puzzle?"

"Honestly, Penny, I do like to chat with you when I don't have a hidden agenda, but this isn't one of those times. We local folk may need an assist from you folks with federal government power. Bobby and I have been trying to research the background of a suspect in the murder of Angela King. We ran into some discontinuities in her history due to unregistered name changes and records that are sealed. I know that you guys are as busy as can be, but could Steve or someone else from your Washington office help us to bypass some legal record blocks?"

"I think Steve would be available. I'll call him and have him contact you. Angela's murder may be a local affair, or it may tie into our broader case. I see no problem if we join your effort. I do see one interesting implication of your crime."

"What's that?"

"There will be no prosecution of Angela for her murder or attempted murder of Charlie King in Canada."

"That had crossed my mind also."

127

"Is there any chance that Charlie killed her for revenge, assuming he survived her earlier attack, or that some friend of his did it on Charlie's behalf?"

"We don't want to close our minds to any possibilities, but so far we're concentrating on possible interpersonal conflicts in the workplace or at some past time. We think we know *who* did it and *how*. We're trying to pin down the *why* of it before Bobby makes an arrest."

"That sounds like good police work, Irma. I'll have Steve contact you right away."

Penny was accurate in her statement. Ten minutes later Steve DuBois and Irma engaged in a long telephone conversation during which she aimed him at several areas of Joyce Jennings' background that warranted additional sleuthing. Some of these involved legally restricted information. Steve promised to call in a few favors their agency had earned along the way. He felt sure that they would be able to get information flowing on Joyce's childhood background.

While she awaited Steve's feedback, Irma would check with Arthur to learn what the Bishop had revealed about Angela's past.

CHAPTER 36 – PAST TENSE

Irma stopped in at Arthur's church office and slid into his guest chair while he completed a conversation with Shirley. The subject was planning a party for the veterans who lived in the group residence on the other side of the lower parking lot.

Shirley touched Irma on the shoulder as she stood to return to her office. "Irma, do you realize that I don't see you nearly as much as I did before you two got married?"

"I miss you too, Shirley. I don't get over here as much because the courtship's over. I always had to be here to defend him against all the other women who were after him, but now that he's hooked, the competition has moved on to other targets."

Arthur said, "I wish you two wouldn't talk about me as though I'm not in the same room with you. I feel invisible."

Shirley said, "We do that just to see whether you're paying attention. Sometimes your concentration is so deep that you don't even notice other people walking in and out of here...I think I just gave myself a cue. Irma, I'll be back in the church office if you want to talk more."

After Shirley left, Irma walked over to Arthur and gave him a shoulder rub. "She's right, you know; I should visit you here in your native habitat. I have to remind myself that you do fulfill your pastoral duties along with everything else."

"My two worlds overlapped today. I had the unusual experience of visiting Bishop Chandler and pumping him for information while I tried to be deferential to him at the same time."

"Knowing you, I'll bet he gave you a lot more information than he realized. Are you ready to share some of it with me?"

"Of course I am. The most interesting part is that I was looking for background data on Angela, and during the process, I learned a fair amount about Joyce."

"Hold it right there, Arthur; I've been hitting snags in my quest for Joyce's history. What exactly did you discover?"

"For one thing, I learned that she was adopted, and her adoptive parents took in five additional children from different ethnic and national backgrounds. Joyce grew up to be comfortable in situations where a variety of cultures and languages were represented."

"Is she fluent in several languages?"

"Howard gave me the impression that she may be, but he didn't specifically say so. He did give me the additional information that she's single and without children."

"He doesn't know everything about her. Bobby and I found out that Joyce had married a man she lived with for a short while. He turned out to have already had a wife, so Joyce had her marriage annulled to keep him from having to face bigamy charges. His name was Robert Carmichael. Now that I have your information from Howard Chandler, I'll ask Steve to check into the details of Joyce's adoption. We think he'll have enough government connections to get around some of the secrecy they place on old adoption records."

CHAPTER 37 – KARL SIMITSKI

They flew to Columbia, Missouri and then drove out to Karl Simitski's home, located just far enough away from Finger Lakes State Park to avoid the almost continuous sounds of motorcycles and all terrain vehicles on challenging trails. Joe and Penny exchanged surprised glances as they drove up to the simple stone house nestled in the woods. It didn't match their expectations for the home of a successful art collector. They also doubted that it contained sufficient space to house the collection that had so impressed Alicia. They parked their rental car close enough to the edge of the long sloping driveway for other vehicles to pass, and climbed the six steps to the front door. The doorbell rang loudly and soon the door opened to reveal a tall, round-shouldered man who looked older than he probably was. He wore a red plaid flannel shirt and blue jeans.

Joe said, "Mr.Simitski? Thank you for allowing us to visit you on such short notice. I'm Joe Gonzalez, and this is Penny Greene. We're interested in the cuneiform cylinder that you're in the process of acquiring."

"Come on in, and we'll talk about it. We can use the front room; it has a good view of the park and all the activities down there."

They sat down and helped themselves to lemonade from a pitcher perched on a coffee table made from an outsized blacksmith bellows.

Karl said, "I don't know how you found out about that piece, but I haven't finalized my bid on it yet. It's not even here. I'm having a consultant in Texas check out its authenticity and history. Even if it were here, I wouldn't want to sell it. It will become a valuable addition to my collection of antiquities from the Middle East."

Penny said, "We definitely would like to see it, but not for the purpose of trying to buy it from you. We're actually from a federal agency, and we're responsible for examining artifacts of this type to determine whether their sale would be legal. We suspect that this particular item was stolen from the Iraqi National Museum during the looting spree early in the war there."

"If it is a stolen item, I would, of course, cooperate by giving it up. However, at this time I'm more interested in examining it to determine its significance than I am in actually owning it. I feel fortunate that you've raised this question before I parted with a major amount of capital for it."

Joe said, "I'm sure that we can work with you on the timing of any possible confiscation of this item so that we may all learn more about it. I do have one question that has been bothering me as we've sat here. Where do you keep your collection? This house certainly isn't large enough to store or display it."

"The house suits my personality, Joe. I may have money, but I don't like to advertize it, and I like this location. It's convenient for appreciating nature and for watching young people at play. These pastimes help me feel younger than my calendar age. As for the collection, that's another reason for this location. Old abandoned underground mines dating back to the nineteenth century honeycomb this part of Missouri. They contain a variety of minerals. I purchased one of them and converted it to a private underground museum. I've improved it with proper structural support, modern interiors, and even air conditioning. Most museums in buildings aren't as appropriate for art preservation. I have a consulting associate who visits it periodically and maintains it for me. I'm free to concentrate on other things."

Penny said, "Do you have other objects similar to the cuneiform cylinder?"

"If you're angling at the question of the backgrounds of my artifacts, I have complete sales history documentation on everything. The cylinder was the first item I've ever considered without such a pedigree. That's why I wasn't particularly surprised when you showed up. I only opened myself up to questions of rightful ownership because of the potential significance of this particular antiquity."

Joe said, "What's so special about it?"

"You don't know?"

Penny said, "I'm afraid we've been playing a catch-up game on this artifact. Outside of feeling sure that it left its proper home in Iraq illegally, we don't know much about it."

"In that case, you'll have to stay for dinner, and afterward I'll enlighten you. I promise you won't be bored by spending a little extra time with me."

CHAPTER 38 – BACKGROUND CHECKS

Irma paced back and forth in their apartment, trying to restart her circulation after sitting for a long telephone session with Steve DuBois. He had presented such a detailed report on what he had found out about Joyce Jennings' family that Irma had given up on taking longhand notes and had switched to entering most of her notes as a document on her computer. After her pacing exercises, Irma called Arthur and asked him to come home to review the new information with her. While she waited, she did thirty pushups and then a variety of stretches. After this burst of activity, she felt ready to apply herself to an analysis session. She was still breathing rapidly when she heard Arthur entering.

"Hi, husband, sorry to disturb your rituals at church, but Steve delivered on his task of peering into the normally opaque world of adoptions."

"Your enthusiasm suggests his delivery contained something useful to us. I'll get my coffee, and we can get right to it. I have a little input too, but I'll save it for later."

"Are you going to upstage me again with even more useful information?"

"Honestly, Irma, I won't know how valuable my contribution is, until I learn more about Joyce and her family."

Arthur filled one of his NASA coffee mugs from his earlier engineering days and sat down at the dining room table across from Irma and her laptop computer. He knew that she preferred to reveal her information in small doses rather than allowing him to read it directly from her computer screen.

Once Irma looked settled, Arthur asked, "What did Steve discover?"

"Joyce's adoptive parents were hippy types or flower children, as they used to call them. They thought that by adopting children from a wide variety of backgrounds, they would contribute to achieving world peace."

"That's a laudable goal. Did their children turn out well and help with international relations?"

"Not very much; the Mexican child, Jose, grew up to get involved in the drug trade, and some of the others turned out worse than he did. Francois from Quebec joined the Navy and deserted his ship in Greece. He joined a cell of Balkan terrorists. Stephanie from England is in prison for embezzling funds from the Los Angeles branch of her UK firm. At least Wieslaw from Poland and Maria from Argentina don't have any criminal records or outstanding warrants against them. They both moved to New York City, where they're actually working for the United Nations in keeping with their parents' goals for their heterogeneous family."

"That leaves Joyce, whom we suspect of murder. What did Steve find out about her specific history?"

"Joyce had no criminal record, but she did euphemistically get into trouble. Following her annulled marriage to the bigamist, she had a brief affair with a sailor. That escapade ended up with her pregnant. She refused to get an abortion and started to raise the child, a girl named Robin, as a single mother. An interesting side point was that the family name of Joyce and all her siblings wasn't Jennings. It was O'Grady. Joyce changed her name, perhaps to that of the sailor who fathered her daughter."

"You said she started to raise Robin. Did anything happen to the child?"

"You caught that phrasing right away. As a single parent, Joyce had to work full-time, so she placed Robin in a preschool as soon as she was potty trained and able to handle socializing with people outside of the family. The Brannigan Preschool had a few complaints registered against it, but it was close to her apartment, and it was less expensive than most. Robin went there for a year or so without incident, but one early December morning, the children in her class were helping their teacher trim the school Christmas tree, and something happened that caused Robin and another little girl named Lisa to be electrocuted while stringing the lights. There was an investigation afterward; it led to a finding of accidental death for the two girls. Most people thought the cause was negligence on the part of the teacher and the school. It turned out that the string of lights was in poor condition, and the tree was out on the front porch. The floor was still wet after an early morning rainstorm, so the children were handling defective lights while walking through puddles."

"I assume from your comments on the investigation that no one was charged in connection with their deaths?"

"That's right, but there were consequences. The city shut down the Brannigan Preschool, and Beverly Brannigan, the founder, committed suicide six months later."

"What happened to the teacher who was in charge?"

"I don't have any information on that one. Steve's contacts thought she had left town."

"Did he include her name in his summary of the situation?"

"Let me check...Here it is; it was Marcia Melrose. Is that significant?"

"I've been doing some background checking on our late District Superintendant. Her birth name was Marcia Angela Melrose. By the time she had begun to prepare for the clergy, she had changed it to Angela Marcia Markham. That was her name when she married Charlie and became Angela King."

Irma said, "Then we have our motive – revenge."

"And not just any form of revenge; it had to be by electrocution."

CHAPTER 39 – SPECULATION

Karl Simitski finished the last sip of his wine. Then he refilled it from the distinctive wine bottle. Holding the glass up against the blazing sunset, he said, "Both blood red; how very appropriate."

He turned to Penny and Joe. "I hope you two like adventure stories. Is it safe to assume that you both saw the movie *Raiders of the Lost Ark?*"

They both acknowledged that they had.

"That movie had it all wrong, but it was entertaining."

Penny said, "That was one of my all-time favorites, but you couldn't take it seriously. It was just an adventure story. What do you mean by saying that they had it wrong?"

"Penny, there really was an Ark of the Covenant. It's described in the Bible and mentioned in many places. It was the portable home for the stone tablets of the Ten Commandments that Moses had received from God. The thing they had wrong in the movie was that they found it in Egypt."

Joe came closer and joined into the conversation. "Where should they have found it?"

"Nobody knows where it is today. Let me give you a little background from history and the Bible too. Nabopolassar founded the Chaldean Kingdom in Babylonia in 612 BC after the Chaldeans defeated the Assyrian kings. When he died in 605 BC, his son, Nebuchadnezzar II, came to power. You read in the Bible about this same Nebuchadnezzar. As the big power in the area, Nebuchadnezzar required payments of tribute from all the smaller states to guarantee that he wouldn't conquer them with his armies. Judah, one of those tribute states rebelled in 597 BC, but was invaded and

137

conquered. They returned to being a tribute payer, but rebelled again in 588 BC under their new leader, Zedekiah. In 586 BC, Nebuchadnezzar reacted to these repeated rebellions by sending the armies of General Nebuzaradan to Jerusalem where they destroyed the Temple of Solomon and most of the city. They deported most of the remaining residents of Jerusalem to Babylon and, according to the Bible in 2 Chronicles, Nebuchadnezzar's forces took away to Babylon *all the vessels of the house of God, large and small, and the treasures of the house of the Lord.* Scholars have never been sure whether the Ark of the Covenant was one of those treasures, but the simplest and most logical answer is that it was. Other scholars have suggested that the Ark remained hidden deep below the ruins of the first temple; or that Jeremiah and his followers took it before the Babylonian armies arrived and hid it in a mountain cave. There is the theory upon which the movie was based, that the Ark was captured in a later Egyptian invasion, and some would have it that the Ark now reposes in Saint Mary of Zion's Church in the ancient Ethiopian city of Aksum."

Joe said, "Where do you think it is?"

"I'm committed to the straightforward theory that Nebuchadnezzar took it back to Babylon along with all of the other treasures of the temple."

Penny said, "What would have happened to it then?"

"Nebuchadnezzar built many palaces and temples dedicated to the Babylonian gods. He recorded the plans and technical details of each building on one or more clay cuneiform cylinders like the one we have been discussing, and he typically stored each cylinder within a small chamber in the corner of its building so that the information on that cylinder might be used when the building needed reconstruction at a later time."

Penny stared out into the distance as the last rays of the setting sun disappeared. "How well were

Nebuchadnezzar's buildings preserved? Are they still there?"

"Nebuchadnezzar died in 562 BC. He was succeeded by several minor kings, and the Chaldean Kingdom ended when they were conquered by Cyrus the Great of Persia in 539 BC. Under his rule, Cyrus allowed most of the Jews to return to Jerusalem and take some of their temple vessels with them. The rest of the temple treasures remained in Babylon. To answer your question, the buildings are long gone, and no one knows where the treasures are, but many of the cuneiform cylinders remain."

"And you think the cylinder you are trying to buy is the treasure map?"

"To be honest, Joe, I have no idea, but I've been in this artifact business long enough to have a hunch, simply because its condition is so good. Over the centuries, many people must have gone out of their way to preserve this particular cylinder. I'm waiting for the opinion of my academic consultant to affirm or negate my theory."

"Would you organize a big expedition to try to find the Ark and the other treasures if your consultant says this might be the key piece of evidence?"

"No, Penny; I'm getting too old for that. I'll settle for convincing myself that I have something unique in my collection that in some way has a linkage to the Bible and God. That would be more than enough treasure for me."

Joe said, "That sounds awesome, Karl, but I have to remind you that this cylinder was probably looted from the Iraq Museum. As such, it would have to be returned; you would not be allowed to keep it."

Karl smiled and patted Joe on the back. "The Oriental Institute at the University of Chicago has been trying to construct a database of the looted items. They have reported that the Iraq Museum's collection of approximately forty-eight hundred cuneiform cylinders remains missing. How is anyone going to determine that this particular cylinder is one of those forty-eight hundred? The destruction of a building during the invasion of Baghdad might have released it from an unknown wall cavity, or it may have belonged to an individual who left no will. I'm not a young man, and I'm sure my attorneys will be able to keep the ownership question open until I die. That will be long enough for me. I'm due to visit my consultant in Texas. You folks are welcome to come along to see how the analysis of this antiquity turns out."

CHAPTER 40 – AUTOPSY RESULTS

Arthur walked out of Miller's Garage on Dalton Street after having dropped off his Saturn Vue for an oil change. He opened the passenger door on Irma's Mustang and was in the process of sliding into the front seat when Irma's cell phone rang. She answered it and heard Chief Bobby Andrews voice in response to her opening greeting.

"Hi, Irma; when I couldn't get any response at your apartment, I thought I'd better try your cell phone. I have autopsy results on Angela King, and I'd like to discuss them with you. If Arthur's with you, bring him along."

"He is, and I will, Bobby. I take it that they found something unexpected."

"They did, but I'd rather wait to discuss it with you folks when you get here. I'll set us up in the conference room. I'll plan on a meeting a half-hour from now. Can you handle that, or do you need more time?"

"Thirty minutes it is, Bobby. Consider us on our way."

Arthur fastened his seatbelt as Irma eased the Mustang away from the curb and into traffic. "What's up, and where are we meeting him?"

"We're headed for the Police Department conference room to examine the autopsy results on Angela, but I'm going to drive to Burger King on the way so that we can grab a bite. We'll have enough time to eat hamburgers in the car before the meeting. Bobby sounded as though the post mortem report surprised him."

Twenty-five minutes later, they entered the Parkville Police Department and waved to Al Gomez at the front desk as they headed for the conference room. When they arrived, they found Bobby finishing his own brown bag lunch.

"Hi, you two; you're right on time. Pardon my eating here, but Renee has me on a tight budget and a calorie counting budget too."

Arthur slid a hamburger across the table to Bobby. "We bought an extra burger for you. Enjoy it; we promise that we won't tell Renee about the additional calories."

"Thanks. I can eat only so many lettuce and tomato sandwiches, but I don't want to be critical of Renee. Now you'll just have to sit and relax while I eat this. There's hot coffee in the pot, Arthur. Irma, you'll find Diet Cokes in the refrigerator next door."

A few minutes later, Arthur and Irma sat relaxed and settled as Bobby cleaned off his end of the table.

"That did taste good. I asked you here because we have new developments relating to the death of Angela King. John Pugh, Irma's successor as County Medical Examiner – he covers two counties – found two burn marks on the back of Angela's neck under her hair. That's consistent with Arthur's suggestion of a shocking device used on the head or neck, burning her corneas. John Pugh also discovered that Angela's body contained high levels of formaldehyde. Irma, I'd like your opinion as to what that means and how she came to have it in her system."

Arthur said, "It sounds as though she was embalmed prematurely. What do you think, Irma?"

"It definitely sounds suspicious. Arthur, you've been in her office and in the Bishop's outer office and conference room. Did you see any hotplates or chafing dishes around?"

'There were two on the counter under the wall cabinets in the alcove where they prepare coffee and store food for lunches and snacks. Why do you ask?"

"Were they the electric kind or the traditional type that uses a can of Sterno to keep the food warm?"

"I didn't see any cords on them. I'm pretty sure they were the kind where you set fire to the stuff in the can underneath the dish."

"The flammable stuff in that Sterno can is made from ethanol, methanol, and a gelling agent. Methanol is also known as wood alcohol. If you drink it, it turns into formaldehyde in the body and affects your liver, kidneys, and heart. They added the methanol because too many down-and-outers were drinking Sterno instead of burning it. The company wanted to be sure no one would drink very much of it."

Bobby said, "Are you saying that Angela had a drinking habit and sipped Sterno when she was at the office because she couldn't get anything else? That doesn't sound reasonable."

Arthur shook his head. "No, Bobby, Irma's suggesting that Joyce had been working to get rid of Angela for a long time. Joyce couldn't get away with murdering her in the office, but she did bring her coffee, and it would have been simple for her to add a spoonful of Sterno to each cup."

Irma said, "Poisoning is a matter of dosage and the state of the victim's body. If the opportunity to get Angela into a separate office for a quick electrocution hadn't occurred, Joyce could have continued the process of killing her gradually. Depending on the dosage and frequency of Sterno in Angela's coffee, it would have taken a few more weeks or months. Eventually, Angela's organs would have started to shut down. At that point, only a multi-organ transplant would have been able to save her. Bobby, it appears that Joyce Jennings wanted Angela dead, and she took more than one approach to making that happen."

"I understand the revenge motive that you two uncovered. Do you think there was any other motive involved based on their working together?"

Arthur said, "That's an interesting twist to think about. Joyce may have also been jealous of Angela's career success. How significant is that, Irma?"

"I think you're getting to the trigger for the murder. Joyce wanted revenge for the death of her child, and she had to be furious when she found out that Bishop Chandler was considering backing Angela to be elected the next conference Bishop."

Arthur said, "The irony of the situation is that Angela had already forfeited that advancement when she admitted she tried to kill Charlie. She was on her way out the door."

Irma said, "That made it even more important for Joyce to kill her now. If Angela left the church hierarchy, Joyce would have no further access to her."

CHAPTER 41 – TEXAS

The taxi pulled up to a building on Campus Drive at the University of Texas, Austin, and three visitors emerged from the back seat. Karl Simitski led the way up the stairs to the front door of the building followed by Joe Gonzalez and Penny, who continued to use her maiden name, Greene, during any introductions. Karl demonstrated his familiarity with the Middle Eastern Studies department offices by winding his way through the building's maze-like corridors without guidance. He stopped at a door and waited for the others to catch up. Then he turned the doorknob and entered, calling out a greeting to the occupant of the office as he did.

"Good morning, Geraldine. We had a smooth flight down here. I brought two associates with me, Joe Gonzalez and Penny Greene. They're into middle eastern antiquities too."

Geraldine Quig backed her wheelchair away from her desk and pivoted it to face the trio of visitors. "Hello, Karl; it's good to see you again. Joe and Penny, I'm pleased to meet you. Any friend of antiquities is a friend of mine...No, Karl, I wasn't referring to you."

"Don't mind her, folks; she likes to throw a few verbal jabs during every conversation. Have you made any progress in examining the cylinder, Geraldine?"

"I have indeed. That's why I'm in such a good mood today. In keeping with all of the other ancient sayings, I have good news and bad news."

Karl said, "We've had a long trip, so let's start with the good news."

"Fair enough; I'm pleased to report that your hunch had merit. The exceptionally good condition of the cuneiform inscription on this cylinder correlates with its importance. It is a partial inventory of the treasures taken from the Temple of Solomon."

"Does it include the Ark?"

"No; the items it lists include menorahs, bronze vessels of various sizes, candle snuffers, and dishes for incense. Don't forget that these cylinders can hold only a limited amount of information. It would have required quite a few cylinders to record the entire inventory. According to the Bible, in 2 Kings Chapter 25, the Babylonians even took large bronze structures and broke them into pieces for removal to Babylon. I'm not sure how they would even describe those on cylinders."

Joe said, "Geraldine, you said that was the good news; what's the bad news?"

"The bad news is that there is absolutely no reference to the location of these items. Even if there were, we could hardly trust it. This cylinder dates back more than twenty-five hundred years. You would certainly expect items to have been moved during that long period of time."

Karl said, "Not if they had been secreted below ground level, and the building eventually collapsed. That's how many of our finest antiquities were preserved. Anyway, Geraldine, you have determined that this cylinder itself is a treasure, because it confirms the truth of the Bible account."

Penny said, "Your findings impress me. I studied the Bible and this ancient history many years ago, but I never expected to see or touch something that was part of it. Karl, I congratulate you for having recognized the significance of this item."

"Thanks, Penny; I appreciate your words, even though I'll have to take legal action if you decide that this item was among the looted artifacts."

Joe said, "You're safe for a while at least. An investigative board of experts would have to study the piece and rule on its authenticity and history. You're an expert, Geraldine. Do you think this was one of the looted items?"

"I'll have to come down on the side that says that Travis Tobias found a recently unearthed artifact rather than a looted one. Its condition is too good. Those looters didn't care for the pieces they took. They threw them into the backs of pickup trucks and stacked everything in garages and sheds. I can also contribute the fact that I visited the Iraq Museum several times, and I never saw a cylinder in such good condition."

Joe said, "I assume that you have continued to give this piece tender loving care here at the university. If you will agree to be its impartial custodian, I see no reason why we should confiscate it at this time. Do you agree, Penny?"

She nodded affirmation. "When we get back to Washington, we'll arrange for additional experts to meet with Geraldine here. This artifact is too valuable to keep moving it around through different hands and processing procedures. Karl, you'll probably never see the treasures themselves, but this cylinder is the next best thing."

"If Travis Tobias, the soldier who found this piece, hadn't died, he might be able to tell us exactly where he found it. That clue is gone forever, but if that panel of experts certifies that Travis, acting as an archeologist, had the right to remove and sell the item he found, his family will benefit substantially."

CHAPTER 42 – PONDERINGS

Arthur had made four false starts on his sermon for next Sunday. He had started to work on the topic of *Spiritual Age*, but that had gone nowhere. Then he had tried *Being a Good Neighbor,* without finding inspiration. His third unsuccessful try was *Sharing Your Gifts*, and the fourth attempt was *Living in Harmony.* Having had no success with originality, he started to study the lectionary for this week's scheduled scripture readings as a scholarly fallback. Irma's entry into his office interrupted his research.

"That's what I need. Irma, you're my inspiration in everything else; how about aiming me toward a great sermon topic?"

"I came here in the hope of sharing some semi-spiritual and semi-ridiculous thoughts with you, Arthur. Are you up for a change of pace?"

Arthur leaned back in his desk chair. "I'm perfectly willing to let you be the preacher today. What's on your mind?"

"We'll have to move into the church sanctuary if I'm going to say what's bothering me. I'll need holier surroundings than your office."

"I see that this is going to be a serious conversation. Head on in there, and I'll stop by the office and ask Shirley to hold all telephone calls."

A few minutes later, Arthur joined Irma in the sanctuary. He smiled when he saw her standing behind the pulpit, as though she would be delivering a sermon. He sat down in the front pew, facing her.

"This must be role reversal day. Go ahead, Irma; I haven't done well at developing a sermon today. I'm sure yours will be better."

"I'm here in part because I'll need the support of this lectern for what I'm about to say. I also need the other religious emblems around me."

"Go ahead; you obviously have something important to say."

"It's less important than heretical. After talking with Penny on the phone about the significance of that cuneiform cylinder, I've become agitated. Forgive me if my voice quivers a bit while I say this, but I don't quite know how to handle what I've been thinking."

"Irma, you can say anything you're thinking to me, whether it's in this place or not."

"Alright, here's my stream of thinking...This case began when Angela told you she stabbed and killed her husband, but that her friend said she saw him alive and well at a meeting later. Then the individual she saw, calling himself Oliver Parkworth, got into a car accident that should have killed him, but walked away from it and disappeared. Every time I look at the original name of our victim, Charlie King, I see C. King, or Christ the King. Where else do we have an individual who died violently and then appeared alive again? In the biblical crucifixion account, someone even stabbed Christ in the side, as did Angela to Charlie. If Charlie King is also Oliver Parkworth, the death event and reappearance alive happened twice. This is not natural."

"I grant you that his name has a coincidental resemblance."

"Did you ever read Dickens' *Oliver Twist*? In that story a poor ragamuffin boy on the streets turns out to have been from a wealthy family and ends up reunited with his family and rich once more. Dickens played with his names, like the Artful Dodger in that same book. He used the name Oliver Twist to signify that the story was *all of a twist* in the life outlook and possibilities for this young boy. I bring this up because by the same logic, Oliver Parkworth becomes *all of a park worth*, which implies a relationship to God's creation that Christ would have. Christ said he would come again. Perhaps he has, and we're witnessing it."

"I'd like to feel that it would be possible to meet Jesus, but so far I have to believe that there's a logical explanation behind all of this."

"OK, Preacher Man, then give me the logical explanation behind a set of birth certificates found in C. King's jacket that lead to a possible revelation of the treasures stolen from the Temple of Solomon, possibly including the Ark of the Covenant."

"I have no answer for that one. I don't even know why my name was on one of those certificates."

"I don't either, but I'm guessing that your role will become evident soon, because all of the other five people have already played their parts in this drama. What do you have to say about that?"

"I don't know how to respond to what you have said, Irma, except to say that it certainly stimulates my imagination, and to thank you."

"Why are you thanking me?"

"I want to thank you for sharing your thinking with me, and for solving my sermon problem. My sermon topic will be *How Would You Recognize Christ If He Walked Among Us?*

CHAPTER 43 – WASHINGTON

Penny and Joe Gonzalez had returned to their agency offices in Washington, DC, to review the case with Steve DuBois and to arrange for additional antiquities experts to visit the University of Texas for study of the cylinder. Now that Penny and Joe lived elsewhere, it was a special event to return to their offices.

They had only had time to review the latest batch of mail when Steve arrived.

"Greetings; it's good to see you two back at your desks. We keep them from getting too dusty by piling junk mail and federal regulations publications all over them."

Penny said, "We missed you too, Steve. Thanks for adding Office Manager to your list of titles."

"My primary title this week is G-man. Ellen and Eric Tobias are vacationing here, and I promised to show them the sights. Eric wants to be a G-man when he grows up."

"How are they doing on their own? Are you joining their family circle?"

"No, Penny, there's nothing serious between me and Ellen, but I do like both of them. They've always been a traditional family, and I've never had one. When you've grown up with a single parent, and that parent is in the military, you keep moving around and spend much of the time as an add-on to somebody else's family."

"Well, we're glad that you've befriended them. They'll need assistance and guidance in the future."

"What do you mean by that, Joe?"

"We're beginning to believe that the cylinder was not looted from the museum, and if Karl Simitski's lawyers can successfully argue against any Iraqi claim that it must be repatriated, the Tobias family will have a substantial amount of money to invest toward their futures."

"Would it be appropriate for me to discuss that with Ellen Tobias while she is in town?"

Penny said, "I don't see a problem, but you'd have to add the disclaimer that there are several hurdles to be leaped before she will see any income."

"That would work. I think she would be able to face the future quite well without any income from the artifact, but she'll be practical enough to accept any benefits that come her way."

"That sounds as though you two have come to know each other rather well."

"Joe, I'll admit that we have been corresponding and exchanging calls since my visit to Paul, Idaho."

"In that case, go off and spend some time with them. You've taken care of the offices while we've been away. We'll catch up with our backlog while you take a break."

Penny said, "Before you go, let me look in the back of my desk drawer. I think I have something for you."

She rummaged through several drawers for about ten minutes. Just as she thought her quest would fail, she found the object of her search.

"Here, Steve, give this Junior G-man badge to Eric. I picked it up at an FBI open house about ten years ago."

CHAPTER 44 – CONTACT

Karl Simitski ran up the stairs to the room he used as his office in time to answer the telephone on its fifth ring.

"This is Karl speaking."

"Karl, this is Arthur Blake calling. I'm a friend and associate of Penny and Joe Gonzalez. I know that they've been working with you on evaluating that cuneiform cylinder."

"I thought her name was Penny Greene."

"I didn't realize that she had introduced herself to you that way. I'm sorry if I confused you. Penny uses her maiden name in situations where it may not be useful to have people know that she and Joe are married as well as agency associates. To give you full disclosure on my identity, I'm in Parkville, Illinois, where I'm the Pastor of the Parkville United Methodist Church. My wife and I also operate ABC Consultants, an investigative entity that frequently consults with Penny and Joe's federal agency."

"That's quite a mouthful of introduction, Arthur. How may I help you today?"

"I think we should discuss how I might help you, Karl. You see, I've become somewhat of a Bible student as part of my ministry. Due to that and my interest in investigations, I've been doing some research homework concerning that cylinder and its significance. If you'd like to visit me here in Parkville, I'd be happy to share it with you."

"Arthur, I can head your way tomorrow. I have a few obligations to clear up today. Will Penny and Joe be in on our meeting?"

"They're in Washington right now, but I'll try to arrange it. To give you some travel planning flexibility, let's meet at my church at three o'clock in the afternoon."

"That sounds good to me. I'll look forward to it."

After hanging up with Arthur, Karl called Geraldine
Quig and the consultant in charge of his art storage
facility to say that he would be out of town and might not
be back in touch with them for a few days. Then he looked
out his window at the dirt bike activities below him and
the sun slowly sinking in the west. He felt that he would
soon be on top of the world.

CHAPTER 45 – JOYCE

Joyce Jennings looked nervous as she sat in the interrogation room across the table from Chief Bobby Andrews. Bobby initiated the conversation.

"Joyce, you are not under arrest; this is only a preliminary interview. Nevertheless, you have the right to have an attorney present to represent you. Shall we proceed with our discussions, or do you want to wait until you obtain legal representation?"

Joyce relaxed after Bobby's statement that he wasn't arresting her. "That won't be necessary, at least for the present. I'm curious about why you brought me here."

Bobby said, "I also have to tell you that we are recording this session and that anything you say may be used against you in a court of law. Do you understand those conditions?"

"Yes, I do."

"Joyce, you may not realize it, but we have done some research, and we know a lot about your history. We know about the death of your daughter, Robin, as a small child, and the circumstances of that death. You have our sympathies for that tragic event. We also know that the teacher at the pre-school, whom you held responsible, avoided charges of negligence in connection with the deaths of Robin and another child. That teacher's name was Marcia Melrose, who later changed her name to Angela Marcia Markham, and then married to become Angela Marcia King, recently deceased while you were acting as her office assistant. We have interviewed Bishop Howard Chandler, and we learned from him that after he had placed Angela on special assignment, you volunteered to be her assistant in the Parkville office, even though he had planned to ask someone with less seniority. You were

155

Bishop Chandler's Administrative Assistant; yet you requested a temporary assignment that an office intern could have handled. Would you like to comment on these statements?"

Joyce had been taking notes during Bobby's background summary. Without realizing it, she continuously tapped the button end of her pen on the table while she responded. "You have been doing your homework. Yes, that woman's negligence was responsible for the death of my daughter; and yes, I followed her to this area so that I could monitor her activities. Neither of those statements means that I killed her. Her death looked like an accident to me."

"Her death was a deliberate electrocution. Your daughter was electrocuted under her supervision, so you decided to end her life the same way."

Bobby's belligerence surprised her. "The similarity of the two deaths is an interesting coincidence, Chief, but you have no evidence that I was the perpetrator, assuming it was a murder rather than an accident."

"That steel chair, faulty lamp wiring, and painted steel plate covering the carpet under the desk all constitute a deliberate electrocution trap in my opinion."

She stood before speaking. "They may have constituted an accident waiting to happen, but that's all. You should also look into the origin of that setup. I made no changes to that office. The furnishings you described were there when we moved in for our temporary stay. Now, before we take this any further, I would like to arrange for an attorney to represent me."

"Of course; that is your right."

"Are you arresting me?"

"Not at this time..."

"In that case, I'm leaving."

CHAPTER 46 – HOUSE OF MING

Penny and Joe had returned from Washington at Arthur's request in order to attend the meeting with Karl Simitski the following afternoon. In order to compare notes in a relaxed atmosphere, they had gathered for a late evening Chinese meal with Irma and Arthur at House of Ming.

Penny finished eating an egg roll and said, "It's good to be back here. We've been traveling too much lately, and I enjoy this place so much."

Joe said, "Arthur, we came as soon as we could get a flight from DC because your action inserts you into the treasure map sequence of the birth certificates. We could hardly believe it when you said you had arranged the meeting with Karl tomorrow."

"I know. While I talked with him on the phone, I heard a voice inside my head telling me my actions were weird. I didn't plan this. It's just my nature to take the known facts and situations to the next logical level. That's how we solve our cases."

Irma said, "I'm still spooked by this whole chain of events. Charlie disappears, presumably murdered. Then he appears again as a different person, and that person disappears. Then we obtain the contents of Charlie's jacket pocket – six birth certificates that turn out to represent stops on a treasure-hunting expedition. When you folks told us about Karl Simitski and Geraldine Quig, I thought we had come to the end of the line. Arthur was the last remaining individual whose birth certificate was in Charlie's pocket, and there was no reason for him to get involved. Why did you change all of that and call Karl?"

Arthur said, "Maybe it was my flair for the dramatic, or maybe I felt left out of the fun Penny and Joe had while following the trail of the cuneiform cylinder. Anyway, I decided to do a little more research, and that led to my deciding to join the game and call Karl. He sounds like a great guy, by the way."

Joe said, "He is that, but are you going to tell us about your research results?"

"That, people, is the subject of our meeting tomorrow. My comments so far were the appetizer, and I've finished them, just as you've finished your egg rolls and soup. The waiter is coming with our main course. You'll get your main course of my story at the meeting tomorrow."

CHAPTER 47 – BOBBY ANDREWS

At nine o'clock the next morning, the doorbell rang long and loud. Irma ran her fingers through her hair and opened the door to find Bobby Andrews on her doorstep.

"You're just a bit early, Bobby, and I'm not used to cops raiding my apartment at daybreak. Come on in and have some toast and coffee. Arthur is still getting dressed. Are we in trouble that you've come so early?"

"I think I'm the one who's in trouble, and I need your help as usual. You and Arthur are beginning to make me realize how much I depend on you."

Arthur walked into the dining room from the bedroom. "What do you mean by beginning to make you realize? I thought we became your necessity a long time ago. Anyway, we'll do whatever we can to help you, Friend Robert."

"Stick with Bobby; I never did care for my formal name."

Irma said, "I'll bet you always wanted to be a British copper."

"That's enough, you two. I came here for assistance, and all you want to do is make fun of me and my name."

Arthur said, "We'll be good. We needed to get back at you for arriving so early. Tell us how we can help."

"After our several discussions, I brought Joyce Jennings into the station for a preliminary interview. I told her we knew all about her background and about the death of her young daughter, and that we knew she had followed Angela to this area because she held her responsible and wanted revenge."

Irma said, "How did she react to that opening salvo?"

"She said that the background information was correct and that she had come here to keep tabs on

Angela but not to murder her. She said that she felt Angela's death had been an accident, and she claimed that all the furnishings in the office where Angela died were exactly the way they had been when they first arrived."

"Are you checking that story with the landlord?"

"We talked with him, but he said that he hadn't examined the premises before Angela and Joyce took occupancy. He said that the former occupant, a tax accountant, moved one day earlier. The landlord didn't even have current contact information for the accountant."

Arthur said, "So the problem is that you can show motive and opportunity, but you have insufficient evidence that she committed the crime."

"Or even that a crime was committed. A good lawyer will get the jury to believe that it was an accident."

Irma said, "Can you charge Joyce with attempted murder for spiking Angela's coffee with Sterno on a regular basis?"

"I'd even have trouble making that charge stick. We found Joyce's fingerprints on the Sterno cans in the Bishop's outer office, but other people handled them too. I'm sure she could argue that handling those cans is a regular part of her hospitality duties. My problem is that I revealed our interest in her before we had sufficient hard evidence."

Arthur patted Bobby on the shoulder. "It's one thing to know someone committed a crime, and another to have the evidence to prove it."

Irma said, "We can prove that she put the coffee on the desk after Angela's electrocution. Arthur, why did your expression just change? You look as though you've just had a shock."

"I have had one. You mentioned the coffee on the desk after Angela's electrocution. Remember that Joyce made that coffee black with two teaspoons of sugar, while Angela actually took her coffee with a little bit of creamer and no sugar. At the time we said that was part of the evidence against Joyce for the murder...She didn't know how Angela liked her coffee. If that's the case, then someone else in the Rockford office gave the coffee laced with Sterno to Angela. If Joyce had been that person, she would have known the correct coffee formula. We'll have to ask Bishop Chandler who made Angela's coffee. We may be looking at two people who were out to get Angela King, a second person in addition to Joyce."

Bobby said, "That also weakens our case against Joyce for the electrocution. That other person could have set up the shock trap. Joyce may be guilty of nothing but getting the coffee recipe wrong and leaving the cup on the desk after Angela was already dead. We definitely need more evidence before we can move against Joyce."

Irma said, there is another possibility within the office situation. If Angela was the type of person who kept a bottle of whiskey in her desk for an occasional drink while at work, either Joyce or someone else could have spiked that with wood alcohol, so that Angela administered the adulterated drink to herself. What about that possibility, Arthur?"

"The United Methodist Church frowns on alcohol, especially in churches and church offices, but we know that many clergy bend that rule a bit. We have more work to do before we can call Angela's murder solved."

CHAPTER 48 – CONFERENCE WITH KARL

Promptly at three o'clock in the afternoon, Arthur heard a car horn in the upper parking lot on Main Street. He walked outside to find a man with a short graying beard climbing out of a red Jeep Cherokee. Arthur walked toward him as the driver retrieved a black backpack from the front passenger seat.

Arthur said, "Karl Simitski, I presume."

"And you must be Pastor Blake. I'm very pleased to meet you."

"You do know how to make a grand entrance. When I received your phone call saying you were about a half hour away, I was surprised because I had expected you to fly rather than drive. You must have been on the road early this morning."

"I actually took it easy. It's about a seven-hour drive, and I stopped for breakfast and lunch. I wasn't sure how long I'd be here, so I drove old Betsy to give myself flexibility. Are the others here yet?"

"They should be along in a few minutes. Would you like to freshen up after your ride before we begin?

"No, I'm good, Arthur. I lunched at a truck stop where I took a shower. Those places have all kinds of facilities for long-distance drivers."

"Let's go inside to the conference room and see whether the others have arrived. Shirley Hadley, my secretary, has set up refreshments for us there."

As they walked inside, Karl said, "I hate to admit this, but I haven't been in a church for quite a while. Maybe our relationship will lead to my improving my spiritual habits."

"That's probably a good idea for someone who's investigating objects that are the subject of biblical writings."

"Touché, Pastor; it's time for me to get into the spirit of these matters."

They entered the conference room where they found Penny and Joe munching on Danish from Shirley's usual assortment of day-old Hadley's Bakery pastry. Irma rose from her seat at the table as they entered.

Arthur said, "Karl, you already know Penny and Joe. Penny, I'm afraid I blew your cover when I spoke with Karl on the phone. He now knows that you two are married. Karl, this stunning and perceptive person is my wife, Irma. She works with me on investigations and is a former medical examiner."

They shook hands all around, and helped themselves to drinks and pastry before sitting down.

Penny said, "Karl, I use my maiden name when we are in a situation where Joe and I assume different functions in dealing with the public. What Arthur didn't tell you is that he and stunning Irma are newlyweds, but you may have perceived that from his description of her."

"The thought had crossed my mind. I also perceived from Arthur's words when we spoke on the telephone that he might have some very interesting information for me. I have to admit that I'm excited by that possibility."

They all gravitated to the table as they completed their snacks and made themselves comfortable for the business of the day. Arthur opened a thick file folder and started the session.

"I've gathered from comments you've all given me that you've reached a consensus that the cuneiform cylinder brought home from Iraq by Travis Tobias is an authentic treasure. Professor Geraldine Quig has certified it to contain a portion of the inventory records for items brought back to Babylon when the army of Nebuchadnezzar II destroyed the Temple of Solomon in

Jerusalem. I further understand that it is in such good shape that it is not likely to have been part of the loot taken from the Iraq Museum. Is that correct?"

Penny and Joe nodded, while Karl just smiled.

"Karl, I take your smile to be an affirmation, in a Cheshire cat sort of way. You have every reason to be proud. However, I'll play the role of the devil's advocate for a second and remind you that the cylinder is not yours until Ellen Tobias decides whether she wants to sell it and agrees to a price for the object. Travis Tobias sent the cylinder to his friend Roger Svenson for evaluation purposes, but from what I've seen and heard, Travis did not sign a written agreement for Svenson to act as his agent. Once Travis died, Svenson could only have acted on behalf of Ellen, and she did not give him any authorization at all. I therefore suggest that Ellen Tobias or her representative should be included in any future meetings where the fate of the cylinder is to be addressed."

Irma said, "That's not a very hospitable way to start the meeting, Arthur."

"Karl, I hope you realize that it's not a question of hospitality, but of objectivity. I'm sure that the question of ownership is a high priority matter to you."

"That it is, Arthur, and I fully intend to do right by Ellen. Can we move on to the additional information you said your research revealed?"

"I'll get right to it...I'm not sure I agree with your theory regarding the location of the Ark of the Covenant. That sacred relic might be in Babylon or Egypt or Ethiopia, or Israel, or it might have been destroyed somewhere along the timeline from 586 BC to the present. However, I do agree that some of the temple treasures remained in Babylon after Cyrus the Great let the Judahites take some of the treasure and return to Jerusalem.

"For those of you who don't know Cyrus, he was a very interesting and astute guy. He ruled Persia, and after

Nebuchadnezzar II died, leaving several weak kings as successive heirs, he decided to annex the Babylonian kingdom to his realm. The last king in Babylon was Nabonidus, said to have mental problems, but in any case, he spent ten of the seventeen years of his rule at a desert oasis rather than in Babylon. He left his son, Belshazzar, behind to rule in his place. One evening, when Belshazzar was having a huge feast, Cyrus had his army divert the water in the river channels that supplied the city. Then he led his forces under the wall and into the city through the now-dry water channels. The city, the Babylonian Empire, and the Chaldean Dynasty that it embodied, fell that night without a fight. Cyrus the Great of Persia became the new king."

Joe said, "I'm impressed that they had such great tacticians that long ago. I thought they just went head-to-head in big battle formations."

Karl said, "That type of battle was primarily a European development. In other regions they were more flexible in varying the tactics to suit the circumstances...You appear to be a fan of Cyrus, Arthur."

"I'm a fan of anyone who uses creative thinking to accomplish goals. Anyway, Cyrus freed himself of the burden of the enslaved Jews by sending them home, and he maintained good relations with them by letting them reclaim part of the temple treasure. However, he kept the major part of that booty for himself. It is likely that the inventory detailed on the Tobias cylinder is part of what he retained. That leads us to the next obvious question. What did Cyrus do with the treasure, and where is it today?"

Irma said, "Those are two questions, Arthur. Are those questions rhetorical, or are you going to do one of your magic tricks and actually answer them?"

Karl said, "I don't think he would have had me come all this way unless he was going to at least present us with a theory."

"You're right, Karl, and the reason I counted the two questions as one is that I believe that the place where Cyrus the Great stored the spoils of Nebuchadnezzar's war is the same location where they reside today. I don't think that anyone has found them. You're more expert on the history of antiquities than I am. Do you have any reason to believe that the treasure has been discovered and removed from its hiding place?"

"No, I don't have any such knowledge, and yes, I do believe that the treasure of Solomon's Temple remains hidden. Are you going to suggest where to look for it?"

"I will, with the assistance of Cyrus the Great."

Penny said, "I've seen your act before, Arthur. You do a pretty good job of pulling rabbits out of hats, but where are you going to get Cyrus?"

"In a manner of speaking, I'm going to the British Museum for him. As you know, there are still a large number of cuneiform pieces of various sizes and shapes in museum collections. We know that looters took forty-eight hundred of them from the Iraqi Museum alone. The British Museum is the current resting place for what scholars call the Cyrus the Great Cylinder, which dates back to 539 BC and the conquest of Babylon. They translated the forty or more lines of Akkadian language cuneiform script to reveal the story of the entry into Babylon and the capture of the last king, Nabonidus, along with details of the strong beliefs held by Cyrus."

Penny said, "That's all very interesting, but does it reveal anything about the items inventoried on the Tobias cylinder?"

"Let me read you some excerpts from the translation of the Cyrus the Great Cylinder:
[Marduk, king of the gods] ...He called Cyrus, king of Anshan, by name; he appointed him to lordship over the whole world...Marduk, the great lord, looked joyously on the caring for his people, on his pious works and his righteous heart...To his city, Babylon, he caused him to go;

he made him take the road to Babylon, going as a friend and companion at his side...Without battle and conflict, he permitted him to enter Babylon. He spared his city, Babylon, a calamity. Nabonidus, the king, who did not fear him, he delivered into his hand...The lord, who by his power brings the dead to life, who amid destruction and injury had protected them, they joyously blessed him, honoring his name...I took up my lordly residence in the royal palace with joy and rejoicing; Marduk, the great lord, moved the noble heart of the residents of Babylon to me, while I gave daily attention to his worship...the gods who resided in them, I brought back to their places, and caused them to dwell in a residence for all time...I caused them to take up their dwelling in residences that gladdened the heart. May all the gods, whom I brought into their cities, pray daily before Bel and Nabu for long life for me, and may they speak a gracious word for me and say to Marduk, my lord, 'May Cyrus the king who worships you...dwell in peace...'"

Irma said, "That's quite an extraordinary document. I'm beginning to understand this Cyrus. He was one of those warriors who firmly believed that his god was on his side so that he had nothing to fear."

Penny said, "I must be dense, because I don't see where you're going with this, Arthur."

"I'll be happy to spell it out for you. I saw Karl nodding as I read the translation, so I think he gets it. The point is that Cyrus the Great took on the role of the god Marduk's chief warrior, and felt that he was safe as long as Marduk was on his side. We know that he retained the bulk of the treasures from the Temple of Solomon. Where would he have hidden them? The obvious answer is in or under the Temple of Marduk. Do you agree, Karl?"

"You very well might be correct. You've done more research on this than I have. I'm sure that nothing remains, but how accurately do we know where the Temple of Marduk stood?"

Richard Davidson

"I'm sure you all know that Babylon was in what is today Iraq. During his reign, Nebuchadnezzar II built a stepped tower called a ziggurat three hundred feet tall, with outside staircases and a shrine on the top. According to maps I've seen of ancient Babylon the ziggurat, also called Etemenanki, was located just about five hundred meters due north of the Temple of Marduk."

Joe said, "Well, Arthur, you won't be able to locate the Temple of Marduk unless you can find the ziggurat, which is long gone. What is its location?"

"I was hoping you'd ask that question. You see, the Google Earth satellite mapping program places Etemenanki at 32°32'10.82" N by 44°25'16.65" E."

Karl said, "Perfect; you have the exact latitude and longitude."

"Not only that, but I can tell you that the elevation of the ground at the ziggurat is one hundred and fifteen feet. There aren't any structures there now, but the ziggurat stood within a large square plaza, identifiable from an airplane or satellite. The question for you, Karl, is: What do you want to do with this information?"

CHAPTER 49 – HOWARD CHANDLER

Bishop Howard Chandler realized that he would have to postpone his plans for retirement, possibly for a very long time. Angela King, his candidate for promotion from district superintendent to the episcopacy, had rendered herself ineligible due to her confession of attempted murder. Later, she had died suddenly, possibly through the action of his private secretary. The police had questioned Joyce Jennings, and appeared to suspect her of committing the murder. He had once thought that he had good talent for judging the character of his associates, but no longer. The actions of the people closest to him revealed serious judgment flaws that he would never have guessed or even believed. He had worked for years with potential murderers.

At least Arthur Blake had remained a reliable although unconventional resource. He would have to visit with Arthur soon to obtain his opinions and, yes, guidance. Strange that he, as Bishop, would have to rely on a relatively new pastor to protect his reputation and shepherd him forward. Arthur understood people's dark instincts for violence and corruption. He certainly didn't. He had even started to wonder how many of his associates had entered the clergy due to personal ambitions and selfish motives rather than in response to a spiritual call.

Howard Chandler had considered himself an optimist for his entire life. He had risen through the ranks of spiritual leadership by trusting in the good that lies within people and encouraging them toward positive outlooks. He had considered this a winning formula for a healthy lifestyle, but perhaps he had just been fortunate. Now his luck had run out. He had found himself surrounded by scoundrels, and he didn't know how to rescue himself from the snare that enmeshed him. It was like trying to speak an unknown language with no rules of grammar. He had prayed that his burdens would soon dissipate; but he knew that he would have to act on his own to move toward personal redemption. He would arrange a visit with Arthur in the morning. It was strange how making even that small decision improved his outlook. With Arthur's assistance, he hoped to achieve a new perspective marked by awareness and cautious optimism.

CHAPTER 50 – MUTUAL ASSISTANCE

Joyce Jennings remained away from her office, thanks to the leave of absence the Bishop had given her following her discovery of Angela King's body. Her absence allowed Arthur to schedule his meeting with Howard Chandler at the Bishop's Rockford offices rather than at the Parkville Church. He preferred this arrangement because it would allow him to search for evidence during his visit. When he entered the outer lobby, he found Bishop Chandler seated on a couch waiting for him.

"Welcome, Arthur; I wanted to usher you in myself and to remind you that we will discuss confidential matters today. Please don't continue our discussions in front of any of the staff."

"Certainly, Howard; everything will be strictly between us. Do you mind if I grab a cup of coffee before we sequester ourselves?"

"I've had an urn set up within my office, so you don't even have to make that coffee detour. I really appreciate your coming over here on short notice. Shirley told me that you've had meetings with out-of-town visitors this week. Go on into my office. I'll stop and instruct the receptionist to hold all of my calls."

Arthur entered the Bishop's office and poured a mug of coffee. Then he sat down in one of the chairs by the fireplace, in keeping with the Bishop's preference at their last meeting. Howard entered, closed the door behind him, and took the other fireside chair.

"Arthur, I would like you to brief me on the status of legal matters involving Joyce Jennings and our late friend Angela King. I'm also looking for your personal advice and opinion about this strange situation. Two of my most trusted associates may have committed violent crimes, and one of those two may have murdered the other. I've never been exposed to serious crime before, and I don't know how to react."

"I do appreciate your feelings, Howard. I study criminals and the reasons for their engaging in antisocial actions, but most positive-thinking people don't know what to do when crime touches them or comes uncomfortably close to their lives. If you'll pardon a light-hearted comment, your situation reminds me of the old entertainer, Jimmy Durante. He used to slap his hands against his thighs and say 'I'm surrounded by assassins!' – Howard, I'm afraid you actually are."

"I take it from that analogy that you do believe that Joyce murdered Angela."

"I'll remind you of your caution that everything we discuss today is confidential. It's a limbo situation right now. The police and I believe that she did it, but we have to gather more evidence before the authorities can formally accuse her of the crime."

"I used to wonder why you took time away from your ministry to pursue investigations, Arthur, but now I'm beginning to understand how it prepares you to deal with those who are sinners in more than the abstract sense. You're not bothered by the evil in people the way I am."

"Oh, I'm bothered by it alright. I'll suggest that the difference between us is that you tend to accept an individual as being good until something happens to prove your opinion wrong. I see both good and evil in everyone. Angela and Joyce may both have committed murders, but I can list many good things that they both have done. Even the most outwardly perfect person has flaws and weaknesses; that's the nature of humanity. We try to be good, but we can never completely succeed at it. If we could, we would be self-satisfied and stop trying. We continually face new challenges and threats."

"What's my problem, Arthur? Am I too naïve about people around me? Have I been too sheltered from evil?"

"I don't believe that for a minute, Howard. When the Jurisdictional Conference elected you Bishop of the Northern Illinois Conference, you had to compete for the position with many other individuals, some of whose motives were far from pure. Along the way, many people probably sought favors from you with dishonest stories and fraudulent claims. You know in your heart that those same people would turn their backs on you if you didn't have the power to give them something. You see shortcomings in people all the time, but you have avoided violent evil in the past. You have to accept the fact that violence exists, and right now, it is existing very close to you. It's part of our lives. Regardless of the United Methodist Church's views on gambling, we do it all the time. We gamble that if we have morality and follow God's way, we will be able to distance ourselves from the unsavory and violent aspects of life. Most of the time we live the kind of life that is our goal, but not always. We pray for the best, but we have to prepare ourselves for the worst. I've chosen to prepare myself by learning to understand the bad in people as well as the good."

"Am I less good because I failed at evaluating the character of those around me?"

"We all fail at something, often many things. You failed to see the evil in people around you because you weren't looking for it. You didn't want those near you to have moral problems. At the same time, they were doing everything they could to maintain their images in order to achieve their ambitions. We see what we want to see. We see others in ways that make us feel comfortable with them. If we can't feel comfortable with those around us, we distance ourselves from them and break off the relationships. A healthy society requires that we learn to live with those who don't meet our standards as well as those who do."

"Arthur, I appreciate what you've said. It does help to realize that we all face the same relationship problems. I also appreciate your outlook because it helps me understand you better. I'd like to have a follow-up discussion with you after we've resolved these criminal matters."

"Thank you, Howard. If you don't mind, I'd like to make a copy of my next sermon and look around the offices for possible evidence before I leave. I had one more question for you. On those occasions when she worked in these offices, who brought Angela her coffee?"

"Usually, Joyce would bring Angela a thermally-insulated carafe of coffee in the morning, and then Angela would fill her cup from it during the day. Joyce didn't work for Angela, but she felt quite willing to supply a full carafe each day. Feel free to ask me any other questions you have about the case or the two of them as individuals, either before you leave, or later on."

"I will, Howard, and thank you. I think we both benefited from this session."

CHAPTER 51 – AFTERMATH

Following the meeting at the church, Irma took charge of showing Karl Simitski around Parkville, while Arthur excused himself to meet with Bishop Chandler. Penny and Joe had gone home to catch up on correspondence that had arrived while they had been in Washington. Irma and Karl used her Mustang for their tour, which covered the two lakes on both sides of the central Swanson Hill, the small downtown area, and some of the countryside surrounding the town.

As they drove, Karl said, "It's very nice around here, small but still adequate resources and not too far from larger cities. That's the feeling I have where I live too. I didn't want the interruptions and noise of the city, but I wanted to be within reach of travel and academic facilities."

"Tell me, Karl, whether that session today is apt to trigger any actions on your part. Now that you have a geographically accurate suggestion for the location of those artifacts from the Temple of Solomon, will you organize an expedition to search for them?"

"No, Irma, field archeology is not my bag. I'll pass the meeting information to Geraldine Quig at the University of Texas. She might want to see whether her colleagues at the University of Chicago's Oriental Institute might be interesting in collaborating on a dig."

"Penny had mentioned that Professor Quig uses a wheelchair. Is she able to do field archeology?"

"Actually, Geraldine is in a wheelchair because a stone slab shifted when she was crawling through a small hole into an Egyptian tomb. It crushed her legs. Despite that, she could and would participate in a dig. Her contributions would be limited to planning, plus the cleaning and cataloging of artifacts dug out by others."

"What do you do with your own collection? Do you loan pieces out to museums and universities?"

"I'm afraid I'm an introvert when it comes to my stuff. I study it up close and try to appreciate the history and creative process for each piece, but I'm not much of a sharer. I have one or two colleagues and consultants I invite to assist me when necessary. Beyond that I simply preserve items for the future."

Irma drove back into the upper level church parking lot and turned off the engine. "Would you allow some of us to visit and view your collection?"

"I'm afraid I wouldn't be able to have visitors there for a while. My underground facility had some leakage and wall cracks due to heavy rains, and I have contractors reworking the walls and ceilings right now. They've sealed my collection into temporary storage units to protect the items from construction vibration and dust. Perhaps we could do something in the future after they've finished."

"I'd like to arrange a dinner outing for those of us who were at our conference plus a few friends whose work might be of interest to you. Will you be staying in town for a day or two?"

"That sounds awfully tempting, Irma, but I do feel I should get back and attend to several pending obligations. I also want to pass the information from our meeting here to my academic friends. I'll try to get back here for a longer stay on my next visit. For now, I'm going to have to just freshen up and get on the road."

CHAPTER 52 – HOMECOMING

Steve DuBois answered his cell phone as he finished his lunch in the Burger King parking lot. He swallowed the last bite and said, "Steve here..."

"Steve; it's Ellen Tobias. We arrived home to find someone had broken into our house and ransacked the place while we were on our trip to DC. We found the file drawers open and file folders all over the place. Our bookcases were emptied also."

"Did they take anything?"

"It's a little early to have the complete picture, but the only thing I spotted so far is that the file on that cuneiform cylinder is missing. I looked for that right away because that thing was the only potentially valuable object we've had in the house recently."

"What papers were in that file?"

"It had some information about these things that I got off of the internet plus the correspondence between Travis and that Svenson guy when he first brought the thing home from Iraq."

"Are you and Eric OK?"

"We're fine. I would have called you anyway to say that we had arrived safely, but the break-in made it more urgent."

"Call the police, and ask them to put a security watch on your house, in addition to searching for clues. Then put new locks on your doors, and make sure they're the deadbolt type. I'll get our agency involved in the investigation. I think they're after the cylinder, and they're following the trail that starts with Travis. I'll let you know what we find."

Steve hung up and called Joe Gonzalez. "Joe, we have a problem. Ellen Tobias had a break-in at home while she was here in Washington. They stole the papers related to the cylinder from Iraq. It could have happened up to a week ago, so you'd better check later points in the trail of that thing."

"Steve, this thing is moving rapidly. I just got off the phone with the police in Austin. Somebody stole the cylinder from its secure cabinet at the University of Texas, and Geraldine Quig is in the hospital with a possible concussion after they pistol-whipped her."

"You'd better check on earlier people along the trail to Texas. The stolen papers only mentioned Svenson. Something may have happened to him too."

"I'll do that, Steve, but the people behind this may have tracked our contacts with Alicia Pavone and Karl Simitski as well. They may have all received unwelcome visitors, although Karl may have been with us in Parkville when all of this happened. Let's split up the effort, Steve. You check on Roger Svenson, and I'll check on the others. Call me when you have results."

CHAPTER 53 – EVIDENCE

Bobby Andrews completed his check-in call to his wife Renee, and rotated his office chair away from his desk to face his utility table. As he did so, he reacted with surprise to see that Arthur and Irma had entered his office during his conversation and had settled themselves into his guest chairs.

"How did you two sneak in here without my hearing you? Are you training to be cat burglars?"

Irma laughed and placed a file folder on his table. "I think we'd rather be considered spies than cat burglars. I didn't want to alert Renee to my spending time with you. Al Gomez has been spreading rumors about the two of us."

"Now cut that out, Irma; you're here with your husband, anyway."

Arthur said, "Would you like me to leave so that you two can be alone?"

"Let's not have you playing that game too, Arthur! You both must be in good moods to tease me like this. Do you have new information for me?"

"Irma and I have been snooping and comparing notes, and we believe that we have at least enough evidence against Joyce Jennings for you to obtain a search warrant and examine everything in her house. I don't think we have quite enough for the prosecutors, but we're getting close."

"That means that you don't think that a second person at Angela's office spiked her coffee with wood alcohol. Is that correct?"

"I found out how Joyce adulterated Angela's coffee without knowing how Angela liked to drink it. The Bishop told me that on those days when Angela was in the office,

Joyce would bring her a thermally insulated carafe of coffee in the morning and that it would supply her for the full day. Angela poured her own coffee and fixed it the way she liked it without Joyce ever seeing her do so."

"Wouldn't Joyce have seen the remains of her coffee when she picked up Angela's cup at the end of the day?"

"Angela used Styrofoam cups and threw them away."

Bobby made a few notes in a notebook. "You're saying that we might be able to make a case against Joyce for attempted murder due to her cumulative poisoning of Angela's coffee over a period of time. Do you have any more evidence against Joyce for the actual murder in the Parkville office?"

Irma said, "I'll take that one, Chief. First, we just explained to you why Joyce incorrectly prepared Angela's coffee at the murder scene. She didn't know the correct recipe, so Joyce lied when she said Angela told her to make it that way. We have something new as well. Remember Joyce's claim that she found Angela's body when she returned from making copies downstairs. We did find document pages that she dropped in the inner office, supposedly when she discovered the body."

"That's true, but is it important?"

"Very much so; Arthur printed out a file and made some copies while he was in the Bishop's office. I have them in this folder. The copier and printer there are loaded with an unusually fine watermarked paper, presumably because Bishop Chandler wants his letters and documents to indicate his status. The documents that Joyce dropped at the murder scene were on the Bishop's paper. Also included in my file are two sheets of paper from the printer at the Parkville office where Angela King died and from the copier downstairs. You can see that they are lighter weight, plainer finish, and have no watermark. Joyce had prepared those copies in the Bishop's offices ahead of time so that she could drop them to show how shocked she was when she found the body."

Bobby said, "That is significant new information. I might have enough to get a search warrant, but I'd have to work through the sheriff or the Illinois State Police because Joyce doesn't live in Parkville. It wouldn't be a problem."

Arthur said, "I have one other item that's not exactly evidence, but it's suspicious. Joyce called Bishop Chandler to tell him that Angela was dead before she called the police or paramedics. She was more concerned about her relationship with her boss than she was with Angela's death. She cried when she called him, but she showed no emotion when we talked with her."

Irma said, "That's unusual, but you never know how people will react when they're in the presence of death. Nevertheless, it's part of the overall picture of how Joyce behaved that day."

CHAPTER 54 – ROGER SVENSON

On the third ring Steve DuBois heard a young girl's voice; "Inland Associated Art Examiners, may I help you?"

"May I speak with Roger Svenson?" He suspected that Svenson would be among the missing, but he played this call straight. Then the unexpected happened.

"This is Roger Svenson speaking."

Steve recovered quickly. "Mr. Svenson, this is Steve DuBois. I work with Joe Gonzalez, and he suggested that I call you to indicate that you might be having unwelcome visitors."

"That sounds ominous. Would you mind giving me some more details?"

"This would be in connection with that cuneiform cylinder you were selling for Travis Tobias. I'm sure that you're aware that Travis died in Iraq after placing the piece with you. His widow, Ellen Tobias has reported a burglary during which thieves stole your correspondence with Travis about evaluation and possible sale of the cylinder. I expect the people who stole those papers will contact you to force you to tell them the current location of the cylinder."

Steve was surprised to hear Svenson laugh.

"So that's how they knew about me. Mr. DuBois, I did receive visitors, but they were hardly unwelcome. Two Israeli businessmen came here unannounced. They knew that I was the agent for the cylinder, and indicated that they wanted to purchase it. I told them that I was in the process of negotiating a sale and that the artifact was at the University of Texas being evaluated by an expert in Middle Eastern antiquities. To my surprise, they responded with an offer to double any price I had been discussing with any other client. They were quite serious about this, and we concluded the transaction. They gave me a cashier's check from a local bank. I gave them a bill of sale and other documentation to use in claiming the item at the university. Ellen Tobias will shortly be receiving a very large amount of money. It won't compensate for her loss of Travis, but it will give her and her son financial security."

Steve remained silent for several seconds while he absorbed Svenson's news. "That is an unexpected development. We thought that these people were likely to threaten you and force you to reveal the location of the cylinder so that they could steal it. Would you mind telling me the names of your clients so that we might contact them?"

"I see no problem with that. Their names were Mordecai Lewin and Yakov Pensky. They said that they had authority to purchase the cylinder for a museum in Israel. They didn't tell me the name of the museum."

"Thank you very much, Mr. Svenson. Your information will definitely alter the way we pursue this matter."

Steve disconnected and immediately placed a second call to Joe Gonzalez. "Hi, Joe; it's Steve. I just spoke with Svenson. He received visitors, but they didn't harm him; they purchased the cylinder at a very high price. He said that they were Israelis acting as agents for a museum in Israel, but given the break-in at the Tobias home, I'll bet they were Israeli government agents. Svenson executed the sale despite lingering questions about his authority to act as agent for Ellen. Have you contacted any of the others yet?"

"No; I wanted to give you a chance to touch base with Svenson, the first link in the chain, before I contacted the others. Don't worry about the agency issue. He has a reasonable legal case for it, and he behaved in character. Svenson is an opportunist with questionable ethics. After delivering the payment, the Israelis, as buyers, had the legal right to claim the cylinder from Geraldine Quig. Her injuries must have been due to her resisting their taking it, even though they had legal documentation. I wonder why she would have done that. Give me the names of these buyers, and I'll check them out."

"Svenson said the men were Mordecai Lewin and Yakov Pensky. Do you want me to go to Austin and check on Geraldine Quig's condition and story?"

"Let's meet there at the airport, and we'll visit her together. She should see someone she recognizes. Call the office in Washington and have the travel people book us on flights that arrive in Austin at about the same time. We'll meet at the airport there. I'll ask Penny to handle the background checks on the Israelis."

CHAPTER 55 – IRMA AND ARTHUR

Irma finished setting the table, brought out the hot food, and added a thin vase with one red rose.

"Arthur, breakfast is ready. It's a special occasion!"

Arthur finished putting on his sweater as he took his chair. "Wow, banana pancakes, basted eggs, and buns. It must be the birthday of the letter B."

"Nope, it's something more important than that."

"How about: At last we're alone day?"

"You're getting closer, but I guess I'll have to tell you. It's our fifty-day anniversary. We've been married for fifty days."

"I have to apologize. I forgot to get you a present."

"That's no problem; you're the present."

"I always knew you were a romantic, Irma. How would you like a trip to Iraq to dig for buried treasure?"

"You're not really thinking of going if someone organizes an expedition. That's a war zone."

"No, I'm not that crazy, and I certainly wouldn't want to expose you to more danger than we frequently have around here. I do think that someone will make a try, though."

"Do you mean Karl Simitski will go after it?"

"I don't read him as being someone who takes chances himself. He would probably pay local Iraqis to do the job for him, if he had people he could trust."

"Who else might try to find it?"

"After hearing from Joe about the Israelis who bought the cuneiform cylinder and disappeared with it, I wouldn't be at all surprised if the original owners of that treasure slipped an undercover team into Iraq to get it back."

"They weren't at your meeting. Would they know where to look?"

"I'm sure they have more clues than I did. They know about the cylinder of Cyrus the Great and they may have been collecting information about these lost items for the better part of three millennia. In addition, they now have the Tobias cylinder. They may find something in its translation that Geraldine Quig missed."

"You may be right. I do want to compliment you on your presentation for Karl Simitski and the rest of us. It was very clever. Based on that meeting, give me your impression of Karl. You had enough contact there to form an opinion of him."

"Then you also sensed that he was hiding something."

"I did have that feeling, plus I found that he was very tense when I took him for a local tour, especially when I asked if we could visit his collection."

"Maybe the collection is part of what he's hiding. What did he say about it?

"He didn't reveal anything about the contents of the collection, but he claimed it was hermetically sealed away during emergency maintenance of his underground chambers. I had the definite impression that he has things there that he doesn't want us to see."

"Well, that might become a topic for a future phase of this investigation, but right now I want to investigate your special breakfast and my romantic wife. Romance in the morning is a great idea."

CHAPTER 56 – AUSTIN

Joe Gonzalez landed at Austin-Bergstrom International Airport and followed the rest of the arriving passengers into the terminal. He found Steve DuBois waiting for him outside the security area with the keys to their rental car, a maroon Ford Focus. Both having only carry-on luggage, they headed for the car and drove directly to the University of Texas. Steve did the driving, while Joe checked in with his police contact to determine Geraldine Quig's condition and location. He learned that she had left the hospital and had said that she planned to return to her office. Joe informed the police that the individuals who had reportedly stolen that item from the university might have only claimed it after presenting documents showing they had purchased it. He promised that he would contact them again after he had clarified the facts with Professor Quig.

Once they arrived at the campus, Joe directed Steve to the Middle Eastern Studies building where he had first met Professor Quig. They parked and headed inside. The note on her office door indicated that she would be in the departmental research library for an hour and gave the room number. When they found the library, Joe and Steve saw Geraldine sitting in her wheelchair with a large book on her lap. A two-by-two gauze dressing secured by tape adorned the left side of her forehead.

Joe waved as they walked in, moving toward her while scanning the room for other occupants. Seeing none, he said, "I heard about your injury. Do you feel better now? Was it a concussion?"

"Hello, Mr. Gonzalez. No, I was fortunate. I have only a large bump on my head and a laceration, but I'll bounce back quickly. Who's your friend?"

"Geraldine, I'd like you to meet Steve DuBois, an associate from my agency, and please call me Joe."

Steve and Geraldine shook hands. Steve said, "What are you studying? That book looks very large and very old."

"I'm learning as much as I can about the Temple of Marduk in ancient Babylon. Following his return from the meeting with Joe and his friends in Illinois, Karl Simitski suggested that knowledge of the temple would be useful. Your friend Pastor Blake impressed Karl with his analytical skills."

Joe said, "He has a knack for such things. We rely on his thinking in many of our investigations...Does your research indicate that Karl is planning an expedition to try to find the artifacts stolen from Solomon's Temple?"

"He hasn't made a decision on that. I suspect that a lot will depend on the amount of detailed information I discover. I suspect that you're here regarding the theft of the cylinder that Karl left with me for evaluation."

"We're here about that cylinder, but Steve has discovered that your visitors purchased that cylinder and came to you with a valid bill of sale and other documentation of ownership. Didn't they present those papers to you?"

Geraldine wheeled her chair over to the study table and placed the book on it before she replied. "Yes, they presented those papers to me, but I questioned their legitimacy, in the absence of any communication from Karl. He had been very sure that he had the exclusive right to purchase the cylinder."

Steve said, "That may have been his impression, and the ethics of the transaction may be in question, but the agent of the artifact's owner received a much higher offer than Karl had discussed, and he accepted it. He told me that he had not considered the price Karl discussed a true offer, both because Karl had refused to put it in writing and because it was contingent upon your evaluation and recommendation. The agent received a higher offer without any contingencies, and he accepted it. It appears to have been a valid contract."

Joe said, "I don't understand why the men who came for the cylinder pulled a pistol on you and hit you with it. If they had presented their documents to a judge, he or she would have ruled that they owned the artifact and could claim it without any conflict."

Geraldine wheeled her chair to face Joe. "It didn't exactly happen that way, but I let the police reach their own conclusions. The truth is that Karl very generously supports my work. I wanted him to have a chance to outbid those men, so I quite literally fought a delaying action. To compensate for my being confined in a wheelchair these days, I carry a handgun in a holster next to my hip. It's hardly noticeable and usually covered by my loose clothing. When those men presented their papers to me and asked for the cylinder, I pulled my gun on them. In the struggle to take it away from me, one of them hit me on the head with it. He was surprisingly strong. In a sense, I deserved my injury for taking such a rash action."

Joe said, "Karl wouldn't have been able to outbid those men. They represented the government of Israel. Their mission was to get a detailed accounting of the items that had been stolen from Solomon's Temple and never returned."

"Karl will be angry about losing this antiquity. He has a terrible temper, and he looked on this cylinder as connecting him to Old Testament history."

Joe said, "He expressed that same sentiment to me. Perhaps he'll decide to go to Iraq and try to locate the treasure represented by the cylinder."

"He knows that Iraq would not be safe for him right now, so I doubt it. Do you think you can straighten things out with the police so that I won't be in trouble for letting them reach the wrong conclusion about my injury?"

"I'll do my best, but the original version will remain in the police and newspaper files. I suggest you remove yourself from indebtedness to Karl or any other client if you want to keep your reputation as an unbiased authority on antiquities."

CHAPTER 57 – SEARCH WARRANT

Arthur and Irma exited the front door of their apartment house two minutes after hearing the horn signal from the black car in the loading zone beneath their kitchen window. Arthur carried Irma's forensics kit while she had a camera bag slung over one shoulder and her purse over the other. Irma accompanied the equipment into the rear seat, while Arthur joined the driver in the front.

As he belted up, Arthur said, "Thanks for the ride, Bobby. I see you decided to go plain clothes and plain car on this mission."

"That's because we're observers this time, with the Illinois State Police taking the lead. Thanks to both of you for the assist. We'll have an advantage over the others because we examined the scene of Angela's death. We'll have a better chance of recognizing significant items at Joyce's house."

Irma asked, "Where does she live?"

"Joyce Jennings lives in a farmhouse in the next county. That's why I worked through the State Police to get the search warrant. It's out of my jurisdiction. A farmer actively cultivates the land on a rental basis while she leases the dwelling. She's been there for several years, so she probably considers it her home."

Arthur said, "It might be interesting to see when her lease expires. If she killed Angela, she might have timed that action for the end of her lease. With Angela gone, Joyce might feel free to move back to California or somewhere else."

Irma said, "That's an interesting speculation, but I disagree. Joyce would have murdered Angela because Bishop Chandler assigned the two of them to work together in a separate office, and that gave Joyce a tempting opportunity to commit the deed."

Bobby said, "The fact that Angela had no qualms about working with Joyce suggests that she had no idea that Joyce was the mother of one of the children who died while in her care. Angela had buried that event deep within her memory, but to Joyce it was still a current issue."

Irma said, "Some people never forgive."

Arthur smiled and turned to look at Irma. "You did it again. Thanks for next week's sermon topic. You inspire me in many ways."

When they arrived at the farmhouse, they found that the Illinois State Police had already entered the home through an unlocked kitchen door and had initiated their search. Bobby, Irma, and Arthur introduced themselves to Captain Sylvia Menendez, put on vinyl gloves, and joined the others. Bobby assisted those working in the basement, while Irma stayed on the main floor, and Arthur went upstairs to examine the bedroom level.

Arthur found nothing remarkable in the main bedroom or the bathroom, so he proceeded to the spare bedroom. He observed that the décor there was less feminine, with furniture and accessories having a solid colonial style. A worktable in the corner of the room showed cuts and gouges on its top, apparently due to its use for crafts and other projects. The left half of the closet housed a set of purchased steel-grid shelves, crammed with a variety of miscellaneous objects. One of them caught his eye. He moved on to check for items stored under the bed. He pulled a large shallow corrugated carton from under the bed, removed its lid, and then he replaced it. He walked to the head of the stairs and called down to those below.

"I think I've found something significant. Irma, would you please bring the camera. I have the rest of your gear up here."

Irma came up the stairs, closely followed by Captain Menendez and a younger officer. Irma said, "What did you find?"

"Several interesting things, but as a test, I'd like you to look into the spare bedroom closet and tell me whether you see anything significant on the shelves."

Irma set down the camera bag on the bed and walked to the open closet door. She pulled the beaded chain to turn on the inside light and scanned the shelf items without touching any of them. She found it surprising that Joyce had stored some paint cans up here rather than in the basement. The photograph albums might reveal some interesting aspects of Joyce's history. She saw a carton full of hand tools and a corded electric drill, and she saw a stack of board games. Then Irma looked on the top shelf and saw what had aroused Arthur's interest. "I think I see what you mean, and I think you're absolutely correct."

Captain Menendez had stood patiently observing this exchange. "You two enjoy cryptic comments, but how about letting us outsiders in on your point? Is there something significant in the closet, and if so, what is it?"

Irma said, "I'm sorry, Captain; Arthur asked me to look without explanation to see whether I would confirm the importance of what he found, and I have. On top of that set of shelves in the closet is a desk lamp that is an exact duplicate of the one that electrocuted the victim, Angela King."

"That is a big coincidence, but the lamp by itself won't convict her."

Arthur said, "I think you folks should see what I found under the bed. It's the rest of the story."

Arthur removed the lid from the under-bed carton and stepped back so that the others could see what it contained."

Irma said, "We have the duplicate lamp in the closet, and in here we have a white sheet of steel, similar to the one that was used as a floor mat in the office. In with the tools in the closet were a voltmeter, and some clip-lead cables. My guess is that Joyce tested out her trap in this room before installing the real thing. I'll bet that lamp in the closet even has a section of its cord with the insulation stripped away."

The young officer took down the lamp from the shelf and examined it. "You're right; this cord is definitely faulty, although it appears to be due to wear rather than any deliberate stripping of the insulation. It would pose a shock hazard. I'll seal this lamp into an evidence bag."

Captain Menendez said, "Mark that under-bed carton as evidence and take the whole thing. This excursion is getting some results. You never know whether a search outing will be fruitful. Take that other stuff from the closet too."

They all headed downstairs to the main floor. As the young officer was about to carry the evidence parcels out to his van, Bobby emerged from the basement stairs. "Hold up; I have another piece of evidence to add to whatever you have there. We found this behind the furnace; it's a combination stun gun and high-power flashlight. Some of my military police cohorts carried them. I suspect that the shocking electrodes will match the marks on the neck of the victim. It could be the weapon used to make sure Angela was dead after she had received the initial line voltage shock."

CHAPTER 58 – REACTIONS

Having returned to Joe's home after their joint trip to Austin, Steve sat with Joe and Penny at their dining room table following dinner.

"I always enjoy visiting you two because both the food and companionship are so good."

Penny said, "You're always welcome, Steve. Your visit to Roger Svenson in Kansas City completely changed our understanding of what happened to the cuneiform cylinder at the University of Texas."

"There's a lot about that event and its aftermath that bother me. How do you feel about it, Joe?"

"I understand what you mean, Steve. If you hadn't found out about the Svenson transaction, Geraldine Quig would have been quite happy to let everyone keep thinking that those men stole the cuneiform cylinder. She's not the ideal ethical academic."

"She's not independent either. She's supported by Karl Simitski, and she'll say and do whatever he wants."

Penny said, "I wonder whether your conversations with Professor Quig might not have revealed more information about Karl. Irma told me that she suspects he's hiding things from us. She told me about his tension when she talked with him and the excuses he gave for not allowing anyone to visit his collection."

Joe said, "I think you're onto something with that line of thought, Penny. Quig told us that Karl has a terrible temper. Yet, we've been back here for a couple of days, and no one has received any contact from him. I would have expected him to rant and rave about the sale of the cylinder to the Israelis when he thought he had the deal wrapped up. What did Roger Svenson say about his relationship with Simitski, Steve?"

"That was the problem. Karl had been so secretive, wanting Svenson to work through his agent, Alicia Pavone, that there was no relationship between Karl and Roger Svenson. Alicia never even gave Roger the identity of the buyer. Then when Karl sent the artifact to Texas for evaluation and translation, Svenson thought they were stringing him along and stretching the time for the negotiation. He was ripe for someone to come along with a higher cash offer. By taking that offer, Roger told Alicia and her secret buyer, Karl, that he didn't need them. He undoubtedly enjoyed that development."

Penny said, "Have you called Svenson since your return, Steve?"

"I did. I called him yesterday to tell him that his clients had picked up the cylinder to finalize the transaction. The real reason I called was to see whether he had received any repercussions from Karl Simitski or Alicia. He told me that no one had contacted him and that he was glad he wouldn't have to deal with them again."

Joe said, "There's something wrong here. Either Karl is acting contrary to his reputation, or some thug is going to pay Roger Svenson a visit in the near future. Geraldine Quig will have told Karl that we visited her, so I don't think that Svenson is in danger. Karl would know that we'd go after him if anything happened to Svenson. Therefore, Karl is being quiet for some other reason."

Penny said, "Maybe it has something to do with my report from Irma that he definitely doesn't want anyone to visit his collection. That collection could contain stolen items, or he might be doing other things in his underground museum."

Steve said, "What kinds of things, for example?"

"He could be trafficking in weapons or manufacturing explosives."

Joe said, "Steve, you took notes when we visited Professor Quig. There was something unusual that she said about Karl when I asked whether he might organize an expedition to look for the temple artifacts in Iraq. What was it?"

Steve pulled out a pocket notebook and scanned its pages. "She stated that Karl knows that Iraq would not be safe for him right now. I took that to mean that he wouldn't want to go into an area where the religious and ethnic factions were still murdering each other from time to time."

"I think it's more than that, Steve. Suppose the Tobias cylinder hadn't been the only item from Iraq that he wanted to have in his collection. If the government there suspected Karl of buying some of the looted items from the Iraq Museum, they would not be friendly to the idea of him going there to look for more of their antiquities."

Penny walked over to her desk and removed some papers from a file on top of it. "If he has been buying looted artifacts, we already have authorization to go after him for them. We have several bulletins describing some of the missing items."

Joe said, "Karl has been thinking about those thefts. When we were at his house he mentioned the work at the Oriental Institute of the University of Chicago to tabulate the looted items. Karl remarked that the total included forty-eight hundred cuneiform pieces, both seals and cylinders. We should contact the Oriental Institute to get better descriptions and listings of those items that are still missing. Then we should visit Karl's collection with a warrant and check for anything suspicious."

CHAPTER 59 – IRMA AND RENEE

Renee Andrews opened her door to admit Irma Blake, and realized that she had sensed correctly the melancholy in Irma's telephone voice. This girl definitely needed a shoulder to cry on and a pep talk.

Irma tossed her jacket onto the hall chair and preceded Renee into the family room where little Thelma Lou lay asleep in her playpen. The peacefulness of the child did coerce a slight smile from Irma, but nothing compared to her usual enthusiasm at the sight of her goddaughter.

Renee broke the ice. "Come on over and sit next to Mother Renee on the couch. We're free to chat for as long as you like. Thelma Lou just fell asleep. She's probably good for a couple of hours, and Momma's out shopping."

"How did you know I wanted a long talk?"

"Girl, it's written all over your face. You gave me plenty of support when the baby had health problems. Now it's time for you to unburden yourself to me. Has Arthur been beating you? If so, I'll have my favorite Police Chief straighten him out."

Irma leaned back and shook her head. "It's nothing like that. I'm just a little blue because our marriage hasn't turned out to be all romance and roses, with Arthur always being excited by the affections I aim at him."

"So that's it. Your fantasy world and the real world collided, and the real world won. Don't look now, Irma, but just about every bride feels this funk."

"I know; I'm supposed to be realistic. The problem is that it took years of creative campaigning for me to get Arthur to the altar, and now he's more interested in his work than he is in me. I waited more than forty years to get married, and now I sometimes wonder whether it was worth it."

"You are in a down mood. Start by opening that box on the coffee table and having some chocolates. They're a new dark chocolate brand that Momma found, and they're great."

Irma leaned forward and did as instructed. "They are good, but I need food for the soul, not the body."

"Now that you're nourished, I'll get personal with you. Are you saying that Arthur isn't romantic at all and that you can't turn him on?"

"No, we have romance now and then, but I expected a more constant diet of it once we got married. Does Bobby get romantic only once in a while?"

Renee laughed and slapped Irma on the shoulder. "Now I see your problem. Bobby is Bobby, and Arthur is Arthur. Bobby is attentive whenever he can break free from police work because he knows I'm the best thing that ever happened to him and because he has a romantic soul. Arthur has never been one to broadcast his feelings. He's a sweet gentle person, and he'll give you attention along with all of his other interests, but don't expect him to dedicate his life to you and you alone. You're asking him to become someone else, and you might not even like that person if he did. You spent years trying to get him to marry you because you loved what you saw in him. Appreciate him; don't try to change him."

"But he has the potential to be so much more."

"More what...Do you mean you want him to be more like the fantasy of him that you've imagined? You'd better drop that line of thought, or your marriage is heading for disaster. Love him for what he is, not for what you would like him to be. As for that continuous romance stuff, get real. Every day we have problems and obligations that we have to face. They're your priorities. Grab the romance when you can fit it in along the way; it will be all the sweeter when you realize you had to overcome the problems of life in order to earn romantic interludes."

"Earning romance...that's a new concept for me."

Renee stood up and looked down on Irma. "And now I'm going to straighten out your muddled thinking. You gave me your la-di-da story about campaigning to get Arthur to marry you over several years. That's a bunch of nonsense. During that those years, you and Arthur worked together and helped each other through tough times. That's what brought you together, not your campaigning. When we help each other through life's problems, we get closer to each other than to anyone who doesn't have those shared experiences. That's where the love comes from, not the romance books. Your marriage doesn't have difficulties, only unrealistic goals. If you want romance from Arthur, then do something special for him. He'll respond to it. Knowing Arthur's restrained emotions, he's not going to keep pushing the romance button on his own."

Irma stood up and hugged Renee. You're right. I've been feeling sorry for myself when I had no real reason for regrets. Thanks for knocking some sense into my head. We're approaching the holidays. It will be our first married Christmas, and I'll make it a romantic one."

Thelma Lou woke up with a shudder and started to cry.

"And now, Irma Blake, you can pay for my wisdom by changing your goddaughter's diaper."

CHAPTER 60 – ELLEN

She had picked up all of the papers and other items that the intruders had strewn all over the floors in the living room and den. Then she had replaced the snap locks with deadbolts as Steve had suggested. Ellen Tobias felt rattled by the invasion of her little house. That event had shown her that danger could even extend to Paul, Idaho. Steve's supporting concern and clear instructions as to the steps she should take to restore her security had reduced her tension.

They hadn't openly discussed anything yet, but she wanted Steve to be a major ingredient in the recipe for her future. Eric wouldn't be home from school for another hour, so she would have privacy for a special telephone conversation.

Ellen arranged the pillows for best comfort on the couch and placed an open beer within reach on the end table. She added a pad of paper and a pen just in case Steve said something that would require taking notes. She surveyed the arrangement and deemed it perfect. Then she wriggled into a comfortable position and keyed in his cell phone number. His clear voice followed the third ring.

"Hi, Ellen; I was just about to call you. Hold on while I get back into my office for privacy...I'm free to talk now. Have you cleared up that mess you found after the break-in?"

"That I have; and many thanks for your guidance on the replacement locks. I feel safe and secure again."

"You won't have to worry about them coming back. It turned out that they were after the contact information for Roger Svenson in Kansas City. They contacted him and convinced him to sell Travis' cuneiform cylinder to them for much more money than he hoped to get from someone else. You're going to be very wealthy because of that sale."

"That is good news, but I treat it as Travis' legacy for Eric. I won't touch that money except in an emergency. Right now, I'm more interested in whether we have a future together."

"You don't waste time in idle conversation, Ellen. That took me by surprise, but I'll admit that I had been wondering the same thing. Now that you're going to have all that money, I have to say that I don't know. That kind of wealth could change you, and it bothers me. My dad used to tell me that it was just as easy to fall in love with a rich girl as a poor one, but I never bought into that thinking. I wanted a relationship where we shared and struggled as equals."

"Steve, I want that too. I never asked for this money, and I'm sure Travis didn't think that cylinder was valuable when he brought it home. He just liked history and wanted a souvenir for Eric. The money will be for Eric, and I'll put it away until he's old enough to appreciate the whole story and to handle wealth. Who knows; maybe he'll put it away for his eventual kids. I'm with you. I feel that we can't let it change us, and I'm including you in that statement."

"Thanks, Ellen; I think I needed to hear that. I do think we'll have to give things some time, to see whether we do change. I also know that this case doesn't end with your receiving that money. We're going to have a lot of work at our agency before the investigation can be marked complete. I'll keep in touch with you, as we get closer to that point. Then maybe our heads will be clear enough to make some decisions. Can you live with that?"

"I'll have to, but it will be a tense period. I haven't even received that money, and I already hate it for changing things."

CHAPTER 61 – DISCOVERY

Illinois State Police Captain Sylvia Menendez watched silently as divers in wet suits pulled the body onto the shoreline from the water-filled depths of Sandy Hollow Quarry. People discarded strange things into the many abandoned limestone quarries in Winnebago and adjacent counties, notably stolen and discarded cars, industrial equipment, and occasional bodies. Unlike the other discards, the bodies were unique in that they sometimes developed buoyancy and rose again to the surface. Willie Sanders had spotted this one while taking his son Jesse fishing. He had wanted their first fishing outing to be memorable, but not in this way. Willie had told Jesse to remain in their car well away from the retrieval effort, while he continued to watch from a respectful distance.

Captain Menendez doubted that they would be able to identify this poor creature from photographs. They would first try to determine whether the cause of death had been murder, suicide, or an accident. Then they would hope to get a DNA match with someone in an available database. She suspected that the identification process would take a long time.

She saw John Pugh bending over the body to begin his on-site preliminary examination prior to removing the remains to the morgue for a thorough autopsy. Sylvia edged a little closer, but she didn't want to intrude on his space or concentration until he was ready for her. After about seven minutes, John turned and motioned for her to join him.

She squatted alongside him and the partially decomposed body. "What happened to this poor guy, John?"

"It's a definite homicide, Sylvia. Somebody stabbed him and then tied his crossed arms in front of him, holding a large rock against his stomach. The murderer thought that no one would ever find the corpse because of the depth of the water in this quarry, but the knots in the rope here are amateurish, and the rock eventually slipped out and sank to the bottom. I think we can eliminate Boy Scouts and sailors from your investigation. They would never have tied knots like these."

"He's wearing pretty common fishing or camping gear. I don't see anything there that would be unusual enough to trace for identification."

"I'll be able to tell you after the autopsy whether he was thrown in while he was still alive, or if he was already dead at that time. It will depend on whether we find his lungs full of water due to his struggling to breathe while submerged."

Sylvia Menendez reached down and rolled the body over. Then she pointed to his back pocket. "Look, John; they're in bad shape, but that's a pack of playing cards in his back pocket."

"He may have liked playing cards, but someone dealt him a dead man's hand...the poor devil."

CHAPTER 62 – ROGER SVENSON

What a crazy turn of events it had been! For ten years, he had schemed, cajoled, and worked angles to make a living from commissions on appraisals and minor art sales. Then he had stumbled onto the cuneiform cylinder just because he had done some camping and skiing with Travis Tobias. They would never have met if their fathers hadn't served in Vietnam together.

He had feared that Alicia Pavone and her secretive buyer would try to muscle him out of a commission on that artifact. Her buyer had to be some kind of nut, thinking he could keep negotiations going forever on a noncommittal basis. Those two Israelis had walked into his shop and had given him the chance to rub Mr. Secretive's face in it. He had even doubled his expectations as far as the final price for the cylinder. The cashier's check had cleared, and now he was sitting on close to a million dollars in his account. His proximity to that amount of money made his fingertips tingle.

Roger wondered whether he needed to part with all of it less the fifteen percent commission he had mentioned to Travis. It had all been verbal and handshake stuff. With Travis dead, he could tell his widow the agreed commission had been thirty percent. Heck, some galleries got away with fifty percent. He didn't even have to reveal the full amount of the sale price since he had handled all of the documentation. He could easily prepare new documents showing a lesser price. Life would treat him very well from now on.

CHAPTER 63 – JOHN PUGH

Arthur entered the Parkville Police Department and stopped to talk with Al Gomez, who was working on assignment charts.

"Good morning, Al; has Bobby arrived yet?"

"You're here early. He's in his office, but he didn't tell me he had a meeting scheduled with you."

"That would be because I'm here to see if I can catch him before he starts his busy day. How does his schedule look?"

"I wish I could tell you. He hasn't given it to me yet. I try to keep things organized around here, but nothing ever goes as planned anyway. Go on in to see him. He can't get mad about your interrupting a schedule he hasn't given me."

Arthur thanked Al and headed for Bobby Andrews' office. Bobby motioned for Arthur to sit down while he finished his telephone conversation.

"...He just stopped in. I'll work it out with him and Irma. I'm not sure whether we have one or not, but we'll get something for you. I'll talk with you soon, John."

Bobby set the phone back on its cradle and turned to Arthur.

"Are you psychic or something? How did you know I wanted to talk with you?"

"I didn't, but there are too many loose ends concerning events around here. I need to compare notes with you. What do you have – something coming out of that telephone conversation? And who's John; do I know him?"

"That was John Pugh. He took over Irma's Medical Examiner caseload, even though he's really the CME in Winnebago County. We haven't had enough in the budget

206

to hire a new full-time person here. Anyway, our friend Sylvia Menendez of the State Police fished a body out of Sandy Hollow Quarry up by Rockford. It's an abandoned limestone dig, filled with water. After working with us on that search at Joyce Jennings' house, Sylvia wondered whether the body might tie in with something I said to her."

"That got my attention. What were you discussing?"

"I had told Sylvia about Angela's possible murder of Charlie King in Canada while they were fishing. It came up when we were discussing evidence against Joyce for killing Angela. I told her that they may have been two of a kind, each striking back at someone who had wronged them."

"What does that have to do with a body in a water-logged quarry?"

"Nothing except for the fact that the body reclaimed from that site carried identification in its inside jacket pocket indicating it was someone named Charles King."

"That is an interesting surprise. Now we have to find out whether it was Angela's Charles King. What address was indicated, and was there a photo I.D. there, a driver's license or something similar?"

"There's a Nevada License with a photo. The body is too far gone for facial comparisons, but we may be able to check the DNA against somebody's database. It will take a while to process and compare DNA. We'll have to do something else for near term follow-up."

"I have an idea, Bobby. At that meeting in Denver, Julie Wyandt thought that Oliver Parkworth was Charlie King. I'll ask Joe for a picture of Oliver to compare with this I.D. shot. There should be some resemblance if it's Angela's Charlie. I'll also ask Irma if she wants to visit John Pugh and inspect the remains. He probably won't mind a little extra assistance."

"And she would probably like to sit in on an autopsy again."

Arthur stood and prepared to leave. "You're right. She needs a mission...The finding of this body may cast a totally different light on Angela King. If it's her ex-husband, she was a determined and violent murderer. There was nothing spur-of-the-moment about it. That story about their trip to Canada may have been pure fiction...I'll get back to you, Bobby, after I get Oliver's picture from Joe."

CHAPTER 64 – COMPARISONS

Arthur arrived at the Gonzalez house two hours after having left the Parkville Police Station. He had first stopped at home and discussed the quarry discovery with Irma, who promptly decided to visit John Pugh and assist in examining the body. He had sensed that this burst of activity would be good for her, and Irma's enthusiasm as she left confirmed his prediction. He made a final stop at the church to ask Shirley to cancel his two afternoon appointments.

Penny opened the front door in response to his ring. The rolled-up sleeves on her flannel shirt signified her readiness to thrash out the issues of the day.

"Good morning, Arthur. We've assembled all of the case files in the dining room. You indicated that we might have a breakthrough, or at least a major development. Come on in; grab some fresh coffee; and brief us on the new developments."

"Thanks, Penny; I think we're about to see things more clearly."

They walked into the dining room, where Joe was in the process of printing a photograph that he had received by email.

"Hi, Arthur; I passed your request to Aaron Foelsch, the principal of the West Minico Middle School in Paul, Idaho. I caught him just after he arrived at school, and he sent me a file for Oliver Parkworth's photograph. I'm printing it out now. I assume you're going to fill us in on why it's a high priority item."

"If I'm not mistaken, that picture may be the key to this whole case. At the very least, it will guide our next steps in the investigation. By the way, Penny, your coffee is outstanding this morning."

"Thanks for the compliment, Arthur, but judging by the excitement in your voice, I probably should have given you the decaffeinated blend."

"When I start to see the different aspects of a case making sense, I do get a little energized, but there's still a long way to go before we solve everything.

"The key new developments are that with the assistance of the Illinois State Police, we searched Joyce Jennings' home and found electrical items that she may have used to test the electrocution setup intended for Angela King in that Parkville office. State Police Captain Menendez, who worked with us on the search and learned about our case, has since been involved in retrieving a corpse from an abandoned quarry near Rockford. That decomposed and waterlogged body carried still-legible identification as one Charles King of Las Vegas, Nevada."

Joe said, "Do we know whether that person was Angela's ex-husband rather than a different Charles King?"

"That's why I requested a photo of Oliver Parkworth. I was sure you could get one from the school where he taught, and Angela's friend Julie Wyandt had said he looked just like Charlie."

Penny said, "I hate to be a spoilsport, but even if Oliver's picture matches the corpse's I.D. photo, how do we know that the body isn't Oliver carrying Charlie's identification? Unless we find Oliver somewhere, we haven't proved that they are two separate people. For that matter, how do we know that the corpse wasn't a vagrant carrying Charlie's I.D.?"

Arthur got up and refreshed his coffee. "You're raising good points, Penny, but we'll have to examine them one at a time. Irma will compare the Oliver Parkworth photo with the license photo on the body. Irma is meeting with the current Medical Examiner to examine the body, and she'll look at the knife wounds to see if they match Angela's story. The preliminary on-scene report at least says that this person suffered stab wounds. They're also going to check databases for a DNA match to the body. We should try to locate a living version of Oliver soon. If he's a separate person, he's becoming important."

Joe said, "If the body is Charlie, then we know that Angela King was a violent scheming woman. If Joyce Jennings killed her by deliberate electrocution, she's just as bad and violent. This is starting to look like the proverbial nest of vipers."

Penny said, "Some of the folks associated with the handling of that cuneiform artifact may be just as bad. We'd better take another look at them."

CHAPTER 65 – STEVE

Roger Svenson had sent his receptionist home early. He never quite knew what was going on in Steffani's mind, and it distracted him from his own deliberations. Today he would make a break with the past. He, his computer, and a few key files would leave Inland Associated Art Examiners and disappear. They would never resurface, at least not in Kansas City or any place near it.

His passport was current and, after a brief stop at the bank to close his account, the first leg of his meandering adventure would take him to Lima, Peru. No one would ever think to look for him there, and the money would last a very long time in that economy. It wouldn't be permanent. As soon as he felt the urge to move on, he would move to another exotic but inexpensive locale. Thoughts of his idyllic new life filled his mind as he walked through the outer rooms, carrying his large attaché case and whistling that old song, *On the Road Again.* He opened the outer office door to find a man in jeans, boots, and a red flannel shirt standing there.

"Are you taking a trip, Mr. Svenson? The tune you were whistling suggests that you're planning to go somewhere."

"Where I'm going is none of your business. The office is closed. Who are you, anyway?"

"I'm Steve DuBois. We spoke on the telephone a while back, concerning your sale of that cuneiform antiquity to those Israelis. I'm here representing the federal government. You'll be interested to know that we have put a hold on your bank account while we investigate the source of the money they used to pay for the item. Money laundering is always a potential problem in international transactions. Should there be no problem with the funds,

212

my friends at the Internal Revenue Service will issue a secondary hold order to guarantee that you pay the taxes due on that large amount. I don't know whether that might change your travel plans, but please don't let me delay you."

"You're acting as though I'm some kind of criminal, Mr. DuBois. I assure you that I'm only taking these materials with me because I have a large amount of homework to do."

"There's no problem with that. I applaud private enterprise and initiative. I should also tell you that Ellen Tobias is a friend of mine. Her attorney expects that a local judge will issue an injunction today, barring you from touching any of the funds in your bank account until you sign an agreement limiting your share to fifteen percent in accordance with the written notes left by Travis Tobias and discussed with his wife, Ellen."

Roger Svenson stared at Steve. Then he smiled and said, "It's good to see that our government is being so businesslike in this matter. Perhaps they'll learn how to balance their budget someday. Do you have any other pronouncements for me?"

"You'll enjoy this one. You're free to go. Although you have highly questionable ethics, you haven't broken the law – yet. However, our agency and the IRS will continue to monitor your business activities for several years into the future. Have a great day."

Steve turned and headed for the elevator without looking back. Although he hadn't mentioned it, he suspected that Svenson's biggest worry might not be the freeze on his funds. Karl Simitski might eventually decide to retaliate for Roger's abandoning their presumed deal.

CHAPTER 66 – PATHOLOGY

John Pugh removed his magnifying goggles and walked over to greet the visitor who had set a technical equipment case on the laboratory bench.

"Hello, Irma; it has been a while since we've been face-to-face. I'll have to remind myself that your last name is Blake now. Married life appears to be doing well by you."

"That it is, John, but as soon as I walked in and caught the lights, sights, and smells, I felt as though I had flashed back to the old days. Are you able to keep up with the work in both counties?"

"So far I'm doing what's required. If we run into large numbers of incidents or deceased, I might have to beg you for some part time assistance."

"You really know how to charm a girl, but let's hope the deaths don't get overwhelming. I'm here to see the victim you fished out of Sandy Hollow Quarry. Have you learned much from the body?"

"That body had to have been in there for months, and even though the deep and cold water slowed down the decomposition process, there were limits to what we could examine. At least he had some identification in his pocket."

"How well did the driver's license photograph match what was left of his face?"

"I'd say as well as could be expected under the circumstances. That kind of picture is never good to start with, and we had to clean it up to get rid of the dirt and at least some of the cloudiness of the laminating plastic. Then we had to compare it to a face that had only partial skin covering plus deteriorating and shredded flesh. It's an imperfect comparison, but the head shape was about right. We'll need a DNA comparison to confirm it. Did this

Charles King have any known relatives that we can use for a DNA family pattern match?"

Irma removed her cell phone from her purse. "We don't know of any relatives, but Arthur sent me a photograph of someone who had been mistaken for the Charles King who is involved in the case we're investigating. I'll bring it up on my phone, and we can compare it to the I.D. photo."

They placed the Nevada License on the workbench. Irma set the phone showing Oliver Parkworth's image alongside it.

John said, "I see a resemblance, but I'd need to see them both at roughly the same magnification. The I.D. photo is much smaller."

Irma put her phone in camera mode and took a picture of the I.D. photo. Then she sequenced the new image to be next to the one Arthur had sent to her and adjusted the magnification. She and John tried to memorize images as she switched back and forth between the two on her camera screen.

John said, "They are quite similar, although someone familiar with both people would not confuse them."

"I think we can conclude that the Charles King in the license photo is the Charlie King that we are investigating. I also conclude that Julie Wyandt mistakenly identified Oliver as Charlie because she had not seen Charlie more than a few times and not recently. That also means that they are two different people. At one time we wondered whether Charlie had recovered from his injuries and had reappeared as Oliver."

John said, "Now let's compare your enlarged camera photograph of the license picture to the corpse." He pulled a stainless steel body drawer out of the wall refrigeration unit and held the camera screen next to the head.

"I'd say it's the same person, given the terrible condition of his face. What do you think, Irma?"

"I'm not quite ready to say it's a match. However, there may be back-up evidence to confirm the identification. Angela King said she stabbed Charlie twice in his left side. Let's look for cuts in what remains of the flesh and knife marks on the bones."

They transferred the body to the autopsy table and arranged their lights to better study the corpse's left side. John viewed it through his magnifying goggles. "Here's a straight line cut, rather than a ragged tear. It's high enough that the blade may have caught the bottom of the rib cage. I'll photograph this cut in the flesh. Then we'll be free to open things up to check the bones."

After completing the photography and the related documentation, John spread the deteriorating flesh to view the lowest rib. "I have a definite knife notch on the lowest rib, Irma. The knifepoint could have extended upward enough to catch the lung, an artery, or even the heart. What kind of knife did she use?"

"If she was telling the truth, she used a fish cleaning knife. There are quite a few types, but most are usually long with a serrated edge, and I've seen some with forklike points."

"That could be the weapon here. It looks as though the knife struck the rib and pivoted upward causing damage to the interior chest organs."

"Would he have been alive or dead when he was thrown into the water?"

"I'd guess that he was alive but unconscious, Irma. His lungs had water in them, so he would have been struggling to breathe under water. She tied his arms to clasp a rock or a concrete block to his abdomen, so he would have had to be unconscious if he didn't resist that maneuver."

"Based on those findings, I agree that this is the Charlie King of our investigation, and he matches the ID photo with a high probability."

CHAPTER 67 – COMPANY

Alicia Pavone dusted her living room end table and surveyed her apartment. The living room and dining room projected an immaculate and inviting image. She had removed a few of her more feminine decorations and enhanced the scene with several abstract sculptures that might appeal to Karl. She doubted that they would get to the bedroom phase tonight, but she had added a few fresh flowers for a romantic touch and the slightest hint of perfume. Alicia had been worried that her interview with those federal agents would mark the end of her relationship, business and otherwise, with Karl Simitski, but his voice had sounded cordial on the telephone. She saw promise in his impending visit. As she returned her cleaning supplies to their cabinet, the doorbell rang.

Alicia straightened the ruffles on her pink dress as she approached the door, reminding herself that a few years of seniority did not negate dreams and romance. She opened the door to find Karl totally dressed in black, from his boots to his jeans, shirt, and leather jacket. The gray in his beard offered the only point of contrast.

"Welcome, Karl; it's so good to see you again. I bought some of your favorite wine to start the evening."

"I'll join you for the wine, but I don't expect to stay the whole evening."

Alicia tensed up at his unexpected comment. She tried to remain calm. "Is there something bothering you? Can I help in any way?"

They had gone into the kitchen where she had the wine bottle and glasses on a silver tray. She tried to uncork the bottle, but her hands shook and didn't cooperate with her intentions.

Karl took the bottle and corkscrew from her. "Let me do that." His bottle-opening technique showed frequent practice. He poured the wine and handed her a glass.

"Alicia, I had great hopes for working with you, but you screwed up badly. You were supposed to control the relationship with that Svenson pipsqueak, and you were supposed to keep my name out of all of the dealings. Instead, I've had to entertain unwanted federal agents, and I've lost that prized antiquity to strangers who bought it out from under me long after you started negotiating. How could you let Svenson get away with that?"

"Karl, I would never have revealed your identity. The problem was that those federal agents already knew your name. They must have had some kind of intelligence unit watching you. I did underestimate Roger Svenson. I took him to be a timid dormouse who wouldn't dare to turn elsewhere no matter how long the process took. He has no class and no initiative."

"You forgot that he also has no ethics. He's street scum and just as willing to stab a partner in the back as not. You're lucky that I'm not a violent person, but I can't let you get away with this failure."

Alicia felt her knees starting to shake. She leaned against the wall for support. "What are you going to do to me? I thought we had a future together."

"I can tell from the scent in this place that you had hopes of seducing me, but that will never happen. I've started to pass the word that you're unreliable as an agent and that you're a poor negotiator. You dropped the ball by sitting back and letting the negotiations lapse for too long. No wonder that worm wriggled off the hook; you failed to take up slack and keep him engaged in the process."

"That's unfair. There was nothing to negotiate while you were having the professor evaluate the object."

"If things had gone properly on this deal, you would have made a lot of money. Contemplate that during your retirement."

"I'm not planning to retire."

"Then you'd better find another career. I have enough connections in the art markets that no one will hire you again as an art agent. If some independent artist has the bad judgment to hire you to represent him, his art won't sell. As I said before, enjoy your retirement...Goodbye!" With that, Karl turned and went out the door. He heard her screaming at him all the way down the hall. As he walked back to his car, he mused: *She's just lucky my mother told me I should never hit a woman. I won't have that constraint with Roger Svenson.*

CHAPTER 68 – SITE SEARCH

Arthur sat sharing coffee and brainstorming with his best friend at church, Wally Sanborn, a retired Army logistics specialist and the coordinator of youth missions at the church. They had covered a variety of theoretical and insignificant topics when Penny and Joe Gonzalez appeared in the doorway of Arthur's office.

Arthur said, "Come on in, you two. We're just entertaining each other by solving the world's problems and indulging in creative thinking."

Penny said, "I hope you don't mind our unannounced visit, but we should compare notes on our current project. Will a quick discussion interfere with your church obligations?"

"Not at all, Penny, and please let Wally sit in with us. His clear thinking and military background have helped us in the past."

"It's fine with me if Wally's interested."

Wally stood and brought over additional chairs for Penny and Joe from the conference table. He arranged them in a semicircle around Arthur's desk.

He said, "I'm very interested. I like to think I contribute at least a small amount to Arthur's investigations."

Joe said, "Before we get started, I'll get one more chair. As we passed through the downstairs door, I saw Irma coming into the driveway."

Joe returned with the fifth chair just as Irma entered the room.

"Your chair awaits you, Mrs. Blake."

"Thank you, Joe. I appreciate both your anticipating my arrival and your use of the Mrs. Blake moniker. I'm still getting used to the sound of my new name. I'm the bearer of some interesting news, but I'll let Arthur run this show." She punctuated her deferential sentence by strolling over to Arthur and giving him a kiss.

Arthur responded with a one-armed hug. "Double thanks, Irma; with regard to discussions, you've earned the right to start us off. What do we conclude from the autopsy and related matters?"

"Unless future DNA tests contradict our preliminary findings, John Pugh and I agree that the body in the water-filled quarry was that of Charlie King. Angela's tale of a trip to Canada was pure fiction, probably designed to connect her to a murder that no one could prove. I suspect she hoped to be tried and found not guilty, so that she would be protected by the double jeopardy rule when the quarry body eventually surfaced."

Joe said, "Then there is no doubt that Angela intentionally murdered him."

"None at all; she lied about the location, but she accurately described the way she stabbed him. Her story contained some truth but mostly fantasy. She appears to have enjoyed rationalizing the bad things she did. She probably did the same thing earlier when those children died while in her care in California."

Arthur said, "I assume we've eliminated the possibility that Oliver Parkworth and Charlie King were two identities for a single person."

"John Pugh and I compared their pictures, and although there are facial similarities, they were definitely different people. Oliver is still among the missing."

Penny said, "I have a feeling that he still has a part to play in this drama, but he's not on our immediate agenda."

Arthur said, "Thanks for the cue, Penny. I'd say that the next item for us to discuss is Karl Simitski's art collection and its location. He was very evasive when Irma asked about visiting it. Penny, when you visited his home, did he give any hints?"

"He showed his pride when he talked about how he had converted an old mine into a modern art museum, but he didn't hint at its location. Do you remember anything about location, Joe?"

"I agree that he avoided that topic, but I've been trying to work it out. I contacted the Missouri Department of Natural Resources. They have a program that aims at finding the locations of abandoned underground mines and mapping them. They've had a bunch of cases where contractors accidently dug their way into a mine, with results of collapsing houses, other structures, and roads. They've also accidentally drained lakes and ponds into some of these mines."

Irma asked, "How well have they done with the project, Joe?"

"They have maps of more than a thousand abandoned mines, but there are many more, especially small family operations, that they haven't located. The one thing they could tell me is that most of the mines are in the northwestern third of the state, because that's where the coal deposits are. They also have locations for other types of mines."

Wally said, "You could pin down the location more closely from his cell phone usage. Even if he doesn't go to the mine frequently, he probably has a caretaker he calls."

Penny said, "Good thinking, Wally; Karl said he had a consultant who takes care of the facility. They must talk by phone, so all we have to do is map Karl's call history and look for geographical concentrations."

Arthur stood and added some hot coffee to the cold liquid in his cup. "You may not even have to do that. Cell phones wouldn't be able to receive calls in an underground mine. Karl would have installed wired telephone service there. Try checking his telephone bills and those of any company he owns."

Penny said, "Those are two good ideas. We'll search for both land line registrations and frequency of his calls through different cell towers."

CHAPTER 69 – INTERROGATION

Arthur glanced at the caller I.D. window on his phone and picked it up. "Hi, Bobby; How are things at the Police Department?"

"Arthur, I just have to share this with someone, and you're elected."

"It's either something amusing or something strange. Which is it?"

"Probably a little of both...We brought Joyce Jennings in for an interview regarding the death of Angela King. She arrived at the Parkville Police Station accompanied by her attorney, Linda Caldwell. Linda said that Joyce would plead not guilty if we filed charges against her. She stated that Joyce had not even been negligent, because she had no reason to have suspected an electrical fault in the office lamp. I had Assistant State's Attorney Glenn Morgan helping me with the interview. When we got together in the interrogation room, all Hell broke loose. I have it on tape, but I don't think I'll ever dare play it for anyone."

"Why, what happened?"

"It turns out that Linda Caldwell and Glenn Morgan had been married. They broke up three days before their first anniversary due to each of them having had an affair with at least one married colleague at work. I checked around after our session here, and I learned that it was a spectacularly messy divorce."

"What happened during the interview? Did they attack each other?"

"Linda walked in looking for a plea deal. She said that Joyce might plead guilty to a misdemeanor charge of criminal negligence because she had no reason to suspect the existence of hazardous electrical wiring in the desk lamp on Angela's desk. Linda knew she would have a hard time negotiating anything with her ex-husband, but she played it straight and tried for it."

"How did Glenn respond?"

"He positively sneered at her. He said, 'Linda, I figuratively let you get away with murder while we were married, but there's no way I'll let you literally get away with it now. We have evidence that Joyce committed premeditated and deliberate homicide, and that's what she'll have to face in court.'"

"How did Linda react?"

"I'm glad she didn't have a weapon, or she might have used it. She said, 'Glenn, you supercilious S.O.B., I trust my client, and you're not going to get away with railroading her for a more serious crime, just to get back at me. If there were any justice in this world, you would have ended up married to that horse-faced broad you preferred to me.' Then he responded by accusing her of having been paid by several people for her sexual favors."

"Did they actually come to blows?"

"No, I kept them separated. Linda ended up pulling Joyce out of her seat and saying that they had made a mistake hoping to simplify courtroom procedures and that they were leaving. As they prepared to go, Glenn's final shot was, 'Ask your client about all the incriminating evidence she had in her house. You never believe the people you should trust, but you accept the words of losers at face value. Good luck to you in court; you'll need it!'"

"Would Glenn be the one facing Linda in court?"

"He was salivating over that prospect. He wants to convict Joyce and make Linda look like a fool at the same time. He even used the old saying, two birds with one stone."

CHAPTER 70 – PREACHERITIS

It would likely be the last fall day with a summerlike temperature. They had completed their usual daily hike around Mallard Lake and were about to cross Jeffers Street and walk over to the church, when Arthur stopped Irma and kissed her.

"Very nice, Arthur, but were you sending me a message with that kiss?"

"I was, but it wasn't a very romantic one. I'm getting frustrated by all of the routine things I have to do around the church, and kissing you makes me feel more energized."

"Not exactly romantic, but not too bad...If you're telling me that I'm a cure for what ails you, I'll accept that as a compliment. Since you're now energized, let's hike another lap around the lake."

"I'm up for it. While we're walking, I'd like you to help me work out my thinking about our two cases."

They started around the lakeshore path again, this time at a somewhat increased pace. Arthur could feel his leg muscles having to work harder. Irma didn't show any signs of fatigue or laboring."

"If you want to discuss things with me, you'll have to keep up with my pace...You said that we're looking at two cases, by which I think you mean that the murders of Charlie and later Angela King are one, and the saga of the cuneiform cylinder is the other. I'm not sure you have the correct number. I could argue that we're investigating four cases, and I could equally well argue that the correct number is one." Irma's muscles were tiring, but she picked up the pace even more.

"I may not make it all the way around the lake if you keep increasing our speed."

"That's fine with me, Preacher; I spotted a flat area surrounded by evergreen bushes about two thirds of the way around. You only have to get that far, and then we can try some in-place exercises, assuming you're not inhibited by that thought."

"That concept has me more energized. See whether you can keep up with me now."

They both increased their walking speed and broke into a jog as they neared the ring of bushes. Giving furtive glances in both directions along the path and seeing no one they slipped through a narrow gap in the greenery and spread their jackets to pad the ground. They were soon shedding garments and writhing their way through a delightful array of energetic pursuits. Their sweat mingled deliciously in the unseasonable warmth and sunshine. After what seemed a very long time to both of them, they relaxed in a prolonged embrace.

Irma said, "As your personal doctor, this was my prescription for your advanced case of preacheritis."

"And just what is preacheritis?"

"It's what happens to clergy when they take themselves and their religious responsibilities too seriously. You don't feel serious and pompous now, do you?"

"I feel seriously in love with you. Whenever the weather and solitude permit, we're going to have to do this again. I christen this place *Arthur and Irma's Cloud Nine*."

"And I pronounce you cured of preacheritis. If you should have a relapse, we'll have to administer this treatment again."

"I never thought a trip to see the doctor could be so much fun."

They relaxed and enjoyed their natural seclusion until the chill of the ground started to bother them. Then they dressed and slipped out through the same gap in the bushes that had been their entryway. Holding hands, they walked more slowly for the remainder of their transit of the lake path, each trying to burn the details of their tryst into memory.

Halfway back to the road, Arthur said, "You think we could call our investigation either one or four cases if we were to analyze it. I'll raise you one more. I think we could consider it either one or five."

CHAPTER 71 - LOCATION

Penny looked across the dining room table at Joe as they worked their back-to-back laptop computers. "My satellite searches are saying that almost all of the active coal mines aren't in Missouri at all. Most are in Illinois, with some in Indiana."

"That's interesting, but we're supposed to be looking at abandoned underground mines. There should be a lot of those in Missouri."

"There are, Joe. The state has a list of maps available for about 1200 abandoned mines. Most of those are coal mines, but others produced other minerals such as lead, zinc, and barium. There are even clay and limestone mines on the list."

Joe stopped what he had been doing. "How do you propose we narrow the list down to the most probable mines?"

"Finger Lakes State Park near Karl's home is listed as being in Hallsville, Missouri. If we run an east to west line through Hallsville for a reasonable travel distance from Karl's home, we pass through Audrain County on the East, Boone County which includes Hallsville in the middle, and Howard County to the west."

"You're assuming that Karl would want to have relatively easy access to his collection. I think that's a fair theory."

"It's more than a theory, Joe. You may not have caught it, but when we talked with Karl Simitski at his house, he said that access to his converted mine was one of his reasons for settling there."

"I did miss that one. That's a good reason for the two of us going out together on these field trips."

"Anyway, by cross-referencing the Missouri Department of Natural Resources mine list with the three counties that would give Karl reasonable proximity to his collection, I came up with a list of six mines that might be our potential target. That's a lot better than twelve hundred."

"Are they all abandoned?"

"They're probably at least inactive. I also found that there are only two active coal mines in Missouri today, and these are at the southeastern edge of the state's coal field. However, two of the mines I'm looking at are not coal mines, so they could still be in business. One is a clay mine, and one is a limestone mine."

Joe jumped up and came around to Penny's side of the table. "That is an interesting finding. Karl did say coal mine, but he may have been tinkering with the truth to suit his purposes. An abandoned coal mine would be harder to find because there are so many of them. Looking at things a different way, a limestone mine is easy to convert for housing an art collection; it's not dirty like a coal mine."

"There's a big limestone mine in Pennsylvania that's used for storing government and industry documents."

Penny's fingered her keyboard with a staccato rhythm. I Googled the limestone mine name, and found the company last listed in an 1897 mining directory. I think it would be safe to consider that mine abandoned."

"Thanks, Penny; now I'll see whether I can find any utilities serving that location. If he had a limestone mine available, I can't see Karl having converted a coal mine and spending so much more money to clean it. I have a very strong hunch that you've found his lair."

CHAPTER 72 – COMPLICATIONS

Arthur had asked Bobby Andrews to arrange a lunch meeting for the two of them with Glenn Morgan, the Assistant State's Attorney, at House of Ming. At the last minute, he had decided that it would be a good idea to ask Irma to join them also. They all arrived at about the same time and exchanged introductions in the parking lot. Once inside, Arthur asked Tony to give them their usual back corner table and to bring them drinks, but delay the food ordering to allow for discussion time.

After the drinks had arrived, Arthur took the lead in starting the discussion. "Thank you for joining me here on such short notice. I wanted to meet informally rather than officially, so that there wouldn't be a record of this gathering. The fact is that there are aspects of this murder investigation and trial that could have some disturbing implications."

Bobby said, "It looks like a good clean case to me, Arthur. We have evidence both from the crime scene and from the search of Joyce Jennings' house."

"The evidence from her house is what led me to think there's more than a simple revenge-motivated murder here."

Glenn Morgan had been wondering why Arthur was even involved in this police business. Now he straightened up in his seat and focused on Arthur. "You don't think her motive was revenge? Bobby told me about Angela King having been in charge of that preschool where Joyce's young daughter died."

"I think that if Joyce had wanted revenge for the killing of her daughter, she would have taken it by going after Angela, or as she called herself then, Marcia Melrose, during the years immediately following the child's death.

At that time, they were both still in the Los Angeles area. That's when she was young and passionate about things. When Angela, or Marcia, was beginning to study for the ministry and having minor initial appointments, Joyce would have had many opportunities to attack her. I think that after the initial shock dissipated, Joyce returned to taking life as it came rather than rigorously planning anything. That's how she came to have her daughter in the first place. The little girl had resulted from a chance liaison with a sailor."

Irma said, "I think you're underestimating the significance of losing a child to a mother, even one lacking goals in life."

"I may be overstating my case, but I just can't see the fire in her that would have kept her doggedly on Angela's trail for all of these years. She's not that dedicated a person."

Glenn said, "Let's say that you're right about Joyce's character and history. If that's so, why would she have come here and worked in the same office with Angela?"

Bobby said, "I interviewed Joyce a while back, and she admitted to coming to this area and getting a job with the church in order to keep tabs on Angela. She said that she wanted to get a better feeling for the kind of person Angela was, but insisted that she didn't kill her. She also said that she hadn't touched the furniture in the office where the electrocution occurred. She said they moved in and left everything the way it was."

Arthur said, "You've probably noticed the importance of everyone's past in the story of what happened at that murder scene. We all have personal histories that we may choose to hide or at least not mention without prodding. For instance, most of you know that I was an engineer for NASA before I started my seminary training. Other people in the ministry also had prior occupations, or occupations they pursue for extra money."

Irma stared at her husband. "I know you don't mention things like that without a reason. Whose background have you been studying?"

"Let's just say that I was a little surprised to discover that Bishop Howard Chandler once worked as a tax accountant. He even prepared income taxes for most of the other students in his seminary."

Bobby said, "The landlord said the tenant who moved out just prior to the murder was a tax accountant. That does raise questions, Arthur."

"And who arranged for the office rental and assigned Angela and Joyce to go there?"

Glenn said, "Are you saying that we can make a strong case against the Bishop as the murderer?"

"I'm at least saying that the case against Joyce is not as clear as we thought, and I suspect that a jury might be persuaded that either one of them might have committed the murder, making a conviction difficult."

Irma said, "They can't get off that easily. The strongest case would be to present facts showing that they were both in it together. When we searched Joyce's house, we found the test setup for the electrocution in the spare bedroom, and Arthur pointed out how that bedroom was furnished in a masculine style while the rest of the house had feminine touches everywhere."

Glenn nodded his head. "I see where you're going. We need to see whether we can prove that Bishop Chandler visited Joyce and stayed in that bedroom. It might be hard to convince a jury that a Bishop would commit a murder, but it would be a lot easier if we could also show that he had been cheating on his wife with an administrative assistant."

Bobby said, "You folks are changing the focus quite quickly. May I remind you that we would need to show a motive for the Bishop to have been involved? What about that, Arthur?"

"That's the easy part. Howard Chandler was about to retire after a highly praised career. His protégé, Angela King, had told him that she was about to confess to murdering her husband. If she did that, her actions would tarnish his reputation. The only way to avoid that blemish on his career would be for Angela King to avoid trial. Glenn, do they usually try people after they die?"

"We generally can't do that because the people on trial wouldn't be able to defend themselves, and it would be a waste of taxpayer money since we couldn't punish a deceased defendant. I agree with you that Bishop Chandler had a motive."

Arthur said, "You can see why I wanted to discuss these issues privately. Unless you conclude that a case against Bishop Chandler would be strong enough for a trial, either individually or with Joyce, the things we discussed today should never become public. If you agree to that, let's order our food."

CHAPTER 73 – RECONNAISSANCE

Joe Gonzalez and Steve DuBois took on the assignment of checking out the abandoned limestone mine that Penny had pinpointed during her mine records search. They would drive together from Joe's house in Parkville, Illinois to the rural area of Missouri where the mine was located. As they prepared to leave and approached the black SUV they would be driving, they heard Penny calling to them.

"Hold up, guys. I did some more checking, and I think you should check out a second abandoned limestone mine while you're down there. The original one is in or near Jamestown, which is in Boone County, while this second mine is near Moberly in Randolph County. If you get onto Route US63 heading south, you'll go through both of those areas. Moberly being north of Jamestown, you'll reach that one first."

Joe said, "Thanks, Penny; you not only gave us a second target, but an itinerary. Did you pick out motels and restaurants for us too?"

"Enough out of you, Joe...Steve, please make sure my husband stays alert on the road and doesn't get into trouble." She kissed Joe and backed away from the car.

Steve said, "I'm riding shotgun to protect him and keep him awake while he drives. We'll have answers pretty shortly if things go well."

They drove away and headed generally south, taking the Interstates to Peoria, and then Route US24 southwest, crossing the Mississippi River near Quincy, Illinois and connecting to US63 just north of their first destination, Moberly, Missouri.

As they approached Moberly, Steve looked up from the map he was studying. "Joe, both of the locations we're checking on this trip are very convenient to Karl's home in Hallsville. The mine near Moberly is northwest of his home, and the one near Easley is southwest from Hallsville."

"The only problem with going to visit an abandoned mine is that there won't be any signs, and most people won't even think of it as a mine. Hence the term *abandoned*."

"That's true, but we know that we're talking about mines cut into a hillside rather than a quarry or an open pit mine, so look for high ground. I'd rather not ask too many people and alert Karl to the presence of nosy people in town."

Moberly, itself, turned out to be on higher ground; the map indicated an elevation of about nine hundred feet. Route 24 continued westbound from there, while US63 headed south toward Columbia. Penny's notes had indicated that the closest town to the mine was Randolph, which was west of Moberly, so they drove west on US24, scanning the landscape as they proceeded. It didn't take them long to notice a parallel unpaved road south of US24 that showed signs of truck usage.

Joe pointed out the window. "Steve, notice the color of that unpaved road."

"It's surfaced with crushed limestone. We're in the right neighborhood."

They slowed their pace, examining the landscape on the left side of the highway. They passed several small farms with gray soil and multiple drainage ponds. Then they saw increased numbers of trees along the side of the road and a low but wide tree-covered hill behind them.

Steve said, "That hill might hide the entrance to a mine. We can't see anything from the highway because of the rows of trees masking the service road."

"We can't get to the farm road from the highway. It looks as though it turns away from the highway up ahead, so we'll have to double back to get onto it from its beginning." Joe pulled off onto the right-hand shoulder, and made a U-turn to head back toward Moberly. He came to a crossroad next to a park complex with baseball fields and turned south to pick up the farm road.

Heading west again, they passed several farms and reached the hill they had seen from the highway. Then they followed a driveway around the hill. Behind it, they saw a concrete-framed arch cut into the side of the hill and recessed steel-slab doors blocking a paved driveway going through the arch.

Steve said, "Joe, don't drive too close to the doors. I can see two video cameras, one mounted to monitor anyone coming close to the doors and the other aimed for a general view of the parking area. They've probably already seen our car, but if we drive away quickly, they'll think we're either lost or sightseeing."

"Good idea; I'm on my way out of here. We've already learned that this place is not abandoned. I can see that camera turning to follow our car. The license plate traces to our cover organization, *Trading Trends Newsletter.* That won't mean anything to them."

"Those are heavy duty steel doors, and they're large enough to admit a big semi-trailer. They're also freshly painted. This place is definitely active and on alert for unwelcome visitors."

"I'd ask why they need such large doors, but that entrance may be left over from mining days, and heavy-duty trucks would justify them. My guess is that trucks go down a ramp to a lower level that might even extend beneath the highway. This may well be Karl's stronghold, Steve, but since they've already spotted us, I'll play it straight and head out of here. We should check the other mine before reaching a conclusion anyway."

"Start driving toward Jamestown, Joe. It shouldn't take us long to get there."

When they reached the Jamestown area, Joe and Steve both realized that this would not be a likely location for Karl Siminski's underground sanctuary. Apparently, Jamestown had been an active mining region, but the mining method had been different. Surface mines where heavy machinery had scraped bituminous coal and other minerals marred the landscape at many points along the road. While the countryside was picturesque, they decided that the Moberly mine was a much more likely choice, and reversed their direction back toward the north.

Joe and Steve felt sure that they had found Karl's hiding place, but how would they gain entry to it?

CHAPTER 74 - TACTICS

Back at the Gonzalez home in Parkville, Joe, Penny, and Steve debated their best approach for gaining access to Karl Simitski's underground sanctuary. Penny started the discussion.

"I'd like to play it dumb and just ask to see his collection, but Irma said she already tried that, and Karl claimed that he couldn't allow visitors due to maintenance and refurbishing activities that had required protective encasing of his art."

Steve said, "I looked carefully at the driveway and parking area outside the mine. I saw no traces of mining dust or construction residues. That place was very clean, more in keeping with housing an art collection than undergoing heavy-duty maintenance. I'm sure the story he gave Irma was meant to dissuade her from pressing the issue of a visit."

"What do you think, Joe?"

"Well, Penny, I see two possible approaches, and they both have pros and cons. We could probably get a search warrant from a federal court based on our instructions to try to locate art and artifacts looted from the Iraqi National Museum. Simitski's quest to purchase the cuneiform cylinder shows that he is interested in acquiring pieces similar to those the looters stole. That might be enough to convince a judge. The problem with that tactic is that it turns us into Karl's adversaries, and he's not likely to cooperate with us. We would also look stupid if it turned out that we have the wrong mine. We're not absolutely sure, after all."

"What's the other approach?"

"We could remain behind the scenes and get someone from the Missouri Division of Fire Safety to inspect the mine for required sprinklers and other fire prevention devices and cleanliness. That individual could be wearing a miniature video camcorder that would record information on the mine's layout and contents without alerting Karl to our interest."

Steve said, "We would still have to get some form of a warrant if we ever wanted to use the acquired information in court."

"You're right, Steve. I don't know whether a judge would be happy about our using the covert videos to justify a search warrant."

Penny said, "If the inspector took videos for documentation of his normal duties, a judge might accept them. In any case, we'd have problems forcing our way through those steel doors to initiate a search."

"The fire safety laws require a second exit, and if we took the official inspection approach, we could specify that the inspector should check and record the location and accessibility of that exit."

"That's a good argument for the inspection approach, Joe."

"We might need to be persuasive to convince the Fire Safety people to work with us, Penny. I think we would increase the likelihood of their cooperation if we communicated our belief that the mine extends underneath the highway. That might even encourage them to include a structural engineer in the party."

"Do you have anyone in mind?"

"No, but Wally Sanborn could get us connected to someone in the U.S. Army Corps of Engineers. That person could play the role of a consultant to state officials while having a federal point of view as to what's going on down there."

Penny said, "I like that approach. How do you feel about it, Steve?"

"I like anything that gets us the information without involving anyone Karl has met. I sense that we should remain unseen as long as possible. We don't want to spook Karl into leaving the country, if he is guilty of something major."

"You're thinking beyond the possibility of looted art treasures."

"Yes, I am, Penny. That's an awfully expensive underground facility to justify based on housing artifacts that would be almost impossible to sell."

CHAPTER 75 – LANDLORD

Detective Hank Robbins had telephoned the owner of the office building where Angela King had died and asked for an appointment to stop in for an interview. The property owner, Stanley Finch, replied that his main job was selling cars at the Ford dealership, and he wouldn't want to meet there. He requested that they meet at the Parkville Police Station at four o'clock that afternoon after he finished work. Hank had set them up in the conference room so that Mr. Finch would feel more comfortable than if they met in the suspect interview room.

Stanley Finch turned out to be surprisingly young for a property owner, a tall man in his late thirties, prematurely starting to go bald, and with an athletic build. He arrived on schedule at four o'clock precisely.

Hank greeted him in the outer lobby and led him to the conference room. "Thanks for being so punctual, Mr. Finch. Many of the people I interview are very casual about their appointments. I hope you don't mind if I tape record our conversation." Hank pushed the record button.

"I've learned from selling cars that potential customers are easily annoyed if you're not there at the appointed time. Besides, I have some cohorts at work who are more than willing to steal my customers if I'm late. What can I tell you, Hank?"

"I'd like to find out a little more about the tax accountant that rented that office prior to the death that occurred there. What do you know about him?"

"Very little...I met him only once, when he first looked at the space. We took care of the paperwork by mail, and we handled the termination of rental by telephone."

"Do you have records of his address and phone number?"

"He used a post office box in DeKalb. I should have that written down somewhere. I'm afraid I didn't keep a record of his phone number."

"We should be able to get that from your telephone company if you give us the approximate dates when he called you."

"He only called once, and it would have been about a week before that woman died there."

"Pardon my saying this, Mr. Finch, but for a person who's so precise about meeting times, you're not much of a record-keeper."

"Please call me Stan. You're right about my not sweating the documentation. It's a matter of priorities. I'm precise about timing because I lose car sales if I'm not. So far, I haven't found a reason to be precise about paperwork filing. Rental tenants come and go. I keep them happy by not requiring a fixed term lease, and they're only required to give me one week's notice when they move out. That's all because my rental income is an extra bonus. I make my living selling cars."

"Fair enough, Stan; if I showed you some photographs, would you be able to pick out your accountant tenant? What was his name?"

"I'm pretty sure I'd remember what he looked like, although he wore a hat when I met him because it rained that day. Car sales people have to recognize shoppers who said they were just looking on a previous visit. His name was Warren Wilson. I use the two W's to remember it. Memory keys are important for keeping track of customers and potential buyers."

Hank Robbins noted that if the accountant had been the Bishop, he had avoided using his own name. He placed five black and white photographs on the table in front of Stan Finch.

"Look at these pictures carefully, and tell me whether you see him here. Take your time before saying anything."

Stan picked up the photographs one at a time going from left to right as spread on the table. He held each in a variety of positions in order to catch as much light as possible. Then he held the edge of his hand over the top of each head in order to give each pictured person the look of wearing a hat. Finally, he pushed three photographs aside and turned the other two to face Hank.

"He was one of these two. I'm sorry I can't pin him down to just one of these, but as I said, I didn't spend much time with him, and he was wearing a hat."

Hank noted that Howard Chandler was one of the two people selected, but the other was his partner, Detective Gene Murphy. He'd need more than Finch's recollection to build a case against Chandler.

"Stan, did you ask for Warren Wilson's driver's license or other photo identification when you signed the papers for the office rental?"

"I'm afraid not, Hank; as I said, I don't use an official lease, and they're free to leave on one week's notice. For security, I have them pay for two weeks into the future. That gives me rent for the notice week plus the cushion of an additional week's rent to offset any damages to the property. Those arrangements don't require anything too rigorous."

"Very well then, Stan; I think you've answered all my questions for now. I may want to ask you a few more as the case proceeds."

They both rose and shook hands.

"Hank, before I leave let me give you my business card. I could give you an outstanding deal on a new or used car. We just got in a new batch of Ford Escapes that would be perfect for you."

"I've enjoyed talking with you Stan, but let me give you a piece of advice. Never try to sell an Escape to a cop."

CHAPTER 76 – KARL SIMITSKI

Karl knew that he had mishandled the negotiations for that Idaho soldier's cuneiform cylinder. He wasn't at all sure how it had happened, but somehow federal agents had ended up following his every move. He realized that those Israelis, swooping in to buy the cylinder during the stalled negotiations, might have done him a favor. That sale had distracted the feds; but he suspected they would soon return, looking for his underground art storage sanctuary. He had made another mistake when he had mentioned the existence of that facility to them. He would have to move quickly to cover his tracks.

His little converted limestone mine had been more than adequate for his needs, but it had been tiny compared to the underground industrial complex created in a huge limestone mine by Hunt Midwest SubTropolis in Kansas City. He had wanted his own private mine for purposes of secrecy, but with that goal about to be meaningless, he would change to plan B and get lost in the underground megaworld.

Karl sat at his computer and sent out two messages. The first alerted his crew in the mine to start packaging all of the items located there for shipment and to do a thorough cleanup of the facility. The second message went to the Hunt Midwest people ordering a block of space for his existing dummy firm, Transforminium, Inc. This order included relocation of warehoused equipment and supplies from his underground location in Moberly, Missouri, and conveyance to that location of the contents of a unit he had previously rented within the SubTropolis facility. After completing these orders, Karl sat back and relaxed. With sufficient expediting, the feds would get nothing but a surprise at the Moberly mine.

Now there remained but one task to complete. He had to kill Karl Simitski.

CHAPTER 77 – TIGHTROPE WALKING

Arthur needed an excuse to visit Bishop Chandler. He had misgivings about what he planned to do, but he felt it was necessary. Howard Chandler had been his friend, protecting him from the slurs and sniping attacks of Angela King, but if Howard had been involved in killing his nemesis, Arthur would have to help convict him. Bobby Andrews had dispatched the electrocution test components discovered during the search of Joyce Jennings' house to the laboratory with instructions to search for fingerprints and other possible residues that might reveal DNA. He had previously done the same with items from the office where Angela King had died. The lab had retrieved partial unidentified fingerprints from that batch of objects. Bobby had also engaged a handwriting expert to compare the tax accountant's signature and notes on his office rental agreement with samples of Bishop Chandler's handwriting from the Parkville UMC files. Arthur would have the added task of finding a way to get Howard Chandler's fingerprints and possibly DNA samples for comparison without alerting him that he was under investigation.

Arthur placed a call to his father, Peter Blake, an antiques expert and dealer in Richmond, Illinois. He gave him a request and then said, "Do you think you could find one for me, Dad?"

"I'm pretty sure I can, and I'll look for other related items also. It may cost you more than a few dollars."

"That's fine. I have a special need for it."

"Very good son; I'll get right on it, but you do realize that both you and Irma will have to visit us to personally claim the results of my search."

"That sounds like a great idea. I'll be waiting for your call or email."

The following weekend, Arthur arranged for Wally Sanborn to preach a lay sermon while he would be out of town. Irma enjoyed the prospect of spending a couple of days with her in-laws. She still remembered their first visit to the little town of Richmond when Arthur had chastised his mother for prematurely saying that Arthur and Irma should get married. Janice Blake was such an uninhibited person that Irma always felt completely relaxed in her presence.

They arrived just in time for Arthur to join Peter in the basement for a beer and an examination of the results of Peter's quest. Irma took their suitcase up to Arthur's old bedroom and then returned to the kitchen to help Janice prepare the dinner and set the table. They chatted as they worked.

"Irma, I know I'm always a busybody, but I'm concerned, and you're part of the family now..."

"What is it, Janice, or should I be calling you Mother?"

"To tell you the truth, I think I'd prefer Janice, because I think we're going to turn out to be cohorts and plotters. Calling me Janice would put us on an equal footing. I don't want you to feel like the junior partner by having you call me Mother."

"Fair enough; Janice it shall be. What concerns you?"

"Is Arthur being his old unemotional self with you? I hope he realizes what a wonderful person you are and treats you accordingly."

"Janice, you really are special! You sensed exactly what had been troubling me. I put that in the past tense because my friend Renee lectured me on how we're all different, and that I can't make him over to suit my wishes."

"How is Renee doing with her little girl? I hope there aren't any more health issues."

"They're getting along very well, and Thelma Lou is starting to grow at a steady pace. I'm sure she'll catch up with children who didn't have her early problems. Tell me, Janice, does Peter tell you everything he is doing?"

"I'll give him a C-plus mark for transparency. We had an animated discussion about that topic during that period when we were trying to help Mandy after Albert's car wreck. He claimed that he wanted to shield me from potentially upsetting matters. He's been better at keeping me informed since I straightened him out that time. Has Arthur been secretive with you?"

"It's not exactly that, but he sometimes withholds information until I become part of his current scheme. It's probably because he wants to try things without seeking my approval first. We're married now, but we're still two separate people."

Janice stepped back and admired her dinner table. "And that's the way it should be...Go fetch those two separate individuals from the basement, dear; it's time for us to nourish and encourage them."

The next morning, shortly after a traditional country breakfast, Arthur and Irma departed following a flurry of parental hugs and kisses. They both felt that this trip had been worthwhile although for different reasons. Irma knew that she belonged to a complete family for the first time in many years, and Arthur had acquired what he needed for the next phase of his investigation. They both enjoyed the return trip to Parkville, now established as a cherished family routine.

After they arrived home, Arthur told Irma that he would like to ask Bishop Chandler to come visit them for tea. She agreed, but hoped that her husband would soon choose to reveal his motive for the planned event. She knew he had a purpose beyond social interaction.

CHAPTER 78 – INSPECTION

Steve DuBois and Joe Gonzalez focused their attention on Louis Krill's oral report at the Missouri Division of Fire Safety. Lou had inspected the converted limestone mine in Moberly, along with Malcolm Harris from the Army Corps of Engineers. Malcolm had since headed back to his office in Kansas City, leaving Lou to summarize their findings and show the video images that they had gathered. Lou connected the miniature digital camcorder to the flatscreen monitor on the wall. "Joe, I really enjoyed using this device you loaned me. I triggered it from the remote control in my pocket and just walked around normally, knowing that I'd have pictures of everything I faced. I felt completely in control. I'll be applying for one of these babies in our next budget."

"We've found them to be very useful whenever we had to keep people from realizing that they were on Candid Camera. Was the facility structurally sound and clean? Give us a brief summary of your findings before we look at the pictures."

"Good approach; to start with, you were correct in your suggestion that the facility is much larger than one might think. The driveway ramps downward and then doubles back before reaching the shipping and receiving area. I would guess that the main floor is fifty feet below ground level. You were also correct in guessing that part of their facility extends under the highway. Malcolm gave special attention to that aspect of their setup and monitored vibrations in the walls and ceilings from traffic passing on the road above. He indicated that the vibrations were too low to cause structural problems. He saw no danger of the highway collapsing due to dynamic traffic loads, but he raised the question of whether they have the legal right to be under the road, and he'll pass that matter on to the highway department. It may depend on whether the original mine or the highway was there first."

Steve said, "The mine dates back to the nineteenth century, so they probably have no problem on that score. When we first checked out the entrance to this mine, we saw no indications of tracks from recent truck traffic. Was it still that way when you inspected it?"

"That's an interesting observation, Steve. When we arrived, we noticed lots of tire tracks and mud in the area of the entrance and on the ramps going down to the dock. I'd conclude that they had significant truck traffic going in and out since your first visit. It was dry until last week. The muddy tire tracks suggest that this was very recent traffic.

"Continuing with my summary, their fire prevention equipment is in good shape. They have sprinklers and the appropriate number of extinguishers placed properly. The second emergency exit is a wall-mounted ladder leading to a steel hatch at ground level. That's minimal and possibly dangerous; I could envision several situations where they might have trouble opening that hatch. Their ventilation system is marginal, but acceptable. I told the supervisor that I'd like to see it improved. At least they didn't have vehicles generating exhaust gases, except for trucks at the loading dock. Their fleet of four lift trucks are all battery powered."

Joe said, "What do they store down there that they need four lift trucks?"

Lou hesitated for a short while before responding. "I apologize for my lack of awareness. I should have caught that. When we did the inspection, we saw only minor art displays and other art pieces stored on shelves. There was very little there that would have required even a single lift truck; yet they had them all on charge for quick availability. Those truck tracks on the ramps probably indicate that they removed the heavy stuff prior to our inspection."

"How many employees did you see there?"

"As far as I could tell, Steve, they had only the supervisor and two assistants. I guess that's another reason to question the four lift trucks. Who would be driving them?"

Joe said, "Well, your summary convinces me that Karl Simitski lied when he told Irma Blake that large quantities of art were sealed up in plastic and that the facility was being refurbished and reconstructed. You said it was clean and contained only a small amount of art."

"That's correct, Joe. I was surprised to find so much empty space. It's obvious that they moved a lot of something out of there. Let me show you the video I took."

They all turned to face the monitor. The video showed the muddy truck tracks on the driveway down to the loading dock. Then they saw and heard a young man greeting Lou and Malcolm and the doors to the main area opening. Once inside, the camera recorded an area with clean tiled floors and partitions separating several small art displays. Beyond those exhibits, the white floor seemed to go on forever.

Steve said, "I'm no art expert, but I do go to museums in Washington, and I'd guess that the quality of the art we've see thus far does not justify a secure underground space. They must have removed the valuable art and left this token collection for window dressing. Karl expected someone to locate and check out his sanctuary, so he prepared this dummy collection in advance."

The others agreed. They continued to monitor the video, watching Malcolm walking as far as he could toward one end of the floor and then holding a sensor wand against the walls and ceiling while he looked at a meter.

Lou said, "He's underneath the highway now. As we approached, we noticed a large amount of heavy truck traffic. Despite that, he measured very little vibration. It's a well-constructed facility."

After Malcolm completed his measurements, the video showed them going toward an office area at the other end of the tiled floor, led by the young man who had met them at the loading dock. When the group reached that area, the video showed the door to the office area opening.

Lou said, "That's the supervisor, Mr. Edward Timmons."

Joe said, "No, it's not. That's Oliver Parkworth. Several separate mysteries are meshing together."

CHAPTER 79 – TEA PARTY

Irma motioned for Arthur to return the reclining chair to its upright position; then she sat on his lap. "When are you going to tell me what this tea party is all about? I have strong doubts that you're simply buttering up the Bishop for a raise."

"I'll give you the whole picture, but first I have to tell you that we're having an extra guest. When I called Howard to invite him, he asked whether he could bring his wife, Margaret, and of course I said yes."

"That's fine; I had a very pleasant chat with Margaret at our reception while you were visiting Angela at Parkville Care Center. She's affable and knowledgeable, but a little too dedicated to supporting her husband in everything he does. She's a throwback to the days when women were subordinate to their husbands."

"I see no danger of that here."

"Getting back to my original question, what's your plan, and what are you trying to accomplish?"

"You're right as usual. I am up to some skullduggery, but we have to be very careful about what we do and say."

"Aha! Now you're saying *we*; you'd better come clean if you don't want me to accidently wreck your scheme."

"You win. Here's the situation. There are some clues that point to Howard Chandler as a possible suspect in the murder of Angela King. It's not likely, and I want to protect his reputation and my job; so I set up this party to gather evidence without his realizing it."

"How will *we* do that?"

"Dad performed a treasure hunt for me, and came up with a nineteenth century copy of a teapot that Josiah Wedgwood gave John Wesley in 1761. He even went beyond this objective and found a set of six cups and saucers from a set displayed in the Canadian Historical Exhibition of 1899. At that time, these white and gold teacups had been in the Sanderson family for more than two hundred and fifty years, and Amy Sanderson certified in writing that John Wesley drank tea from them often. All of these items are in that carton I very carefully brought back from the folks' house."

"How much did they cost us?"

"So far, they haven't cost us anything. They are on loan from Dad's antiques shop on condition that we get Bishop Chandler to write a note including his opinion about their authenticity. That will increase their sales value for Dad. However, we do have the option to buy them at a considerably reduced price."

Irma moved from Arthur's lap to the couch. "What kind of trap are you setting with this bait?"

Arthur moved over to the couch and sat next to her. "The most magical words in the world for United Methodist clergy are *John Wesley*. With your help, we are going to have an authentic Wesley tea party, during which we will obtain Howard's fingerprints as he examines the teapot, and we will obtain a sample of his DNA when you preserve whatever remains in his teacup. By taking this party approach, we won't alert him to any form of investigation at all. We are simply having a social event."

"You are a schemer. What time are they coming?"

"They'll be here at four o'clock."

It really did qualify as a social success. Arthur and Irma found Howard and Margaret Chandler to be quite charming and relaxed when they settled into home rather than church surroundings. The Chandlers especially appreciated sharing tea and outlooks for the future with newlyweds.

Margaret said, "We've been married more than forty years, and it's so refreshing to be with a couple who are in the first phase of that marriage marathon. We've seen plenty of ups and downs along the way and had to overcome obstacles, as will you; but those bumps and dips in the road are what make a successful marriage. The key is your overcoming them together."

Howard reached over and patted Margaret on the knee. "I would never have reached my present position without Margaret's support. She has championed my talents all the way. Without her, I would have settled for a lot lower position."

Irma said, "I'm beginning to realize the many mutations that love assumes over the years to sustain a marriage."

"Spoken like a true forensic scientist. I'll say amen to that statement, and thank you, Howard, for agreeing to supply my dad with the testimonial about the teapot and cups."

Howard raised the empty teapot to examine it. "I especially enjoy the inscription on it:
We thank the Lord for this our food
But more because of Jesus blood
Let manna to our Souls be given
The Bread of Life sent down from Heaven
Be present at our Table Lord
Be here and everywhere ador'd
These creatures blefs & grant that we
May feast in Paradise with thee"

Howard passed the teapot to Margaret to inspect. She spent several minutes turning and appreciating it. "I always feel very special when I am holding something that is so old. On this pot, I enjoy the outdated spelling of *bless*. It gives me a feeling of permanence. Items like this will be here long after we're gone. I understand your father's enjoyment of antiques, Arthur. My guess is that it's both a career and a love affair for him."

"It is that, Margaret, and I'll bet that my mother wouldn't even object to your phrasing. The thing that bothers me the most about antiques shops is that many of the things that look so good there, are items most people throw away after a short period of use."

Irma said, "You're right, but where would our economy be if everyone kept things forever rather than replacing them after their normal useful life?"

Arthur stood up. "I'm not going to dispute your statement. The problem is that there's no easy answer to the question of permanence or disposability as a way of life. People, of course, should be as permanent as possible." Arthur watched his guests for any sign of a reaction to his statement, but he saw none.

The Chandlers both stood in response to Arthur's standing. Howard indicated that they felt honored to sip tea from cups John Wesley had shared, but that it was time for them to return home. They had a long ride ahead of them. Howard and Margaret thanked Irma and Arthur, collected their outerwear, and departed.

After their guests had left, Arthur and Irma carefully packaged up the teapot and the cups for lab analysis, labeling each cup container to show its user. Then Irma sealed each parcel in an official evidence container and turned to Arthur.

"I hope this won't offend your pastoral sensitivities, but I'd rather let your father sell these cups and the teapot. I wouldn't feel comfortable dining with John Wesley on a regular basis."

Arthur said, "I'm glad you feel that way. John Wesley intimidates me at church through the *Book of Discipline*. I don't need to have him do the same to us at home."

CHAPTER 80 – CONFRONTATION

Lou Krill had arranged for a second visit to the converted limestone mine. He stated that he needed to discuss two minor fire prevention problems revealed from his first visit data. His companion on this second visit was Steve DuBois, dressed in Corps of Engineers coveralls. Per Joe's suggestion, during his first visit, Lou had studied the control location and operating procedures for opening the ground level access doors.

Upon arrival, Lou positioned his pickup truck for video identification and waited for the steel doors to swing open. Then he drove the truck down the ramp to the shipping and receiving dock. The same young man greeted them. Steve shook his hand, as they all entered the main area through the loading dock door. The young guide continued to walk forward, but Lou lingered behind and reopened the loading dock door as it neared the bottom of its closure travel.

Their guide turned and started to object to Lou's action. Then he noticed three armed uniformed men climbing out from under the tarp that covered the back of the pickup truck.

The young man started to run toward the office area. The first armed intruder ordered him to stop. As that man stepped forward, the overhead lights revealed the face of Joe Gonzalez. His two armed companions joined the group. Lou walked over to the control panel and pushed the button to open the outer steel doors at the top of the ramp. As the doors opened, they heard distant car and truck engines. Soon, three more vehicles parked in front of the loading dock. Fifteen additional armed people in uniforms filed in; most took positions around the perimeter of the main area. Two of them handcuffed the young guide and took him out to one of the vehicles.

Joe, Steve and two associates walked toward the office area after cautioning Lou to remain behind in case they met with resistance.

They opened the outer office door and found a woman working at a computer. Joe gestured with his rifle for her to back away from the keyboard. A female associate led her out to the open area. Then Joe and Steve opened the inner office door. Oliver Parkworth rose quickly from his chair and started to reach into a drawer.

"Don't reach for a gun unless you want to be shot, Oliver. We're federal agents, and we want to talk with you peacefully." Joe showed his credentials.

"I thought you guys were terrorists. We've received threats. My name's not Oliver; it's Edward Timmons."

"Well my name's Joe Gonzalez, and it has been ever since my birth. I'm beginning to understand what you people have been doing. When we looked at the background of Oliver Parkworth, we could only find a short period of history. It looked as though you had appeared out of thin air. The same thing happened when we looked at Charlie King's background. Now you say you're Edward Timmons. You manufacture new identities for people. You look a lot like the photos I've seen of Charlie King, and on at least one occasion, you were mistaken for him. Are you or were you related in some incarnation?"

"May I sit down? I won't do anything stupid."

"Sure, right after Steve, here, checks your desk drawers."

Steve moved between Oliver and the desk and checked its contents. He removed a pistol from the left top drawer and a camera from the right bottom drawer. Then he nodded to Joe and stepped aside so that Oliver could sit down.

"My birth name was Gerald Taylor. Charlie's was Daniel Taylor. We're brothers, hence the resemblance. Throughout our teens and early twenties, we were inseparable, even though we fought a lot when we were young children. During our close period, we each picked up the others habits and tastes."

Steve asked, "Why did you need new identities?"

"We grew up in a poor area of Baltimore, and we knew we could never afford to go to college. Since you know us as Charlie and Oliver, I'll use those names. At times, it even confuses me. Anyway, we knew that we could outthink most people our age, and we used library and other research sources to learn a lot of information that was college level and beyond. We sharpened our computer skills and decided to bypass the cost of college by generating new names and credentials to match our skills. Charlie and I took engineering and teaching jobs, and we kept testing each other to assure that our skill levels exceeded those of our degreed colleagues. We didn't cheat anyone except the system."

"What about taxes and social security numbers?"

"We have official numbers for each identity and pay all of the taxes. I won't go into our techniques for becoming official, but many people establish multiple identities in some respect. The old comedian, W. C. Fields, would travel from city to city performing in vaudeville, and each time he stopped, he'd open a bank account under a made-up name and deposit a few dollars into it. He never cashed in those accounts, and they're all out there in the official records, probably on the various states' dormant accounts lists. Paper trails are not hard to generate."

Joe asked, "Are you saying that you created a replacement identity process and then only used it for your brother and yourself?"

"That was our original intent, but then we ran into some other young people who had the qualifications for degrees, so we helped them out. Later, we met people who had done stupid things to damage their reputations and make them unemployable, so we assisted them too. One thing led to another, Joe.

"Charlie stopped checking in with me during his last trip back to see his wife, so I guessed that something had happened to him. I knew it was time for me to disappear when that woman in Denver mistook me for him. With Charlie missing, I sensed danger. That's why I staged the car accident. I figured that I should check on Charlie's welfare. I telephoned his wife Angela, and she told me she hadn't seen Charlie in years. When she said that, I realized I'd probably never see Charlie again. If she had told the truth, my brother never made it to Parkville; if she had lied to me, Angela had probably done something to him."

Joe said, "Did Angela know you or know that Charlie had a brother?"

"No, our deal on the new identities was that no one except us should know about our relationship."

"Why did you conclude that Angela might have done something to Charlie?"

"Charlie considered her dangerous. He once told me that she had gotten away with killing two little kids when she was younger. I didn't know the details, but he told me that she had confessed that crime as part of a threat before he left her the first time."

"Your suspicions were correct. Charlie did die by Angela's hand, but she has since died also. We're sorry to have to tell you about his death."

"She really was as dangerous as he said. I'll miss him. Charlie was the only person in the world I could trust totally."

"Did Karl Simitski bankroll this underground sanctuary? How did you get involved with him?"

"That was both an opportunity and a path to disaster. After a few years of doing our improved identity business on a small scale while we maintained our own mainline jobs, Charlie and I met Karl, who had a different name at the time. He was a refugee from Iraq who had been a member of Saddam Hussein's staff. He left Iraq during the early stages of the American invasion, taking with him a large chunk of one of Saddam's secret bank accounts. He didn't look Arabic thanks to his English mother, so he sought us out to help him become an eccentric American art collector. He figured that buying and collecting art would serve as the perfect process for laundering his stolen money. He talked us into forming a partnership, expanding the identity business and developing this place with his plentiful cash resources. That cash later led to threats from other Iraqi refugees who knew about Karl's past. That's why I reached for my gun earlier."

"You mentioned that involvement with Karl was a pathway to disaster. How so?"

"Some people are greedy, Joe. He decided that if we could generate high-quality identification documents, we had the skills to counterfeit money as well. Charlie and I refused to go along with that phony money venture, but on his own he started to set up a plant for it in the back of this cave. He moved all his equipment and paper supplies to some other location within the last couple of weeks. He also took his art collection and substituted these lower-grade works. I was glad to see all of that stuff go, and I hope it means I'm no longer associated with him or subject to threats from his pursuers."

Steve stepped forward to draw Oliver's attention. "I assume you learned about the Tobias cylinder while you spent all that after-school time with Eric."

"So you're acquainted with the family – good. I want you to know that Eric was one of my favorite students. He's very bright and has a vivid imagination. I expect that he'll be very creative in whatever career he tackles. He told me about the cylinder, and I asked him to write a detailed description of it for me. He did a thorough job on that assignment and brought me a photograph too. When I passed that documentation to Karl, I realized I had made an error."

"In what way was it an error, and what did you do about it?"

"Steve, I was pretty sure that Karl would try to get that cylinder without paying the Tobias family for it. He might have gotten away with it if those Israeli buyers hadn't stepped in. He was angry about that development. You asked whether I did anything to try to rectify things. Charlie had been keeping up with events in Parkville through some friends back there. He told me about Pastor Blake and his investigating talents. I figured that Blake would want to solve a mystery if I immersed him in one. When Charlie went back to see his wife, I gave him a set of birth certificates to pass to Blake, including Blake's own certificate. I hoped that Charlie completed that mission before he died, but I had no way of knowing."

Joe nodded. "We wondered about the source of those documents. Charlie died before delivering them, but they later found their way into Blake's hands. I won't go into all of the details. We followed the chain of certificates and the cuneiform cylinder to Karl Simitski's doorstep plus other stops along the way; I guess that was just what you intended us to do."

"I had hoped it would work out that way. I couldn't let Karl think I was working against him. It would have been too dangerous. He killed several people in Iraq in order to obtain his getaway money, and he wouldn't stop at murdering a minor business associate if he thought he'd been double-crossed."

Steve said, "Getting back to Karl's activities, I assume that he bought those four lift trucks for his counterfeiting operation."

"He did, and I'm not sure why he left them behind. Either he didn't have enough room on the moving trucks, or he expected to have lift trucks available to him at his destination. He purchased them to move his printing equipment and the rolls of special paper. He also planned to use them to move pallets of printed bills, but he hadn't completed a production run before he left here. I have no idea where he went, Steve, and I doubt that I'll hear from him again."

"I think you gave us a good clue, Oliver. He must have moved to a warehouse or other plant where they have lift trucks available to him. We know approximately when he moved, so we'll look for Karl's having leased space in a big building during that period."

"That won't quite work."

"Why won't it?"

"Karl used my system to change his identity before he moved everything out, and then he corrupted my software in a way that keeps me from being able to discover which identity he assumed."

CHAPTER 81 – FORENSICS

Wally Sanborn, Shirley Hadley, and Pastor Arthur Blake had completed a review of the church's plans for Advent and Christmas events when Irma opened the conference room door partway and stepped into the room.

"I don't want to interrupt your church planning session, but I need to steal my husband for a few minutes. Would you two be willing to continue without him?"

Wally pushed his chair back and stood up. "It won't be a problem, Irma. We've just about completed things, and Arthur has given Shirley and me more than enough assignments. You can have Arthur in here, while we go out and get to work."

Shirley gathered her materials and stood. "You may actually have kept this boss of mine from giving us still more work to do. Come in here, and I'll bring refreshments."

Irma said, "You two are very gracious. Shirley, if it's not too much trouble, I'll have a cold drink instead of coffee."

As soon as the door closed behind Wally and Shirley, Arthur said, "I detected urgency in the way you phrased your intrusion. What's happening?"

"I called Bobby Andrews to see how his technician is doing with the tests on the teapot and cups plus the crime scene evidence from the office where Angela died. I thought that he might ask me to assist with the lab work, but his voice sounded unusually official during our conversation. He also said that the in-house tests had been completed, but that he had sent all the evidence to the State Police Forensic Sciences Lab in Rockford for confirmation of their results."

The door opened, and Shirley put a tray of drinks and pastry on the table. Then she turned and left, closing the door behind her.

Arthur poured his coffee from the pot. "It sounds to me as though Bobby received some unexpected results from his in-house lab, and he wants to see whether an objective and sophisticated lab will duplicate them. He didn't want you involved in the testing because you did the analysis at the crime scene."

"I felt a little put down by his attitude. Do you think he feels that I made mistakes or that I'm not objective enough?"

"He's recently spent a lot of time with Glenn Morgan from the State's Attorney's office. My guess is that Glenn's been pushing him to do everything by the book in order to build a strong case. I'm sure he'll inform us of the results from the State Police tests."

"You're being too calm about this. I feel left out of the loop. Forensics is my specialty."

"Bobby doesn't want to insult you, but he wants a conviction. That means he has to think like a lawyer, and not reveal much to those not officially connected to the case. We're outsiders. The good side of that is that we can and do shortcut the normal investigative process. The bad side is that they don't have to give us all the information we'd like to have."

"Why are they being extra careful this time?"

"Investigating a Bishop can be playing with fire. As a pastor and the Bishop's subordinate, I'll be happy to take a back seat on this one."

CHAPTER 82 – PURSUIT

After their interview with Oliver Parkworth, Joe directed his armed associates to arrest Parkworth and the other two employees and place them in federal custody in Kansas City. He thanked Lou Krill for his help and told him they would fill him in on the outcome of this case. Lou left, and Joe's team began to search for clues to the current location and alias of Karl Simitski.

Steve phoned Penny to tell her what they had accomplished and to suggest that she have people check out Karl's Missouri house and interview Professor Geraldine Quig. He had a feeling that the Texas professor was so close to Karl that she would know about the next phase of his activities. Penny said that she would handle those steps and contact a colleague at Secret Service to warn them about a possible new manufacturer of counterfeit money.

When he returned to the office area, Steve found Joe looking frustrated.

"What's wrong?"

"Karl was too thorough. I thought I had a shortcut to finding him, but he destroyed the time-lapse video surveillance tapes for the last two months. We can't view images of the trucks that carried his equipment and supplies to his new location."

"Do you think that Oliver would remember anything about the trucks?"

"We should definitely ask him and the two assistants. The assistants appear to be Oliver's people and probably wouldn't have been overly loyal to Karl, but they also may not have paid attention to his activities."

"Joe, what's your opinion of Oliver? Is he a criminal, or does he just take advantage of flaws in the system? He strikes me as amoral rather than immoral."

"I see him as a puppeteer, Steve. He arranged for us to receive the birth certificates so that we would investigate the cylinder and eventually, Karl. He also uses identities as keys to opportunities. I'd say he's a very clever person who wants to use the world to his own advantage. The same description applies to many people who invest on Wall Street. He could be considered more than technically a criminal, but not necessarily so."

"In other words, we're not done investigating Oliver. You had him arrested along with the others."

"We'll let him out on bond, but we'll keep him under surveillance. He's too interesting to merit a single-category label at this point, and I want to see what he does now that he's no longer hiding behind Karl Simitski."

CHAPTER 83 – STATE POLICE

Those present at the meeting at the Illinois State Police Forensics Sciences Lab in Rockford included Jane Ferguson the Lab Supervisor, State Police Captain Sylvia Menendez, Glenn Morgan who would make prosecution recommendations, and Bobby Andrews as Police Chief in Parkville, where Angela King's murder occurred.

Jane Ferguson opened the meeting with a statement. "Our Rockford Lab serves as a consulting body on this case to confirm and extend the initial findings of the Evidence Technician at the Parkville Police Department. Obviously, our laboratory has better equipment and more sophisticated techniques than could be justified by a local police department in a small municipality. There is also greater objectivity in having two independent analyses of the same data. We did not review the Parkville findings before we performed our own tests, but I am able to say at this time that our findings substantially concurred with theirs."

Glenn Morgan said, "Before we go into the specifics of your joint findings, I'll ask you to be both accurate and cautious in reporting your results. The slightest rumors of improprieties and crimes could adversely affect careers and reputations. Please be very careful that matters discussed here remain confidential and hidden from the public until we announce official legal action decisions. With that in mind, please summarize your conclusions, Jane."

"We did find several sets of fingerprints on and around the electrocution apparatus in the Parkville office where Angela King was murdered. Most of the fingerprints were those of suspect Joyce Jennings and of the deceased, Angela King. One unidentified set remained.

269

"We checked the lamp and the painted steel plate taken as evidence from the home of Joyce Jennings. They had only Joyce's fingerprints on them. We also checked that combination flashlight and stun gun against the photographs of the marks on Angela's neck. Our finding was that this unit could not have made those marks because its prongs are more widely separated. The damaged insulation on the lamp taken from the home of Joyce Jennings appears to have resulted from ordinary usage, whereas the insulation on the lamp that electrified Joyce indicates removal by a sharp blade. No fingerprints from individual H.C. were found in the office where the murder occurred."

Glenn Morgan said, "Your conclusions weaken but do not negate our case against Joyce Jennings. On the other hand, we don't have to worry about any involvement of individual H.C. All in all..."

Jane interrupted Glenn's discussion. "Excuse me, Glenn, but I can't let an incorrect statement pass. The fingerprints of individual H.C. were not found at the crime scene, but they were found on the paint cans and tools removed from the spare bedroom of Joyce Jennings."

The room was silent for what seemed like a long time. Then Glenn said, "The finding of his fingerprints there is not likely to be a criminal matter. The motive for him to have been there may be a matter of innocent maintenance assistance, or it may have been something else. I doubt that we should pursue that line of inquiry further."

"Do you have any other significant conclusions for us, Jane?"

"We have one more that you should consider important."

"What is that?

"We have identified the extra set of fingerprints at the crime scene. They were located on the desk lamp and on the back of Angela's chair."

"Whose prints were they?

"Those prints belong to individual M.C."

"Do we have an individual M.C.? I don't remember anyone with those initials on our list."

"Individual M.C. is Margaret Chandler, the wife of individual H.C."

Chief Bobby Andrews had concentrated on every detail of Jane Ferguson's presentation. He relaxed against the back of his chair when she finished speaking.

"Jane, I appreciate your corroboration of our findings and the additional details that your analysis provided. Frankly, we were worried about possible errors that might have tarnished reputations. Having multiple laboratories reach the same conclusions should allow us to pursue the guilty individual without fear of significant adverse publicity."

Glenn Morgan stood and shook his head. "Hold it right there, Bobby. Public opinion and facts are two different things. If we give the appearance of being out to crucify individual M.C., we could find that we're on the receiving end of bad press and opinions. We need to build a strong case that goes beyond circumstantial evidence, including determining whether she had motive and opportunity. Even then, we may have to consider a plea bargain to keep all of the disturbing details out of court proceedings."

State Police Captain Sylvia Menendez said, "You're right, Glenn; I know quite a few reporters who would grab this information and sensationalize it. The involvement of a Bishop's wife, and perhaps him too, in a murder would be fodder for the news mills and the celebrity churns as well."

Glenn said, "How did we get the fingerprints of these two individuals for comparison with the crime scene evidence? Did we do our evidence gathering by the book?"

Bobby tensed slightly in his seat, and leaned forward.

"Chief, do you have something to say on the subject of procedures?"

271

"Glenn, we were very careful to get a search warrant for Joyce's house in gathering evidence items from there. Sylvia worked with us on that one. We obtained the fingerprints and DNA samples for possible use in laboratory comparisons from Arthur and Irma Blake. They gathered those samples in their own home."

"A good defense attorney might question the Blakes' participation in this, but I think we could argue that they weren't acting as agents of the police. I requested this meeting to review the lab reports. I'll be available to take further action if and when you feel you have motive, opportunity, and enough other evidence to prosecute individual M.C."

CHAPTER 84 – MOTIVE AND OPPORTUNITY

Bobby's somewhat gruff voice on the telephone had summoned Irma and Arthur to a meeting in his office, and the two of them had complied without questions, expecting that their friend and colleague had something to tell them that would reveal the causes of his recent unusual behavior.

When they arrived, they found a cup of coffee and a glass of iced tea already set out for them. Bobby wanted to get to his agenda as soon as possible.

"Welcome, you two; I need to caution you and seek your assistance at the same time."

Irma said, "Hello to you too, Bobby."

"I'm sorry, Irma, but I'm beyond pleasantries right now. You two gathered evidence in a way that was arguably entrapment. I spoke on your behalf with Glenn Morgan, saying that you didn't act as agents of the police and that no one would pay you for your activities. Was I correct, or is this an official ABC Consultants case?"

Arthur said, "There's nothing formal in what we've done. Our only official act was to inspect the crime scene where Angela died. We did that at your request. We're strictly off-the-books in everything else we've contributed."

"Good, at least I told the truth. Irma, I had to leave you out of the meeting at which we reviewed laboratory results because you had a potential lack of objectivity. You had maneuvered people into giving you evidence. You didn't just observe and collect it."

"That's not fair, Bobby. Arthur arranged the gathering in order to get Howard Chandler's fingerprints and DNA. I

273

packaged the teapot and the cups for your lab to examine. I didn't analyze anything."

"You're married now, so you share responsibility with Arthur."

Arthur asked, "Aside from the peeves about procedure, may I assume that they're important because Howard's prints did match those found at the crime scene?"

For the first time Arthur saw Bobby display a hint of a smile. "No, Arthur, they're important because Margaret's prints match those found at the crime scene."

Arthur and Irma showed surprise on their faces. Then she said, "They always say you should look at the least likely person as a possible culprit."

Arthur said, "So Howard Chandler's prints weren't a match. That's a good development for the church."

"His prints showed up on some items in Joyce Jennings' spare bedroom. He's not completely out of the picture, Arthur."

"Well, if Margaret murdered Angela, she would have a very good motive. Killing her would eliminate Angela's trial for murdering Charlie. That would protect Howard from scandal for having selected such an unworthy potential successor. At the same time, she could frame Joyce for the murder and eliminate competition for Howard's affections."

"No wonder you frustrate me, Arthur; you said *if* she did it."

"I did, Bobby, because Joyce also had a motive. Angela had negligently caused the death of Joyce's daughter. You'll have to prove beyond a reasonable doubt which one did it."

Irma said, "There's also the possibility that they worked together to kill her."

"That's possible but not likely. Joyce was at least potential competition for Margaret, and they weren't close friends."

Irma said, "If we consider them individually, Joyce had opportunity. Did Margaret?"

"Possibly; Bobby, you should ask Howard Chandler how much time elapsed between his decision to send Angela and Joyce to that office and Joyce's report to him that Angela was dead. Assuming Margaret knew of the plan, did she have time to set up the trap before Angela and Joyce arrived?"

"Arthur, I'll do that, but I'd suggest that you keep your distance from the Bishop. At some point he'll realize how we obtained the fingerprints, and then you might find yourself looking for a new job."

Irma said, "I'm not sure you should take the direct approach of questioning him about Margaret. She is a quiet, behind-the-scenes sort of person whose primary goal in life is to enhance and preserve her husband's image. The longer you refrain from overt investigation techniques, the more information you will get from both of the Chandlers. You should be able to pin down the timing of the temporary office acquisition from the property owner. Then you'll be able to calculate Margaret's window of opportunity without arousing their suspicions."

"Irma has a good point, Bobby. You also don't want to point to Margaret as a suspect until you're clearer about Joyce's role. If Joyce is the murderer, and she learns about this development, she and her attorney will prepare a defense based on the equal possibility of two different perpetrators. You need more certainty before you make accusations."

"And who is going to do this additional investigation work? You two have already caused trouble and may have hurt our court case."

"Give us a few days to determine the more likely culprit; that's all I ask."

"Fair enough, Arthur, but don't violate legal ethics, and remember that I won't protect you if you get into trouble. You are unofficial in every sense."

Richard Davidson

"Thanks, chief, we'll do our best to clarify things."

CHAPTER 85 – KARL AND OLIVER

Joe had sent Steve back to Paul, Idaho to learn more about Oliver Parkworth's activities during the period when he had been Eric's teacher. Steve had welcomed this assignment as a vehicle for helping him to clarify his own thoughts and feelings for Ellen Tobias and her son.

Now, back at home in Parkville, Joe sat with Penny and the Blakes summarizing their efforts to find Karl Simitski.

"I like the way we manage to have our meetings at the dining room table, supported by Penny's brunch offerings. It's very different from the limited cooking she did at our apartment in Washington. We grabbed franchise food and ran to the office for our conferences. This is much better.

"It looks as though Karl has temporarily slipped out of our reach. By the time we discovered that he had moved his equipment, supplies, and art collection to that underground office complex in Kansas City, he had reshipped it to some other location. We haven't been able to sniff out his trail."

Arthur finished making notes in a pocket memo book. "He has a new name and identity now, but I have a strong feeling we'll meet up with him again. Karl is too convinced of his own capabilities and too greedy to fade away. He'll show up on the radar again, perhaps when he tries to get even with Roger Svenson."

Irma said, "He'd be dumb to take that bait. Karl won't reappear until he's chasing a big prize or he's threatened by someone chasing him."

Penny passed the tray of warm muffins around the table. "At least the Secret Service hasn't discovered any new surges of counterfeit money since we lost his trail."

Irma took a blueberry muffin. "I don't think they will. We found out from Oliver that Karl was an Iraqi who had been involved in the old regime's financial manipulations. I suspect that he'll counterfeit Middle Eastern currencies, or that he'll put counterfeit U.S. money into circulation in that part of the world. Scrutiny of our currency isn't as intense there as it is here. Iran has been passing counterfeits of our money in that region for a long time."

Penny said, "That's an interesting theory. If Karl does something like that, he'll be wealthier and more powerful when we next encounter him."

Arthur refreshed his coffee from the pot. "Tell me more about Oliver. You haven't lost track of him, have you, Joe?"

"That almost sounded like a criticism, Arthur. We're maintaining tight surveillance of his movements. If he hasn't told us the whole truth, he may do something that would lead us to Karl. We also want to decide whether he's an opportunist, playing the system to his own advantage, or if he's something more dangerous. He and Charlie were clever enough to learn how to create new identities for themselves and others. It wasn't identity theft; they hacked into the medical and government databases, taking nothing, but inserting additional documents. They didn't disturb anyone's existing record, and they paid all of their required taxes, so they didn't feel that they hurt anyone. We even found records of Oliver serving on a jury twice. They projected themselves as upstanding citizens, but not the ones they were from birth."

"Still, they broke the law and deserve punishment for it."

"You're right of course, Arthur, but it would be a long and difficult case to prosecute. For the time being, we're going to keep an eye on Oliver and any possible associates. I'd like to see whether potential terrorists approach him looking to establish new identities. If so, we'll have early warnings of their activities, and at the appropriate time, we'll grab them all. I personally don't think Oliver is dangerous. What do you think, Penny?"

"You surprised me with your decision to just keep monitoring Oliver's activities, but I have to agree that he might lead us to more important prey. From what you said earlier, Arthur, you and Irma are taking a similar approach. You talked Chief Andrews into giving you more time to determine which of two suspects is more likely to have murdered Angela King."

"I wouldn't exactly call it monitoring. He only gave us a few additional days. We'll need some luck and very clear thinking to wrap things up within that short interval."

CHAPTER 86 – ELLEN AND ERIC

Steve pulled the rental car into the now-familiar driveway and started to walk toward the front door of the small blue-roofed house on Doris Avenue. He had only gone a third of the way to the front door when it opened and two people ran to meet him. Eric reached him first and shook his hand.

"Hi, Steve; it's good to see you again. Mom talks about you all the time."

"Don't tell on me, Eric." Ellen caught up with Eric, threw her arms around Steve's neck, and gave him a warm and lengthy kiss. "I've missed you."

Steve took a few seconds to absorb his greetings. "I've missed both of you. Eric, I brought you a hat from when I was down in Texas. It's in the back seat of the car. I guessed your size, but it should fit."

Eric ran toward the car while Ellen and Steve kissed again. He emerged from the back seat wearing his new prize.

"Wow! It's a Stetson, and it fits perfectly. I'm glad you picked out a brown one. I don't go with that movie tradition of black hats for villains and white hats for heroes. This brown hat says that I can be my own self when I wear it."

Ellen backed away slightly from Steve. "You're my hero, Eric, whatever color your hat is."

"I thought Steve was your new hero."

"He is, but I need my old reliable hero too." She went back to kissing Steve.

After another long kiss, Steve parted with Ellen, but kept his arm around her. "One thing's for sure, I've never had a greeting like this before. Let's go inside and chat for a while before I drive down and check into the hotel."

Ellen said, "Go grab your bag. This is your hotel from now on."

Steve pulled Ellen closer. "What do you think about my staying here, Eric?"

"You might as well. You're going to get mushy with Mom anyway. Besides, if you stay here you'll have more time to do things with me."

Steve moved toward the car. "I guess that settles it. I'll get my stuff."

Steve followed Ellen and Eric into the house. When he entered the front room, he felt the warmth of the fire in the fireplace and enjoyed the way it brought out the highlights in Ellen's reddish hair. The room looked different from the way he remembered it.

"Did you rearrange the furniture or add something new? This room seems different to me."

Eric said, "We got a reclining chair and a new bookcase. Mom's been reading up on how the government works, and she wanted you to have a comfortable chair when you came to visit."

Ellen glared at Eric. "That's enough out of you young man. I'll explain my own actions in the future. I think it's time for you to clear the other side of the garage so that we can put Steve's car in there."

"Can I wear my new hat while I work?"

"Sure. Do a thorough job of cleaning up. I don't want to see you back in five minutes."

Eric left, wearing his hat and whistling a cowboy song.

Steve picked up his suitcase. "Where do you want me to put this? I can sleep on the recliner, but you'll probably want me to get my stuff out of the way."

"You and your stuff are going upstairs to the bedroom, Steve. No arguments; I've been waiting for you to come back."

They climbed the stairs to the front bedroom. Its ceiling had cut corners on two sides where the slanted roof intruded on its squareness. Steve put his bag down next to the closet and turned toward Ellen.

"I have missed you."

"As I have you...What are you going to do about it?"

"Eric's coming back soon."

"There's enough time for a quick sample. We'll save the main event for tonight – and I've already fastened the lock on the bedroom door. You told me to get new locks following that break-in, so I made the bedroom secure too."

"You have planned ahead..."

Actions instead of words followed Steve's comment. A short while later, when Eric returned to the house from the garage, he heard sounds coming from the bedroom that he hadn't heard in a very long time. He decided to take a bike ride and went back out.

CHAPTER 87 – OLIVER

He had enjoyed teaching eighth grade science, especially when he had learned that several of his rural students had gone on to earn advanced degrees in engineering and science in college. He knew that he had taught well. He had trained them to question statements that people presented as facts unless they had experimental proof or documentation to justify them. He had required his students to duplicate many of the classic experiments from great physicists and chemists. By the time they completed his courses, his students had learned to understand the scientific process; they had not simply memorized dates and facts.

As Oliver Parkworth, he had been a good counselor and friend to many adolescent students, helping them to select their future goals. After leaving West Minico Middle School and getting involved with Karl Simitski, he had lost his independence and had become Edward Timmons, a technician and subordinate to a wealthy man with questionable ethics. The odd development now was that he yearned to resume his previous identity as Oliver, even though he had created that person out of thin air when he had first used that identity in Indiana. Perhaps he craved simplicity and had a drive to lead rather than follow.

Most people have only one identity, but multiple roles in life. He had multiple identities, but his main roles had become protecting his identity-creation process and learning to act consistently in his current guise. There had to be more to life than this. Maybe he should give it all up and return to his birth identity, Gerald Taylor. Funny, that name didn't sound familiar or even appropriate any more. He laughed as he thought of that old Sammy Davis,

Jr. hit song, *I've Gotta Be Me.* He wondered aloud, "Who am I?"

CHAPTER 88 – CHRISTIE REVISITED

"Arthur, I feel a little silly doing this. Are you sure you want to be so melodramatic?" Irma and Arthur had spent the morning rearranging the living room of the parsonage for an afternoon gathering. Their modifications had included bringing a few of their favorite antiques from their apartment to the parsonage in order to create a more old-fashioned ambiance.

"This place will comfortably accommodate a larger group of people than our apartment, and it suits the mood better, being an older building. Just humor me for today."

"You're supposed to be yourself, not pretend to be someone else."

"You're never too old to pretend. Today I will be Agatha Christie's Hercule Poirot, gathering the people connected to a crime and determining in front of all of them the identity of the murderer...I've long been a Christie fan, and I've always wanted to try this technique."

"If you say bucket list, I'll throw one at you."

"Is that any way for my charming assistant to talk?"

"I'm not your charming assistant; I'm your wife, and a trained forensic scientist. I won't let you forget that."

"Do you mind if we separate those identities? It's difficult for a man to get romantic when he knows he's in bed with a trained forensic scientist who's studying his every move."

Irma walked over and gave him a warm hug. "I give up. Today you can be Hercule, and I'll be Miss Lemon, your secretary. At least I won't have to be Captain Hastings."

"Of course not; that's Wally Sanborn's job."

They completed the room setup, including arranging the John Wesley tea service on the low coffee table in front

285

of the couch. Peter Blake had shortened that antique, once a taller dining room table, by removing the upper sections of its legs. The resulting low slab, massive and oval-shaped, lent substance and formality to the scene.

By two o'clock the guests began arriving, many of them not sure whether they had been invited to a social event or an inquisition. All had agreed to come, in order to defend their interests and personally present their individual stories.

Once everyone had selected seats, Irma and Wally distributed snacks and beverages to those who wanted their appetites to proclaim their innocence. Then Irma welcomed them.

"Thank you all for coming. I'm Irma Blake, and this is the largest gathering we've hosted since our wedding. Arthur will lead the discussions today, but because some of you do not know each other, I'll provide the introductions.

"First, I'd like to welcome Bishop Howard Chandler and his wife Margaret. I'm pleased that you were able to modify your busy schedules to allow for this meeting. Bishop Chandler's secretary, Joyce Jennings, has come, accompanied by her attorney, Linda Caldwell. Parkville Police Chief Bobby Andrews and Assistant State's Attorney Glenn Morgan represent local law enforcement. Penny and Joe Gonzalez are federal government investigators. They have no jurisdiction over the local crime we will be discussing, but they have joined us in order to provide relevant background information, as needed. Wally Sanborn, the new Lay Leader of Parkville United Methodist Church, will assist Arthur. Two other members of our group are coming from out-of-town, and will arrive shortly."

Irma greeted each of the guests individually and then sat down in a dining room chair set back slightly from the main circle of seats. She had completed her initial task, but she would have the critical assignment of observing and noting the reactions of her guests to each nuance of Arthur's analysis.

Arthur stood and waved a welcoming gesture to all of the guests. "Thank you for joining us today. This parsonage is well suited to a gathering of this size. I hope that you are all comfortable.

"Today, I will attempt to summarize the steps that have been taken by several cooperating individuals and agencies in order to determine who was responsible for the murder of District Superintendent Angela King."

Bishop Chandler interrupted. "Arthur, is everyone completely convinced that her death was not an accident?"

"Thank you for raising that question, Howard. Reviews of the facts by both local and state agencies indicate that Angela was murdered. The person or persons who committed that murder attempted to convey the impression of an electrocution accident, but crime scene analyses and medical examinations have ruled against that possibility.

"I'll start by requesting that all who are present consider our discussions today to be confidential except for legal purposes. Please do not pass any personal information relating to those present or the victim to those who have no need to know it.

"Angela King was my supervisor as a pastor, but she also knew that my second vocation is that of a student of crimes and the criminal mind. After Irma and I were married, thanks to the Bishop's last-minute assistance, she told me a strange tale of a Canadian fishing trip with her estranged husband, Charlie King. It started with the planned goal of reconciliation, but ended with her having murdered him in the course of a violent argument. She claimed to have abandoned his body in the wilderness. Her confession to this bizarre crime led to the involvement of Penny and Joe Gonzalez whose agency would attempt to locate the Canadian crime scene, and Bishop Chandler's changing Angela's status to special assignment while her crime was under investigation. I should also mention that the Canadian fishing trip tale turned out to be fiction. We subsequently learned that Angela actually murdered her husband deliberately and dumped his body in a water-filled quarry near Rockford, Illinois."

Several people exchanged muffled comments upon receiving this new information.

Bishop Chandler said, "I put her on special assignment because I felt that we needed to eliminate her involvement with church members and the public during the investigation and expected trial."

"It was a wise and objective move on your part, Howard. Unfortunately, it also put her into the office location where she was murdered. I'm sure you selected that Parkville office because you had used it to operate your second vocation, that of tax accountant."

Again, a few of those present murmured comments to their neighbors.

Bishop Chandler said, "I thought that Margaret and I had managed to keep that information secret. The truth is that even a Bishop has to consider moonlighting to supplement his income, and I enjoy tax accounting. It lets me understand people's goals, motivations, and ethics. You and I are similar in having two vocations, Arthur."

"Thank you, Howard. Why did you use Warren Wilson as your name when you offered tax accounting services?"

"I didn't want my clients to know about my church position. Warren is my middle name, and Wilson is Margaret's maiden name. Both names reflect the truth. I formed a corporation under that name, so I operated legally."

"Now I have to ask you an important question. When did you remove your tax accounting business from that Parkville office?"

"That won't take much calculating. My accounting business had decreased so much that I had decided that I could no longer afford the office. I decided to move that business to my home the week before I assigned Angela and Joyce to that office. I completed my move out of the office the day before I put Angela on special assignment and had Joyce contact the property owner. That's why I knew the space would be available."

"And did Margaret assist you in moving out of that office?"

"Margaret and I have assisted each other for a very long time. Of course, she helped with the move. Why do you ask?"

Arthur glanced over at Glenn Morgan and Bobby Andrews. They both nodded, and Glenn made a slight hand gesture to indicate that Arthur should continue his line of inquiry.

"Howard, your statement clarifies one question about the crime, but it raises another. The police found Margaret's fingerprints in that office, but they didn't find yours. Given your statement that you worked together to move you out of the office, why didn't they find fingerprints from both of you?"

Margaret, looking more petite than ever sitting between Chief Bobby Andrews and her husband on the couch, raised her hand. "May I answer that question, Arthur?"

"Of course you may, Margaret."

"Men and women have different priorities when they work together. Howard was concerned with the actual moving of files and equipment. My main objective was to be sure we left the office clean and neat before we left."

Penny and Irma both smiled and applauded Margaret.

Irma said, "Women rate cleanliness higher than men do."

"Please continue, Margaret. Apparently my wife is one of your fans."

"Anyway, the point I was going to make is that after Howard removed the last load from the office, I washed the desk, chair, and other remaining items before joining him in the parking lot. I didn't wear gloves while I did the final inspection and cleanup, so I probably left a few of my fingerprints behind."

"That's very useful information, Margaret. Since you were the last one out of the office during that move, would you mind describing the office contents and arrangement as you last saw them?"

"Not at all, Arthur; the desk was in front of the window, and the chair was pushed back a little so that someone could sit down without having to move it. I never did understand why the landlord supplied such a heavy chair on legs instead of one with wheels. I think there was a second chair against the wall for use by a visitor."

"Was there a lamp on the desk?"

"Yes, I believe it was a small blue gooseneck type, the kind you bend into a convenient position."

"Did you notice whether there was a floor mat under the desk, and if so, what was it made of?"

"There wasn't any, so I can't describe it. There was just the bare wooden floor."

"Thank you for your information, Margaret; you obviously have a good memory."

Margaret relaxed and sat back on the couch. Howard took her hand and smiled at her.

Arthur walked to the other side of the room and approached Joyce Jennings and Linda Caldwell, sitting on adjacent chairs.

"Linda, this is just an informal gathering, so I hope you won't object to Joyce answering a few questions as we continue our discussion."

"Go ahead, Pastor, but I'll stop her if I think legal issues require it."

"Fair enough...Joyce, you told the police that you and Angela left the furnishings in that office exactly the way they were arranged when you moved in. Is that correct?"

"Yes; I only moved the side chair so that we could face each other for discussions and my taking notes."

"When you arrived, did you find the office clean, and was it set up the way Margaret said she left it?"

Joyce thought for a moment. "It was clean and neat. The only difference was that there was a metal floor mat under the desk and chair."

"Are you sure of that? Did you notice the floor mat when you first arrived?"

"I definitely did, because I remember wondering why it wasn't plastic or rubber. I hadn't seen a metal mat before. It looked like one of those white magnetic bulletin boards that you use with refrigerator magnets. I have one of those at home."

Arthur exchanged glances with Irma and Bobby. "Where do you have the one you have at home?"

"I used it in the kitchen for a while, but I took it down and it's now stored under the bed in the spare bedroom. Why do you ask?"

"I didn't see it described that way in the police report on the search for evidence at your house."

Linda Caldwell said, "There wasn't any incriminating evidence found in Joyce's house. I saw no proven connection to the crime of anything they mentioned in the report or took with them."

"Getting back to the floor mat, Howard, are you certain it wasn't there when you worked in that office?"

"There was no mat of any type in that office when Margaret and I moved my accounting business out of there."

Arthur turned to Irma, "Would you please call the landlord and ask him whether he added that mat to the office between the two occupancies?"

Irma went to the kitchen to make her call.

"Joyce, the police considered you to be their prime suspect because you had the greatest opportunity to commit this crime with only you and Angela working in that office. You also had a clear motive. Angela had been negligent in causing your young daughter's death in

California. The facts that you followed her to Illinois and took a job for the same organization suggest that you had not forgiven her. Was her murder your act of revenge?"

Linda Caldwell put her hand on Joyce's arm. "You don't have to respond to that. This isn't a courtroom."

Joyce said, "I really don't mind, Linda. It's time to clear the air about my feelings toward Angela. I did not kill her, but I had not forgiven her for Robin's negligent electrocution. I did follow her to Illinois. I also took a job in the Rockford Conference office so that I could monitor her activities and make her life a little miserable whenever I had the opportunity. When Bishop Chandler requested a volunteer to assist Angela in Parkville, I stepped forward because he needed someone with diplomatic skills in case the media learned of the special assignment. I owed Bishop Chandler a favor because he had helped me with repairs and maintenance at my house."

"And did you do anything specific to adversely affect Angela and make her life miserable?"

"It was a petty act, but when Angela was working in our Rockford office, I added something into her coffee supply from time to time to make her feel sick."

"What did you give her?"

Joyce pushed Linda's cautioning hand off her arm. "I mixed some Sterno from the chafing dish warmer into her coffee carafe on three occasions. I'd read that it would make her feel sick, but that it wouldn't kill her. I needed to feel that I'd done something to her for killing Robin. Angela changed her name before coming here. That proved that she knew she'd been negligent and felt guilty about what she had done to the children."

Bishop Chandler studied Joyce's face as she spoke and realized that he didn't know very much at all about his secretary's past and her feelings.

Arthur walked toward Joyce. "The documents you dropped in the inner office when you discovered Joyce's body had been printed on special high-quality paper that

Bishop Chandler uses in the Rockford office. Did you bring those documents with you from there? The copier in the office building contains lighter weight plain paper."

"No, Arthur, I added the special paper to the copier in Parkville for reproducing Angela's resumes, and I used it in the printer for her other documents. She wanted to make a good impression when she applied for another position and when she documented her past duties as district superintendant."

"One final question, Joyce: why did you lie about when you put the coffee on Angela's desk?"

"You caught me on that one, Arthur. After I made the copies, I went out into the parking lot for a cigarette. When I went back upstairs, I figured I'd better bring coffee as well as the copies to show Angela that I'd been doing something useful during my long absence. I put the coffee on the desk after I discovered her body, not before as I had previously stated. I just wanted to look efficient and not neglectful of my duties."

Irma walked back into the room. She stopped where everyone could see her and said, "I've just spoken with Stanley Finch, the landlord of that office building. I asked him about that metal floor mat and described it to him. Stanley told me that he had used white sheet metal to cover two workbenches in the basement of that building and that he had stored two extra sheets of that material in a maintenance supplies closet three doors down from the copier room on the first floor. He keeps both the closet and the copier room unlocked and open to anyone in the building."

Arthur said, "Therefore, the murderer would not have had to bring the mat into the building from somewhere else."

The doorbell rang, and Joe Gonzalez answered it, returning with Steve DuBois and Oliver Parkwell. He introduced them to the others.

Arthur said, "Steve and Oliver are the two guests from out of town that Irma mentioned earlier. To summarize our discussions to this point, we have pinned down the details of the condition of the inner office prior to Angela King's murder there.

"What we have learned so far is that Margaret Chandler's fingerprints were in the office, an unexpected development, while Bishop Chandler's fingerprints were not, even though he had been the last prior occupant there. Margaret's description of their moving-out cleaning procedures have satisfactorily explained the fingerprint evidence and removed them from suspicion."

Howard and Margaret Chandler both smiled and leaned back on the couch.

Arthur continued. "We then turned to Joyce Jennings, who worked with Angela in the office at the time of the murder. Joyce had a strong motive because many years ago, Angela had negligently caused her pre-school daughter's electrocution. We have to consider Joyce a strong candidate for killing Angela by electrocution. It would be poetic justice for her to strike back at Angela that way.

"After listening to Joyce's responses to my questions today, I consider her less likely to have been the killer. She has a reasonable explanation for the unexpected paper type of the documents she dropped. Her statement that she found the metal mat on the floor when she arrived fits with the property owner's statement that he had stored sheets of that metal in an accessible closet. Joyce's admission that she adulterated coffee in the Rockford office to sicken Angela makes me wonder why she would make Angela ill if she planned to murder her. Why do both?"

Glenn Morgan interrupted. "Arthur, as a prosecutor, I've appreciated your logical way of reviewing the evidence. My problem is that you appear to be eliminating all of the suspects that we've previously discussed. Who else had opportunity and motive?"

"Thank you, Glenn; you make a valid point. We'll respond to it shortly. First, I'd like Wally Sanborn to tell us about some experiments and consultations."

Wally stood up and took Arthur's place in the center of the ring of seated people. "For those of you who don't know my background, I'm Lay Leader at Arthur's church, and I'm also a retired Army officer, having specialized in logistics and special weaponry. I took photographs of the electrocution setup in Angela's office to one of the Army's laboratories that deals with identification and disarming of booby traps. Their conclusions after duplicating and testing the circuit formed by the combination of the lamp, mat, chair, and a person's body, was that it would reliably deliver a shock, but would be unlikely to cause death. The paint on the mat, chair, and lamp would not be a good conductor; the person's reflexes would tend to have her pull back, breaking the circuit; and the steel chair had glide pads on the legs that would not conduct well. This is an issue that should be addressed before this case goes to court."

Arthur nodded and exchanged places with Wally. "Thanks for that confirmation of something I suspected from the beginning. I'll address it again. First, I want to point out that there is one more person here with a strong motive for murdering Angela King. Oliver Parkworth, who came in with Steve DuBois, was Charlie King's brother, even though they used different names. Oliver, can you give me any reason why we shouldn't conclude that you killed Angela to get revenge for her murdering Charlie?"

"I can give you the simplest reason in the world. I was in Missouri when she was killed."

"That's a very strong statement, especially since Steve had instructions to avoid telling you the date of her death while he brought you here. Steve, what do you know about Oliver's location at the time of the murder?"

"When we found Oliver in the Missouri facility where he had been working with Karl Simitski, he identified himself as Edward Timmons, a new alias. Our search of flight records for the period including Angela's murder indicated that an Edward Timmons flew from Kansas City to Chicago two days before the murder and flew back on the morning after that event. He must have allowed time after he arrived for locating Angela and planning his attack."

Arthur said, "That brings me to the statement by Joyce Jennings that she saw the floor mat under the desk when she and Angela first arrived. That would indicate that the killer was already in the building at that time, probably hiding in the closet where he had located the mat. He saw his opportunity to act against Angela when Joyce passed the closet, heading for the copier room."

Oliver stood, and Bobby Andrews repositioned himself between Oliver and the exit door.

Oliver said, "You have no case against me. Wally Sanborn reported that the shock setup in the photograph of that office probably wouldn't have killed her. Her death was an accident."

Arthur responded to Oliver's statement by walking over to Irma. "Oliver, my wife is a former medical examiner who joined me in examining Angela's body right after she died. Irma, would you care to comment on what you've heard from Wally and Oliver?"

"I'll be happy to do that if you'll admit that you reached an incorrect conclusion right after the murder when you said you knew who had committed the crime."

"Fair enough; I admit that I took the bait and saw what the murderer wanted me to see. I had a few misgivings about the scene of the crime, but I repressed them."

"Arthur and I both studied the crime scene, but we may have given improper weights to certain pieces of evidence. As he suggested, we went along with the clues the killer had deliberately left. Oliver's protest that Angela died an accidental death is similar to a magician inducing you to focus your attention in the wrong place. At the crime scene, we treated an observed medical condition as being secondary when it was actually primary. Angela's corneas had been burned during the electrocution. This effect on her eyes should not have happened unless the locus of the electrocuting device was on or near her head. We accepted the setup of the desk, chair and lamp as being the trap that shocked her to death. We observed two marks on her neck and concluded that the murderer had used a high-level stun gun device to assure that she had died in case the initial shock from the lamp had not been fatal.

"From what I've heard today, I believe that the killer reversed the procedure. He or she stood behind Angela and electrocuted her with the device that left the two marks on her neck. Then that person stripped the insulation off her lamp cord and positioned her body, chair, and desk to make it look as though she had electrocuted herself. The killer may have held her hand to the lamp to give her an additional burn mark."

Arthur said, "Thanks, Irma. Your description of the way the killer arranged the shocking apparatus reminds me of the way someone might set up a science experiment. Oliver Parkworth worked as an eighth grade science teacher in Idaho. That's one more reason to suspect the man who wanted to avenge his brother's murder."

Oliver approached Arthur until Steve restrained him by grabbing his arm. "My being a science teacher proves nothing. These are idle speculations. You don't have a shred of physical evidence to connect me with this crime."

Penny nodded to Joe, who walked into the kitchen and returned with a long white box. He held it under his arm as he faced Oliver.

"When we searched your underground sanctuary in Missouri looking for clues to Karl's whereabouts, we found this device. It has your fingerprints all over it." Joe removed the cover and displayed an oversized stun gun.

"We tested this and found it to have more than enough power to be lethal when in contact with a person's neck. Its prongs also have the same spacing as the marks on Angela King's neck."

Bobby Andrews stood and took out his handcuffs. As he secured Oliver's hands behind his back, he asked, "I have to ask you why you held onto this incriminating device?"

"I had a strong feeling that I would have to use it on Karl before he decided that I was of no further use to him. That man scared me. He'll turn out to be an international danger before he's through. Before we go, let me just say that I've always tried to be on the side of righteousness, even though I gave people a shortcut to the mainstream through identity enhancements. I prepared my students well for their adult careers. I've always considered myself one of the good guys; but I couldn't let that bitch named after an angel, get away with killing my brother."

Bishop Chandler said, "Vengeance is mine, says the Lord. She would have paid the price eventually."

Joe said, "And with regard to Karl Simitski, don't worry; he'll pay also. Several federal agencies are already searching for him. We'll find him soon."

Bobby Andrews led Oliver out through the front door, intoning the Miranda rights speech as he formally arrested him. As they left, Bobby thought he heard several loud sighs of relief behind him.

CHAPTER 89 – BISHOP CHANDLER

Arthur and Irma remained to clean up the parsonage after the others had left. They found it an easy task because the summarizing session had been so intense that most people had forgotten to take snacks and drinks. The result was a large quantity of refreshments that the Blakes would take home to avoid spoilage.

After they had rearranged the furniture for normal meeting uses, Arthur asked, "Do you have any comments about how that went, Irma?"

"You were impressive but scary."

"How was I scary?"

"There were moments when you sounded like Hercule Poirot except for the accent."

"You were a cross between Miss Felicity Lemon and Miss Marple. It was fun to wrap up the case the way Agatha did in many of her books."

"I saw Bishop Chandler talking with you before he and Margaret left. What did he say?"

"He requested that I visit him in his Rockford office this afternoon before he returns to Chicago."

"That development could be either good or bad."

"That thought had crossed my mind also."

At precisely two o'clock, Arthur entered the Conference's branch office in Rockford. Naomi, the receptionist, asked him to have a seat while she told Bishop Chandler that he had arrived. She mentioned that the Bishop had given Joyce Jennings a two-week vacation to recover from her recent ordeal of suspicion and involvement with the police.

A few minutes later, Bishop Chandler came out to escort Arthur into his office, where they took the two comfortable chairs in front of the fireplace for their discussions.

"I have coffee on the side table for you, Arthur. I know that you function best with cup in hand."

Arthur was tempted to forego his plasma beverage, but he decided to take it in the hope that coffee would increase the sociability of the session.

"Thank you, Howard; I hope the parsonage meeting wasn't too stressful for you and Margaret. I arranged it in order to complete the investigation of Angela King's murder, including the many side issues, as rapidly as possible."

"Margaret actually enjoyed your drawing together of all the different aspects of the case. Margaret is an avid mystery reader, and she said she felt as though she was in the midst of an Agatha Christie novel in a country manor house."

"That was the model for our gathering."

"Arthur, I was not as favorably impressed by what transpired there. I was not pleased to discover you and the police had considered Margaret and me to be suspects."

"You were suspects only in the sense of our having to understand the activities of everyone who had been at the crime scene at some time."

"I'm pretty sure I know how you obtained our fingerprints as part of that elimination process. You could have just asked me."

"I was trying to be subtle, hoping to never have to mention anything about suspicions, expecting that your fingerprints wouldn't match any found in the office. Once we found that Margaret's fingerprints were there, we had to ask why. Margaret's explanation last evening was both logical and enlightening."

"We'll put that behind us, Arthur. However, my overall impression of that meeting, with your summarizing and analyzing the case, showed me that there's a big difference between the two of us. I've kept up a side business of doing tax accounting to bring in a little more revenue and to learn more about people's thinking and lifestyles. I have a lot more talent for clergy matters than I do for accounting. While you are a successful pastor, your real talent lies in your logical thinking and deductive powers. In the past, I had thought you just dabbled in this detective business. Now I realize that it's time for you to rearrange your priorities."

"Are you about to fire me, Howard?"

"No, but I'm going to reassign you to be a consultant to the Northern Illinois Conference working with any local church that has a disturbing event that requires investigation without necessarily involving the police. Many times, we don't want to air our dirty laundry in public, but we know that we can't just ignore unpleasant developments. You will be our troubleshooter. We'll pay you a reduced salary except for times when you are actively working on one of our projects, but you'll have a lot more time available for your outside investigations. You also won't have a steady diet of obligations to a congregation."

"Who will be taking over Parkville UMC? I know there is a tradition that former pastors have nothing to do with their old churches, but I would like to continue attending there when I'm not involved elsewhere."

"I have no problem with that, so long as you let the new pastor run the church. I suspect that you won't find yourself there on a regular basis anyway. We'll try to accommodate your wishes, but if you develop a conflict with the new pastor, we will have to suggest you worship elsewhere."

"When will you announce this change?"

"I'll give you a month to prepare your congregation for it before I make any announcements. That will also give us time to line up your replacement. This is not a demotion. It's simply a way for us to allow you to pursue your true vocation while being able to call you back for religious or secular troubleshooting. May I assume that this arrangement is acceptable to you?"

"It is a welcome development, Howard, and thank you for allowing me to remain within the Conference structure. I was not looking forward to eventually having to choose one career over the other."

CHAPTER 90 – ARTHUR AND IRMA

When Arthur returned to their apartment, he found an empty ice cream sundae dish on the dining room table alongside a note from Irma that she had gone out for a jog. He put the dirty sundae dish in the sink, took a clean dish, and added a scoop of chocolate ice cream. When he heard the front door open, he took his snack with him and went out of the kitchen to meet Irma.

"Hi, jogger, were you craving exercise or just feeling nervous?"

"Nervous is the correct answer. I've been up tight thinking about you and your session with Bishop Chandler. I pigged out on ice cream and then had to get some exercise to make up for it."

"I thought you had a great idea, so I took ice cream too."

Irma stared at him as he ate a spoonful of chocolate. He put the dish with the remaining ice cream on the table.

"What's wrong? You had ice cream; can't I have some too?"

"This isn't about ice cream."

"What is it about?"

"I've been worried about you getting fired or worse, and you won't even tell me what happened with the Bishop. I bet he was livid over our taking their fingerprints during our tea party."

"He was sharp enough to realize what we had done, and he wasn't particularly happy about it."

"Did he get angry at you?"

"I think he would have been angry if it weren't for Margaret being a mystery fan. She thoroughly enjoyed being in on the solving of the case and the arrest of the murderer last night."

"Did you get fired?"

"Not exactly..."

"What does that mean? Are you still going to be the Parkville Pastor or not?"

"I'm still going to be an ordained elder, but I won't be pastor of a local church. Instead, they're making me the Conference Troubleshooter, charged with investigating and making recommendations whenever a church has a problem that warrants outside assistance."

"What does all of that mean to me?"

"It means that I'm not going to be reassigned to another church in a different location, so we are free to upgrade from renting an apartment to buying a house, anywhere we want. It also means that I'm free to do investigations without obligations to a local church and that I get paid by the Conference for doing their investigations."

"In other words, you no longer have to make a choice between your clergy duties and your investigations."

"Add to that the freedom to work anywhere when a case requires it. I'm optimistic that we'll be able to handle almost anything that comes up."

Irma unzipped her sweat suit jacket. "I'm glad you said 'we' instead of 'I'; let's always keep it that way."

CHAPTER 91 – DINNER PARTY

Joe opened the door and greeted the Blakes. Irma handed Joe a salad bowl, while Arthur walked toward the kitchen, carrying an angel food cake and a potted Christmas cactus with five red flowers on it. After Joe helped Irma with her jacket, they also headed for the kitchen.

Penny greeted them and said, "The food is ready. I thought we would eat in here instead of the dining room. We deserve to relax and enjoy each other's company informally. Our latest joint effort is marked: *Case closed*, and it's time for us to have fun."

Joe cleared his throat to get attention. "I have two announcements. The first is that I called the Washington office to check for developments and emergencies. Steve informed me that our contacts in Iraq say that an archeological expedition working in the area of the ancient city of Babylon triggered some improvised explosive devices or mines in the area. Our contacts there think that everyone in the expedition died. They didn't see any footprints or tire tracks leading away from the site. One of the victims was a woman in a wheelchair. The Iraqis have identified her as Professor Geraldine Quig. No one knows whether she was there with Karl Simitski, using his latest identity. However, he had many enemies in Iraq who may have gone after him. We don't know whether he's alive or dead."

Penny said, "Geraldine deserved a better fate, but at least she died in an ancient city she had researched for many years. If Karl died, I'd have little sympathy for him."

Arthur said, "I predict that we'll find he's still alive. I expect that we'll run into him again...Joe, you said that you had two announcements; what else has happened?"

"You are all invited to join me on January fifteenth in Paul, Idaho. Steve and Ellen are getting married, and I'm going to be Best Man."

Irma said, "Raise your wine glasses for an outstanding future for Steve, Ellen, and Eric. May they live in love and peace, free of evil people."

They all clinked glasses and sipped their wine. Then Irma said, "Too many apparently good people have the capacity for doing evil things, and too many bad people convince you that they're good when they're not."

Arthur said, "That's because they're neither good nor bad. They're just people. We all carry the potential for both good and evil. We have to consciously choose the better path many times along the way."

-END-

ABOUT THE AUTHOR

Richard Davidson is the author of the self-help guidebook: *DECISION TIME! Better Decisions for a Better Life.* He has written four novels: *Lead Us Not into Temptation, Give Us this Day our Daily Bread, Forgive Us Our Trespasses,* and *Thy Will Be Done,* which are the first four volumes of the planned five-volume Lord's Prayer Mystery Series. He is Past President of Off-Campus Writers' Workshop, the oldest ongoing group of its kind in the U.S. and the founder of the ReadWorthy Books Book Review Blog. He is also the founder of the Independent Mystery Publishing Society (IMPS). Mr. Davidson is a Certified Lay Speaker and a former Lay Leader in the United Methodist Church. He is also an aeronautical & astronautical engineer and a businessman.

OTHER WORKS BY THIS AUTHOR

NONFICTION:

DECISION TIME! Better Decisions for a Better Life, VBW Publishing, Inc.
ISBN 978-1-60264-063-4 (soft cover)
ISBN 978-1-60264-064-1 (hard cover)
ISBN 978-1-4581-8395-8 (Smashwords Edition eBook)
ASIN B0052GOZEO (Kindle Edition eBook)

Where you are in life today is the result of all of the past decisions you have made or which have been made for you in response to the various situations and events that have impacted your life. The decisions that you will make from this point forward will determine the degree to which your future will be positive or negative. *DECISION TIME!* gives you insight into the subjective decision-making process as applied to both small and large choices you will face. It includes dynamic aspects, cultural effects, and morality as applied to decision-making for individuals, teams, corporations, and societies. *DECISION TIME!* prepares you to face the continuous impacts of decision situations confidently and without hesitation.

FICTION:

Lead Us Not into Temptation (The Lord's Prayer Mystery Series, Volume I),
VBW Publishing, Inc.
ISBN 978-1-60264-407-6 (soft cover)
ISBN 978-1-4581-7381-2 (Smashwords Edition eBook)
ASIN B0052MGI6Q (Kindle Edition eBook)

Arthur Blake, former NASA engineer turned minister, receives an emergency appointment to be pastor of the United Methodist Church in Parkville, a distant suburb of Chicago, following the bizarre sudden death of the church's unusual former pastor. Pastor Blake's attempts to unravel the mystery that shrouds his predecessor become involved with tracking the child of a possibly bigamous soldier in World War II England, art and jewelry treasures plundered by the Nazis and their sympathizers, and the eventual results of childhood sibling conflicts in combined families. Arthur's allies in his investigation include Parkville Police Chief Bobby Andrews, County Medical Examiner Irma Custis, and the married team of Penny and Joe Gonzalez who work for a clandestine government agency. During the course of *Lead Us Not into Temptation*, the reader discovers how seemingly minor historical events lead to major present-day dislocations in church, village, and family relationships.

Give Us this Day Our Daily Bread (The Lord's Prayer Mystery Series, Volume II)
RADMAR Publishing Group
ISBN 978-0-9829160-0-1 (soft cover)
ISBN 978-1-4580-6717-3 (Smashwords Edition eBook)
ASIN B0052MQI66 (Kindle Edition eBook)

Arthur Blake, Pastor of Parkville United Methodist Church, has to deal with the aftereffects of a traumatic communion incident. He works to assist the authorities in investigating the cause while doing his best to convince members of his congregation that it is safe to return to church. Working with the police and federal agencies, he discovers that the terror of the initial event is minor compared with the potential chaotic impact of future disasters being planned by the perpetrator. The investigation is interwoven with several relationship situations that affect the final outcome.

Forgive Us Our Trespasses (The Lord's Prayer Mystery Series, Volume III)
RADMAR Publishing Group
ISBN 978-0-9829160-1-8 (soft cover)
ISBN 978-1-4657-3739-7 (Smashwords Edition eBook)
ASIN B005SULQ6Y (Kindle Edition eBook)

Arthur Blake, Pastor of Parkville United Methodist Church, tries to assist his father to resolve his trauma after learning that his best friend, recently killed in a car accident, may have been an imposter with a heinous background. The investigation reveals that the presumed accident was but one link in a chain of murders. Blake works to determine the true identity of his father's friend, while also discovering the man's past activities and affiliations. Arthur works to solve the murders in conjunction with his colleagues at ABC Consultants. He also draws on assistance from associates at a covert government agency with which he has worked before. The coordinated effort to solve the puzzle examines incidents that span the period between World War II and the present in order to defuse the personal, national, and international dangers resulting from them.

Thy Will Be Done (The Lord's Prayer Mystery Series, Volume IV)
RADMAR Publishing
ISBN 978-0-9829160-2-5 (soft cover/paperback)
ISBN 978-1-3013-4293-8 (Smashwords Edition eBook)
ASIN B009JU6EZM (Kindle Edition eBook)

The sudden death of a young woman attending Parkville United Methodist Church infuriates her brother and leads to congregational outrage over his outburst and subsequent murder. The investigation of that slaying by Pastor Arthur Blake and his associates leads to revelations of a previously undetected criminal organization operating in the area. Unraveling the mystery and scope of this group entangles Arthur and his associated investigators in a web of conspiracies extending from Illinois to both U.S. coasts and through Mexico to Guatemala.

Deliver Us from Evil (The Lord's Prayer Mystery Series, Volume V)
RADMAR Publishing
ISBN 978-0-9829160-3-2 (paperback)

Arthur and Irma's wedding day has finally arrived, but an unexpected interruption leads to their need to investigate a possible murder committed by someone close to them. With the aid of friends and federal agents Penny and Joe Gonzalez, they follow a series of clues, crisscrossing the United States to learn more about the murder, related subsequent events, and the significance of a rare object brought home by a veteran of the Iraq War. A second murder close to Pastor Arthur Blake's church involves them in a new investigation, assisting Parkville Police Chief Bobby Andrews. Are these murders and the tracking of that strange object connected? Will marriage deteriorate or improve the relationship between Arthur and Irma? Character flaws in many relationships color the outcome.

Overcoming: An Anthology by the Writers of OCWW
Edited and with an Introduction by Richard Davidson
RADMAR Publishing
ISBN 978-9829160-4-9
ASIN B00E80NN4I (Kindle Edition eBook)

Learn more about the writings and random thoughts of Richard Davidson at: davidsonbooks.blogspot.com davidsonbookshelf.com betterlifedecisions.blogspot.com Richard Davidson's author page is on Amazon at https://www.amazon.com/author/richarddavidson and on Facebook at https://www.facebook.com/pages/Richard-Davidson-Author/211578652220873?ref=hl Follow him on Twitter @mysteryimp

www.ingramcontent.com/pod-product-compliance
Lightning Source LLC
Chambersburg PA
CBHW051240260626
47162CB00002B/530